He's Just A Friend

BOOK YOUR PLACE ON OUR WEBSITE AND MAKE THE READING CONNECTION!

We've created a customized website just for our very special readers, where you can get the inside scoop on everything that's going on with Zebra, Pinnacle and Kensington books.

When you come online, you'll have the exciting opportunity to:

- View covers of upcoming books
- Read sample chapters
- Learn about our future publishing schedule (listed by publication month *and author*)
- Find out when your favorite authors will be visiting a city near you
- Search for and order backlist books from our online catalog
- Check out author bios and background information
- Send e-mail to your favorite authors
- Meet the Kensington staff online
- Join us in weekly chats with authors, readers and other guests
- Get writing guidelines
- AND MUCH MORE!

**Visit our website at
http://www.kensingtonbooks.com**

He's Just A Friend

Mary B. Morrison

KENSINGTON PUBLISHING CORP.
http://www.kensingtonbooks.com

Dedicated to all my children. When each of you are ready, love yourself first and choose your friends carefully.
I love you

Jesse Bernard Byrd, Jr., my son
Rachelle Isadora Davis, my niece
Lauren Nicole Davis, my niece
Angela Dionne Davis, my niece
Delisia Noel, my niece
JoVanté Morrison, my niece
Janard "The Preacher" Morrison, my nephew
Roland Morrison, my nephew
Christina Morrison, my niece
Omar Noel, my nephew and godson
Marianna "Tomorrow" Morrison, my niece
Joseph Henry Morrison, II, my nephew
Annissa "Ladybug" Rickerson, my niece
Derianna "Muffy" Morrison, my niece
Ulalila "Lady" Lee Morrison, my niece

Acknowledgments

I render all praises to God. I'm thankful for my parents, the late Joseph Henry Morrison, Elester Noel, Ella Beatrice Turner, and Willie Frinkle. I don't know what I'd do without the love and support of my siblings, Wayne, Andrea, Regina, and Derrick Morrison, Margie Rickerson and Debra Noel.

Thanks to my wonderful son, Jesse Bernard Byrd Jr., one of Northern California's Super 100 basketball players, one of the top three sophomore ballers in Northern California, one of the elite Slam-N-Jam Soldiers basketball players, and most importantly, a brilliant academic achiever on track to becoming an NCAA Division-1 basketball player.

Continued love and appreciation to the greatest editor, my editor, Karen Thomas. Thanks to my agent, Claudia Menza, for also being my friend. To my entire Kensington Publishing family, thanks for your hard work and support.

Thanks to Felicia Polk, my publicist and friend. I love you and attribute a great deal of my literary success to your untiring efforts. Thanks to L. Peggy Hicks, my publicist, for working so diligently on my tours.

A special thanks to my guardian angels, Howard and Ruth Kees, Andrea and Regina Morrison, Malissa Tafere-Walton, Vyllorya A. Evans, Shannette Slaughter, Michaela Burnett, and Gail Fred. You guys stood behind me, believed in me, and supported me.

Thanks to all the bookstore owners, readers, radio and TV hosts for supporting my work.

A woman's first orgasm
Should be by masturbation
Or maybe from oral copulation
But never strictly penetration

She doesn't need permission
To explore herself
By herself
She should try herself

And hold on to her virginity
Not for infinity
But until he can prove
He's the one she should choose

Because penetration the first time hurts
Then she'll bleed
And perhaps end up on her knees
Praying to a porcelain bowl
Through the eyes of her unborn soul

Because he's left her holding his seed
Instead of a deed
Of trust
Signed joint partners

She doesn't even know what an orgasm is
Or how it feels
But oh well he's got his
And she's got his kid

He'll probably jump ship
Before he's burdened with a child

A *child* who has the same smile
She had when he first met her

Now that she's pregnant
She's no longer smart enough
Pretty enough
Pure enough
Nor good enough
To be his stuff

He'll leave her with a load of chores
Because he's out to score
With someone else
Who's willing to help
Add another notch to his manhood belt

Maybe it's the good girl
Whose parents merely said don't have sex
Or maybe it's the curious girl
Who was beaten for having a passion mark on
    her neck
Or maybe it's the loud girl
Who doesn't understand self-respect
Or maybe it's the shy girl
Who couldn't talk openly to anyone about sex
Or perhaps it's the quiet girl
Who no one suspects

If only she knew how to please herself
A baby didn't have to be left behind
She could have taught him
How to stoke her mind

A woman's first orgasm
Should be by masturbation
Or maybe from oral copulation
But never strictly penetration

If someone had told her to spread her thighs
Look into her own eyes
Eyes that would not lie

Her vagina is a beautiful flower
Smile
Look
Look
And lick her fingertips
Then tease her clit
And don't be afraid to touch her tits

Oh there's so much
Her precious temple should learn
Before feeling the burning sensation
Of his manhood's penetration

He should kiss her lips
The moist ones closest to her eyes
Like it's his favorite dish
And his only wish
Is never to make her cry
Or degrade her womanhood to his boys
By creating a bunch of lies

Then she could return the favor
And they both could savor the flavor
His manhood would be intact
Because he knows his girl has got his back
With a smile
Instead of a child

Not my daughter one might say
Well like or not
The girl will someday
Have sex anyway
Ignorance does not prepare

A lover who's unaware
Will learn from someone out there
Someone who probably doesn't care
And despite the parents' good deeds
Someone is willing to share his seeds
With a female harboring unfulfilled needs

A woman's first orgasm
Should be by masturbation
Or maybe from oral copulation
But never strictly penetration

She doesn't need permission
To explore herself
By herself
She really should try herself

And hold on to her virginity
Not for infinity
But until he can prove
He's the one she should choose
To carry his last name
Before carrying his baby

She must be taught to respect herself
Love herself
No if but and or maybe
Because far too often she's still somebody's baby

It's a new generation
And boys masturbate all the time
Let's teach our girls about masturbation
Let's empower our girls with alternatives
To unhealthy situations

A woman's first orgasm
Should be by masturbation

Or maybe from oral copulation
But never strictly penetration

Talk to your child(ren) about sex
Please

CHAPTER 1

"**H**ow could you be so stupid?!" Fancy yelled in the mirror at her reflection. *Swish. Swish. Swish!* Her fists chased the July summer night's breeze blowing through the patio screen into her lonely bedroom. How could she have not known that Byron Van Lee was a married man? A man she'd done everything with. A man she was willing to do anything for. What was she going to do? Fancy swiftly turned, landing three blows against her shadow. Mimicking Laila Ali she struck faster. Harder. *Swish! Swish! Swish!* Long strands of black hair whipped around her neck and clung to her sweaty face.

Fancy massaged her heaving breastbone in an attempt to give her aching heart relief. Maybe if that were the first time a man had lied to her about his marital status, she'd forgive him. Not this time. Not this one. This kind of shit was supposed to happen to other women.

"Why me? Why? Why? Why? Why? Why me?" Fancy questioned herself repeatedly. Why was it so difficult for her to find an honest man? Byron would definitely regret playing with her emotions.

Perspiration beads gathered on her feverish forehead. The salty streams burned her cheeks. White lines remained where tears once flowed. The angrier she became the more she perspired. The more she cried. New salty lines replaced old ones as Fancy recalled the lies Byron had told on their very first date.

Byron had unmistakably said, *"Actually, I'm happily single. Thirty going on thirty-one. Never married. Would love to have two kids, a boy and a girl, but I hardly have time for myself."*

That night over dinner his roaming brown eyes traveled from her face down to her cleavage and back to her glowing smile. Then he had proclaimed, *"And so far I love what I see, Ms. Taylor."* Following his statement, Byron gradually fed her a large chocolate-dipped strawberry. Setting the green stem aside, Byron eased his manicured nail between her lips.

Fancy shivered at the memory. She felt foolish as she visualized sucking the juices off Byron's finger, pretending it was his dick. "Fuck you, Byron! I hate you! I hate your lying ass!" Fancy hugged herself so tight the only thing missing was a straightjacket.

Maybe if Byron hadn't lavished her with everything she wanted. Maybe if he hadn't spoken all the right words. Maybe if he hadn't spanked her with his colossal dick. Maybe. Just maybe she could think straight and delete his phone numbers from her cell phone book like the rest of her rejects. Tears flowed. The red squiggly veins in her eyes doubled. Tripled. Quadrupled. She hated the thought of letting Byron go, but did she hate Byron enough to let him go?

Rocking back and forth on the gold padded stool, Fancy snatched the red washcloth from her vanity and vigorously dried her tears. Sniffles accompanied short quick breaths that escaped her runny nose. Byron had recently dropped her off after another one of their sizzling dates in the city. Again, he'd taken care of her, showing her off to his rich male friends. And in return—just moments ago—Fancy leaned in Byron's lap while he drove across the San Rafael Bridge, en route to her apartment in Oakland. She sucked his head, because that was all she desired to fit into her mouth. Fancy stroked Byron's shaft long and hard until his cum became hers. With each suck, she'd hoped Byron would change his mind and spend the night at her place, but the screeching sound of his tires as he pulled out of the circular driveway still echoed in her ears.

Removing her tan designer minidress, she tossed it across the foot of her bed. Fancy enjoyed prancing around her apartment in the nude and as soon as she made it home, her clothes made it to the bed. This time all except her neutral-colored thigh-high stockings, a thong, and a garter belt. She forced her fingernails inside the runs she'd created shuffling back and forth on the white carpet and ripped a larger hole.

"Why couldn't he just tell me the truth?"

Even if Byron had told Fancy he had a wife, she still would've fucked him. But she wouldn't have fallen madly in love with him.

Snatching the cordless phone from the charger, Fancy punched in the home number she'd memorized earlier from Byron's cellular ID. After he'd hung up from that call, suddenly their night, which was just getting started, was over. "We've gotta go," was all he said, because Byron never offered an explanation or an excuse. He wasn't slick. He was the one who was stupid! Not her. If he lived alone, who'd call him from home?

Shaking Byron from her thoughts, Fancy dialed the number. A woman's voice muttered, "Hel-lo," as though she'd been awakened.

Faster than a Polaroid snapshot sliding out of a camera, a million thoughts flashed in Fancy's mind. The sun rays peeping through her vertical blinds were fading. Fading right along with her undeveloped hopes and dreams for a future she'd fantasized about for well over six months, with Byron. Friday night happy hour at the

Pacific Heights members only club that Byron had taken her to wasn't over until eight and according to her clock it wasn't quite seven. Maybe his conniving ass had returned without her so he could fuck the black Amazon goddess with the London accent all the other men were idiotically hounding and drooling over. Beads of sweat resumed popping out on her forehead. Fancy watched as a thin liquid necklace formed in the crevices above her collarbone.

"Hello?" the woman's voice repeated.

Sitting quietly at her vanity, Fancy pressed the mute button, then rocked back and forth, staring at her reflection in the oval-shaped mirror. "Why do you keep choosing the wrong man?" She rocked faster. Not adoring herself at the moment, Fancy rolled her eyes so hard her green contacts shifted, revealing her natural brown eyes. Green. Gray. Hazel. Violet. Fancy owned a pair of lenses in every color except blue. She flipped the swivel mirror horizontally so she could no longer see how pitiful she looked.

This was insane. What was she going to do if the woman was his wife? Stalk her? Harass her? Make her divorce Byron? Shoot her? Maybe Fancy could beat the woman with the belt she used to spank Byron with during role-play.

"Hello? Is anybody there?" the woman asked with a tone indicating if someone didn't speak up this time, she would hang up.

Suddenly Fancy stopped rocking, pressed the mute button again, and delightfully said, "Hi! Is this the lady of the house?"

Fancy wondered many things about the woman on the other end of the line. Was she the same woman who was with Byron the night they'd met? Was she Byron's wife? If so, how long had they been married? Did the woman have a nine-to-five job? Maybe they weren't married. Maybe they were separated. And in the process of getting a divorce. That's probably why Byron hadn't mention he had a wife.

"Yes, this is Mrs. Lee." Mrs. Lee's voice was choppy and faint, like she should have cleared her throat but she didn't.

Fancy spoke happily. "I'm calling from the *Chronicle Tribune*. We have an introductory special that your family is guaranteed to enjoy. We're combining the best articles and advertisements, and we have a fabulous sports edition I'm sure the man of the house would love! Instead of ordering two papers or missing out on both, your family can be among the first Bay Area residents to get all the news in one paper! Delivered to your front door! For an unbelievable price of twenty-nine ninety-nine for an entire year."

"Really?" Mrs. Lee spoke slightly louder. "I'm sure my husband would love that. But then again . . ." she hesitated. "We—"

"Your husband is a sports fan, isn't he?" Fancy asked, already knowing Byron sat on the Board of Directors for the Oakland Coliseum. Byron had suite tickets for the Warriors, Raiders, and the A's games. He also had season tickets for the Sacramento Kings. He'd taken Fancy to enough games for her to know if she ever met Chris Webber face-to-face again she'd become Mrs. Webber. What sense did it make for her to be loyal to Byron's lying ass?

"He's the biggest sports fan. Okay, why not. It's only thirty dollars." Mrs. Lee had finally spoken in a normal tone. "We'll sign up."

Nervous, still wondering if Byron would arrive home soon, Fancy said, "Wonderful! All I need is your name, delivery address, phone number, and credit card number with the expiration date. And you'll start receiving the paper in three to five days."

"Can you hold for a moment?" Mrs. Lee asked. "I was trying not to wake the baby but he's crying."

Fancy pressed her ear to the phone and listened carefully.

"Waa. Waa." She heard crying in the background.

Oh, hell no! Fancy jumped up from her vanity stool and began pacing the floor. What baby? How old was this wailing kid that sounded like a lamb? Byron was a father, too! Maybe Mrs. Lee was baby-sitting. Or the bitch had Byron's baby, trying to trap him so he wouldn't divorce her ass.

"Hello. Are you there?" Mrs. Lee questioned.

"Of course I'll hold." Fancy smiled to brighten up her voice, then said, "After all, we are a family oriented newspaper group." Fancy hit the mute button and screamed, "Hurry the fuck up!" then pressed the same button again.

When she reached the patio door, Fancy turned around. This time she was too angry to cry. When she reached the bedroom door she turned back around. Too pissed off to sweat. She turned back around again. Too upset to stop moving. She turned again.

"Thanks for waiting. Here's our information."

Racing to the stool, Fancy grabbed her pen. Her naked shoulder pressed the phone to her ear while she listened carefully. She drew a bold letter X across the front of one of her business cards, then wrote Mrs. Lee's information on the back.

Byron could be replaced, perhaps by her boss, Harry, but definitely not by her friend Desmond. Finding a man of Byron's caliber, great looks, and dick stature would be virtually impossible. Byron's six-foot four-inch, two-hundred-thirty-pound frame appeared to have zero-percent body fat. His dark brown skin was smooth. Each time Byron came to her apartment he drove a Benz, a BMW, a Cadillac, or he was escorted by a driver. Whenever he opened his wallet, all Fancy saw were Benjamins and platinum credit cards.

Begrudging Mrs. Lee, Fancy said, "Thanks for your

subscription." Fancy gazed at the address so long that her vision blurred. Byron's address in Oakland Hills— the house he'd given her keys to, the house where they had spent many nights and almost every weekend together, the house she'd partially decorated—was different from the one she'd written down. Mrs. Lee lived in one of the most prestigious areas in Northern California. Cupertino.

"Excuse me, but isn't a supervisor supposed to call me back to—"

Fancy's inner voice yelled inside her head, *Fuck you!* right before she hung up the phone. If Fancy had had an ounce of religion, between Byron and Mrs. Lee, she would have truly lost it instead of losing her mind. Fancy ruled out killing Mrs. Lee because of the baby. *The Nanny Diaries* would read completely different if Fancy Taylor had to care for another woman's kid. Fancy loved Byron too much to just let him go. But another woman was living under her future roof, married to her future husband. One way or another that bitch had to go!

CHAPTER 2

Fancy sat on the edge of her bed staring out her patio window at two Canadian geese flying over Lake Merritt. Her friends thought she was strange because she used her sunken living room as her bedroom. Fancy seldom cared about what other people thought. Both bedrooms combined were smaller than her living room and each bedroom had a morbid view of the Scottish Rite Temple's asphalt parking lot.

Mounted next to Fancy's bed was a silver pole wrapped in red velvet. Fancy had danced on that pole countless times. Sometimes for her male friends. At other times she practiced new moves or simply entertained herself. Fancy taught herself to dance and move like women in the music videos on BET's 106th and Park because rich men—the only kind she'd date—became bored a lot faster than the men who lived paycheck to paycheck.

Ruffling her down-feather comforter, Fancy scurried across her king-size bed in search of her ringing phone. One more ring and her voice mail would turn on. SaVoy's name registered on the display so Fancy quickly answered, "Hey, girl! What's up?"

"Just called to see what you're doing tonight." SaVoy

always sounded happy. Fancy could picture her best friend's bright smile.

"Going out. To a gala at the Ritz. With Desmond."

"You really need to quit using Desmond. One of these days he's going to get tired of you playing with his emotions and God only knows what will happen. He's so nice to you, Fancy. And he's perfect marrying material—for somebody else—so you should quit before you ruin him. Besides," SaVoy pleaded, "you've partied with the pagans three hundred and sixty-four days this year. Surely you can give one day to the Lord. Forget the gala. Come go with me to church tonight and praise God."

Since Fancy didn't go to church any other time of year, New Year's Eve was definitely not the time to start. And as far as Desmond was concerned, the way Fancy saw it, she couldn't use anyone who didn't want to be used.

"Girlfriend, you know I love you but this is New Year's Eve. And from now on, remember this. You've only got one life to live. So stop wasting yours trying to live mine. Gotta go. Bye. Call me tomorrow. After three. Oh, yeah. Say a prayer for me."

"I always do. By—"

Fancy hung up the phone and rubbed her growling stomach. There was still enough time to order delivery service on-line from ezdineinn.com so Fancy raced up seven steps—into the should-have-been bedroom that was her office—over to her laptop and charged one dozen oysters on the half shell from Spenger's to her boss's American Express card.

Fancy didn't cook or sew but her apartment was immaculate. Making her way to the adjacent bedroom that she'd converted into a closet, Fancy stood inside a space that resembled a miniature Saks store. Roll-away racks filled with expensive clothing were scattered about the room.

Name brand shoes were stacked high on shelves. Fancy removed the frequently used stepladder from behind the door, and scanned the photos stapled to the front of each shoe box. "Ah, there you are. Come to Mama," she said, choosing her designer stilettos with the rhinestone-covered heels.

More shoes—jogging, hiking, aerobic, cross-country— and her Roller Blades, lined the floor, neatly flush against the baseboard, sorted by color. The two thousand dollars for her rent was paid. This month. Her hair weave and nails were freshly done, and her car was tuned up. Fancy's men paid for everything, including the new pearl-white headboard and footboard, lingerie dresser, armoire, pillow-top mattress set, and the new vanity that had been delivered on Christmas Eve.

Entering her master bathroom, smoke swirls hovered above a tub filled with hot water and her favorite black cherry bath salts. A homemade body scrub—one-half pound brown sugar stirred into milk and honey body wash—sat in a crystal bowl atop the white porcelain tub. "Ahhh," Fancy exhaled as she nestled her head above the inflatable pillow and closed her eyes.

"Starting tonight, I, Fancy Taylor, proclaim next year as my year for finding the right man. I *am* going to get married and I *am* going to have a baby."

Twenty minutes later, Fancy drew herself from the comfort of her bath and toweled off. Carefully she styled her hair, smoothing each layer of every track, then tossed the soft jet-black tresses behind her neck. The layered edges dangled below her shoulder blades. Sparkles shimmered in the silky platinum of a deep V-cut halter gown that delicately clung to the shapely curves of her breasts, hips, and thighs. Fancy turned around, admired herself in the full-length mirror, and smiled. "Now that's a fabulous ass if I must say so myself." Adding the finishing touch, she brushed on her M.A.C. Chai lip gloss.

The cordless phone rang again. This time exactly at ten. The programmed number from the building's call box registered so Fancy buzzed Desmond in and grabbed her full-length white mink.

"Hey, you look great!" Desmond said, stepping inside.

Fancy closed her eyes and enjoyed Desmond's warm embrace. Careful not to snag her diamond earrings on her coat, she tilted her head and whispered in his ear, "Thanks, baby." She meant thanks for being her friend. And thanks for taking her out again this New Year's Eve.

"You look extra handsome tonight, baby. I'mma hafta claw those desperate divas off my man." Fancy placed her fingertips on Desmond's forehead. Slowly she traced over his temples, along his jawbone, down his neck, and tugged his tuxedo lapel. Fancy smiled, because in order to take her out, Desmond had canceled plans with his so-called girlfriend Carlita.

Fancy hated being alone on New Year's Eve and harbored no remorse that Carlita wasn't the one going out with Desmond. Fancy also hated blue. Blue jeans. Blue sherbet. Blue nail polish. Contacts. Robin eggs. Bubblegum. She especially disliked dating blue-collar workers, which was the main reason why Desmond could never be more than just a friend.

"What's *your* boy Tyronne up to tonight?" Fancy asked, focusing on the beautiful holiday lights outlining the buildings along San Francisco's skyline. Tyronne was another man with big dreams and no money. As long as the cola company kept producing beverages, Tyronne would continue delivering sodas. Fancy's stomach growled, disrupting her thoughts. Damn, the oysters. Oh, well, she'd put them in the refrigerator so she could eat them for breakfast. It was probably best she hadn't eaten them because she definitely would've ended her platonic relationship with Desmond and fucked him real good after the gala if she had.

"You know Tyronne. Probably the life of the party at somebody's house," Desmond said, holding Fancy's hand tighter while driving with his other hand on top of the steering wheel.

In a special way, Fancy admired Desmond. He was tall and good-looking. Desmond's innocent brown eyes shone under his long curly lashes. Whenever his thin mustache stretched across his face, Fancy saw the dimple in his right cheek. The seat belt was tailored to his flat stomach. Desmond was one of five men Fancy kept on her carry-over list for next year. She couldn't imagine life without Desmond yet she couldn't envision being his wife. Was money and prestige really that important? More significant than a man's character? Or his willingness to love?

Breaking the silence, Desmond asked, "What're SaVoy and Tanya doing tonight?"

"SaVoy, church. Tanya—she's going out with some guy she just met named William." Fancy smiled at Desmond and reverted back to her thoughts.

The men who were fortunate to be on her regular dating schedule were now Fancy's sponsors. Adam sponsored her rent, Tony sponsored her Top Notch hair weaves, manicures, and pedicures, and Steven sponsored her wardrobe. That's how Fancy balanced her budget. She determined what needed to be paid, and then calculated which guy was wealthy and worthy enough to pay her bills. If she didn't insist that her men take care of her, they certainly wouldn't volunteer. And if they did volunteer, Fancy knew they'd assume a movie and a meal every once in a while was fair exchange for tasting her pussy.

Fancy also had disposable sponsors. Those were the ones she'd date only once knowing she'd never have sex with them, but she could usually persuade them to pay a bill or two before she blocked their numbers on her home phone. Taking care of herself had become such a full-time job, Fancy seriously considered quitting her nine-to-five. She was willing to trade in all of her sponsors but not until after she was married.

Easing her hand from Desmond's constant massage, Fancy asked, "Made any resolutions yet?"

"Yeah." Desmond nodded as he exited the freeway at Embarcadero. "To go to law school. A brotha don't mind gettin' his hands dirty working on cars, but that's not my destiny. Johnnie Cochran, watch out! Desmond Brown, Esquire, is coming to your town!"

Every town was Johnnie's town. It might help if Desmond at least took the LSAT and submitted a few applications. "That's nice," Fancy said, trying not to encourage his illusion. "At least you have a resolution. I haven't thought much about mine yet."

Desmond drove up to the hotel entrance and valet parked. Fancy's neck whipped side-to-side as she scanned the men getting out of the nearby limousines. Several prospects stood out. Especially the tall, stunning clean-shaven gentleman. The top button of his wingtip shirt was unfastened. A black bow tie dangled about his neck. That was a good sign. A nonconformist with class, and judging from his Rolex watch, lots of cash.

"Isn't this wonderful!" Fancy sang, strolling inside the grand ballroom.

"Yeah, this is cool," Desmond replied, bobbing his head while accepting two half-full champagne flutes. He handed one to Fancy and chugged a gulp from his.

Fancy slapped his hand. "Don't drink it all at once."

"Are you kidding? As much money as I spent on these tickets I might take a bottle home."

"Let's check out the silent auction," Fancy said, maneuvering to get closer to the guy she'd seen outside and to see how much he had bid for the golfer's package.

"Desmond, look at all these arrangements." Fancy pointed at each display. Football. Travel packages to different countries. Basketball. "Oh, my gosh! Can you believe this golfer's package is donated by Tiger Woods?" Gliding her finger underneath the last bid, Fancy looked at Desmond and thought, *Twenty-seven thousand dollars! No way. He must need to get a last minute tax write-off.*

"Damn! I don't care how much money I make, I'd never throw it away like that. Some company, probably Nike, donated all this stuff in Tiger's name. Yeah, that's how the rich get richer. They don't pay for jack. That's exactly how I'mma be, watch. And you gon' be my lady. I'mma spoil you, girl. Buying you that six-hundred-dollar gown was nothing."

That's true, Fancy thought as Desmond reminded her for the fourth time. She rolled her eyes, then scanned the room. The man she wanted was standing on the opposite side of the ballroom with someone else.

"Let's see what's over there," Fancy said, taking the shortcut across the hardwood dance floor.

The emcee announced, "Ten minutes to countdown! Make sure you've got your spirit, spirits, and credit cards."

"Ha! That's a good one," Fancy said, shaking her ass to wedge a deeper arch into her lower back. The woman hanging on to her future man was cute, but up close Fancy assessed the woman was clearly no competition.

Sounding like Lou Rawls, the emcee said, "Five minutes to countdown."

The jazz quartet resumed playing Kenny G's "Songbird." Desmond hugged Fancy so she pulled him closer and was grateful she'd worn her high heels because a real man was now facing her. Thick black eyebrows—with scattered hairs connecting his brows—were his only facial hair.

Fancy's eyes locked with the stranger's as she stared over Desmond's shoulder. Her admirer winked. Fancy batted her eyelids, then seductively smiled at him.

"One more minute folks!" The emcee interrupted the music once more.

The handsome man blew Fancy a kiss over his date's shoulder. Fancy's heart had throbbed when he'd gotten out of the stretch limo, but now her heart pounded. She gently puckered her lips as Desmond held her tighter. The stranger massaged the nakedness of his date's back—the same way Desmond was caressing hers. This man gazed into Fancy's eyes as if they were making love to one another. Fancy's body quivered. Desmond pressed his lips against her ear and inhaled.

"It's time to ring in the new year! Ten! Nine!" the emcee shouted along with the crowd. While the emcee counted, lovers locked into one another's arms, quietly swaying while the single people yelled along with the emcee.

"I can't believe I'm holding you in my arms again this year," Desmond whispered in Fancy's ear. "You know we were meant to be together."

"Six! Five!"

The stranger smiled again. This time he licked his lips as though he could taste her. Fancy's thong became moist and hot. Her breathing became heavier, so she looked away.

The crowd yelled, "Three!"

Got damn, his ass was fine. Fancy's eyeballs eased into the corner sockets. He was still staring. Then he mouthed, "I want you."

"One!"

Fancy shouted, "Happy New Year!" and tooted her horn well after everyone else, including Desmond. The paper flap rolled in her new man's direction, motioning her thoughts, *Come to me, Daddy.* The energy stirring between them formed a lump in her throat. Fancy couldn't ask Desmond to get her a drink because she was just handed flute number five.

Fancy quickly said, "I'll be right back." Swaying her

hips, she gracefully waltzed through the crowd, set her glass on a table by the door, and then exited into the brightly lit lobby. "Whew!" Fancy exhaled loudly. As soon as her hand pressed flat against the ladies' room door, she heard someone say, "Excuse me."

Please, oh, please let it be him. Her heart raced for a man she didn't know at all. She turned gracefully on her tiptoes like she'd learned in ballet class years ago.

"Do you have a moment?" he asked, fondling his dangling bow tie.

Fancy smiled and replied, "For you? Yes, I do." And she meant that because her January dating calendar was overbooked, with three standbys awaiting confirmation.

"Wow," he gasped, then shook his head. "You are amazingly beautiful. I'm Byron Van Lee." He extended his hand. Gently he held Fancy's hand but didn't shake it.

"Hi. I'm Fancy. Fancy Taylor." Fancy wanted to touch him so she said, "Would you like for me to fasten your bow tie?" Holding his tie, she rested the back of her hands on his chest. Byron's muscles were pleasingly solid.

"This is my conversation piece and trademark. Never fails," he said. Raising her hands to his lips, he kissed them.

Desmond walked up to Fancy. His eyes bucked, then his forehead buckled. Desmond stared at Byron, then at Fancy.

Pointing at Byron, Desmond questioned, "Who's this?" Desmond's chest protruded as he continued staring at Byron. Fancy eased her back toward Desmond. Desmond stood directly behind Fancy and firmly secured his hands on her hips.

Byron extended his hand to Desmond and said, "My name is Van. And you are?"

Fancy stepped aside, looked at Byron, and smiled.

Desmond grabbed Fancy's biceps and firmly said, "Let's go."

Fancy kept smiling. Byron smiled at her, then walked away. Fancy really wanted to curse Desmond out for acting so damn childish. When she turned toward the ballroom, instead of letting go of her arm, Desmond tightened his grip.

"No. I mean it. Let's *go*. I spent two whole paychecks to bring your ass here and this . . ." Desmond's voice trailed off, then picked up again, ". . . is the thanks I get. You up in some rich dude's face grinnin' and shit," Desmond grumbled. "Fuck that. I shoulda took Carlita out. Let's go. I'm taking your ass home."

Fancy moved Desmond's hand and walked outside, but not before looking over her shoulder to see if Byron was watching. Byron was gone. The back of Desmond's jaw clenched several times as he ground his back teeth.

Desmond's mindset confirmed why Fancy refused to date blue-collar workers. His mentality and attitude didn't fall far from his profession. Fancy smiled to avoid creating a scene. Desmond wasn't her man. He was her friend. But somehow Desmond had gotten the two confused. Again.

Fancy waited for Desmond to get in the car, then said, "Oops, I forgot my coat." Fancy raced inside before Desmond could offer to get the coat for her. She hurried into the ballroom searching for Byron.

"Looking for me, I hope," she heard a voice from behind.

Fancy smiled with relief when she saw Byron standing near the doorway.

"Here's my card," Fancy said. "Call me." She gave Byron a quick endearing hug. Byron held her coat as she eased her arms into the sleeves. Fancy strolled outside and got in the car. Desmond's jaw was still clenched so Fancy sat quietly as he drove.

Desmond was always getting upset over nonsense. He could keep his negative energy on his side of the car. Fancy's new year was definitely starting out good. She reminisced the moments she'd shared with Byron on the dance floor, then fantasized about how passionately she'd make love to him after their first date. As soon as Desmond parked in front of her building, Fancy got out of his car and didn't bother to say bye or thanks. Figuring she'd give him a real reason to be pissed off, Fancy slammed Desmond's car door.

She stood in her foyer. Easing her hands in her coat pockets, Fancy pulled out a card and frowned as she read, *Byron Van Lee*. Fancy kissed the card and smiled. Then she untied the red velvet ribbon from her dance pole.

CHAPTER 3

Desmond was Professional Auto's "go to" man to fix their toughest mechanical problems. Although he made decent money repairing cars, the rich sophisticated women he adored loved him but not his occupation. His charming physique generally appeased women long enough for him to get a date and repair their cars. Once the females were tuned up, he didn't hear from them until thirty thousand miles later or when they needed servicing again, whichever came first. Lounging in his boss's office, Desmond spent his lunch break talking on the phone with his best friend Tyronne.

"I ain't never called no woman no ho, and I don't plan to start now, but, man, some of 'em sho are triflin'. And the more money they make, the more they act like men. Fuck ya. Don't call ya the next day. And when I call them, they act as though I'm interrupting them and shit. 'Who's this? Is everything okay? You all right?' And most of 'em don't even remember my name. The moment I say yeah I'm all right, before I can add anything else they say, 'Let me call you back.' Man, they don't give a damn about my background or upbringing. And the more I go down on 'em the less they wanna know. Needless to say, I never hear from 'em again. That is, unless I call them back."

Desmond couldn't recall ever breaking up with a woman. He didn't have to. He knew, even the ones that did like him, eventually they'd find something about him that they either didn't like or couldn't change. Then they'd complain about how they never should've given him the pussy—as if he'd asked—and how they lowered their standards trying to raise his. As if they had a better man or any man waiting for them to walk through their door and say, "Honey, I'm home."

Desmond peeled the foil on his overstuffed chicken burrito from Las Pomas. His lips surrounded the warm tortilla as he held the phone in his other hand.

"Desmond, you a fool, boy. Why you feel the need to be so damn analytical about females? Don't you know women aren't as complicated as men think? Women are simple. So keep it simple and stop trying to raise the bar for their asses. You gon' make me call you Jesse B. Simple because that brotha couldn't figure women out either. Besides, some of these females, you don't wanna waste your money or your time on 'em. You see the shit you did for Fancy New Year's Eve and how she back-kicked you in the damn teeth like a jackass. Dude you gon' go broke fuckin' around with these females. I'mma school ya, boy. Here's what you need to do. Show them a little attention. Invite yourself over to her place. Don't tell her where you live. And if she asks, give her a city. Any city. Oakland. Richmond. Vallejo. Like that. And when you get to her place, chill for a minute. Give her a few compliments and conversation. Ask her 'How was your day?' They really like that shit. Then give her the Big Daddy kiss and she becomes your little girl. Eager to please. The next thing you know she's giving you a lap dance. Tap that ass. Then tap your ass right out the mutherfuckin' do'. Whatever you do, after you get the pussy, leave."

Desmond and Tyronne had opposite opinions about women. Desmond believed a woman deserved honesty, love, and affection. But he had a difficult time finding a woman who met his standards. Beautiful. Intelligent. And preferably wealthy or at least well enough off to take care of herself. Except for Fancy. Desmond would do anything for Fancy.

Tyronne felt women served a purpose. Mainly to stress him out. So since women created his stress, Tyronne used them to relieve his tension.

Desmond couldn't resist saying, "You remember Lisa, dawg?"

"Aw, nigga, there you go. You just had to bring her up, didn't you? Man, I put that sistah high on a pedestal and let her move into *my* place . . . The second she caught me kickin' it with someone else Lisa lost her got damn mind . . ."

Desmond did remember Tyronne's horror flick chick. How could his boy have missed the warning signs that that feline was certifiably mental? One day Lisa just walked into the restaurant, spray painted Tyronne's hair, food, clothes, and date. As if that wasn't enough, she cursed him out, insulted his dick—loud enough for everyone in Kincaid's to hear—then she walked out, leaving Tyronne looking like a blue smurf. How could his boy Tyronne, the pimp master, let something like that go down? Desmond shook his head.

". . . Lisa slept with my dick in her mouth like it was a mouthpiece. That's probably why she lost her damn mind. And man, how did she know where I was?"

If Lisa would've asked, Tyronne said he would've told her that the woman was one of his clients. That she was organizing a major conference downtown at the Oakland Convention Center and wanted Tyronne to get credit for sealing the deal with his beverage company.

Tyronne lamented, "Hell, a sistah can't even help a brother move up without his woman getting jealous.

The same damn woman who expects me to pay the bills and wine and dine her ass . . ."

From that day forward, Tyronne swore to Desmond women were no more than sperm receptacles. Mouth. Titties. Pussy. Ass. Of course, he couldn't openly treat them that way. But Desmond knew Tyronne couldn't trust another woman with his heart. Tyronne's ex was drop-dead gorgeous and seemed so happy and accommodating when Tyronne first introduced her to him, but Lisa's ass was perpetrating. Desmond chuckled at how upset Tyronne got whenever he mentioned Lisa's name.

Tyronne's voice escalated. ". . . With the quickness of the Blue Angels jets flying over the Golden Gate Bridge traveling faster than the speed of sound, Lisa's ass sped through her side effects."

Desmond mouthed along with Tyronne because he'd heard the story so many times he'd memorized it.

" 'I'm crazy as hell will fuck you up if I ever see you with another bitch. I don't forget shit because I have a memory ten times better than a got damn elephant trained all the Central Intelligence agents. I'm wanted in forty-eight states and a few foreign countries, too, by fifty plus pissed on and off men and I will kick your ass if I ever catch you cheatin' on me.' But dawg, I swear, her titties were so big all I heard was, "Hi, my name is Lisa."

Changing the conversation, Desmond said, "Check this out." Desmond paused at the sound of oncoming footsteps. After the thumping faded in the distance, he continued, "You have to have an opinion on this. You know dude who got my next-door neighbor pregnant. She met this guy and gave him keys to her house, her car, and she gave him money. In less than one month she was pregnant and he was gone. I mean gone, dawg. Without a trace. Took off in her car! The name he gave her wasn't real. She didn't know his peeps. With the few dollars he overlooked in her savings account, at least she was smart enough to abort the baby."

"Man, that's what I'm talkin' about. Simple. She should've at least made him wear a condom. You won't believe how many females beg me not to slide a jimmie on 'lé cheval.' Once they lay eyes on the foot-long master, they start acting like they done won a got damn award and shit. Holding it next to their cheek. Kissing it. Smiling. One chick gave an acceptance speech. And check this out. Another feline said grace before she . . . ouu, I get hard just thinking about that church girl."

Desmond and Tyronne laughed together.

"Women are desperate, Dez. Desperate. Lonely. Crazy. Putting on that 'I'm so happy to be with you' smile. Trying to act all sophisticated. The first opportunity they get they sneak through all your shit. Cell phone book. Glove compartment. Two-way. Pants pockets. PalmPilot. E-mail. And the second they find something, they flip the fuck out. And I don't even want to start on the married women who give out their cellular and business numbers. They gettin' worse than us, dawg. That's why I stopped inviting 'em to my spot."

Desmond placed his boss's invoices back in the in-box and said, "I want an intelligent woman—"

Tyronne objected. "What? Why? Who gives a fuck if she's intelligent as long as she looks good? 'Cause they all crazy, dawg. We just got to figure out how crazy before they fuck up our—"

Desmond interrupted, "See, that's where I disagree. If a woman can't hold a decent conversation before making love, I don't want her in my bed."

"Making love? Man you got jokes. Give me her digits. I'll wax that ass for you," Tyronne laughed, then said, "Women want to know they've been fucked. They don't give a damn about making love. Most of them don't even know how to make love. Fuck her good and she'll never forget you. She'll even brag to her girlfriends, 'Girl, Tyronne ate my pussy so good I'm still cumming.' Make love to her. She'll bottle that up inside and won't say shit to you or her girls."

"Man, check this out and tell me what you think," Desmond paused. Took a deep breath and started rapping.

"I'm trying to wrap my head around females these days. And although I'm learning the ways of women, I don't think I'll ever understand them. So I flow like this . . . She says I'm just a friend. Was that before or after she let me slide the head in? She says I'm just a friend until another fe-fe is on my dime, commanding my time, then she bumps it up a notch with attitude. Step off, bitch, he's mine. Funny, she didn't feel that way when dude cruised by in his Benz. She rubbed the back of her neck. Then took a step back. And smiled at dude's ass, making it clear she wanted his time. Not mine. Yeah, yeah. I'm just a friend. But last night she was bucking and sweating trying to wear a brotha out!

"Females. Sometimes I want to tell all of them to go straight to hell. But then I'd have to stroke my own ego and my own dick. So I've concluded it's best not to have expectations. Just kick it. Stick it. Penetration. But they won't let me be. Venting their frustrations. They want a commitment. At least that's what they say. When the shit is convenient for them. When they think I'm the best they can do. Then as soon as someone better comes along they wanna upgrade. But when the guy degrades her, then she wants to trade him in, for the brotha she claims was just her friend."

"Whoa, Dez. That's tight man. Look, I gotta deliver these beverages to SaVoy's daddy's store. Now if she wasn't so conservative and nice, I'd ride that sweet ass from the back all night long."

"Man, ask her out. That way you can kick it with SaVoy. I can kick it with Fancy. And we can hang out together since they're friends and we're friends; that'd be cool."

Tyronne instantly replied, "Forget it. I'd ruin that girl for life. I'll have her singing that Erykah Badu song about my ass. And Fancy? Man, fuck that fake gold-diggin' bitch. Friends, man. Just call all of 'em friends like they do us. Peace. I'm out."

Desmond continued sitting in his boss's office, thinking. Maybe Tyronne was right. About the friends part. But he was wrong about Fancy. Desmond slurped his soda, thinking about the girls he'd met. Recently he had stopped telling females the truth and started saying whatever he figured they wanted to hear. Especially Carlita.

Desmond reflected on when he'd met Carlita a year ago. Shortly after New Year's Eve. Shortly after Fancy had convinced him to spend more money than he wanted to attend an affair he didn't like. But he was in love with Fancy so it was worth it, he guessed. But two days ago Fancy had messed up big time. Desmond had a plan for Fancy. If she ever let him hit it, Fancy was going to fall in love with him. And when she did, well, he'd have to wait and see how he felt. He might pay her back. Twofold. For playing with his emotions.

It had been a year ago when Carlita had pulled into the driveway at his job on Martin Luther King Jr. Day and left her engine running. Luckily for her, Desmond had forgotten to borrow his boss's tools to tune up Fancy's car. Carlita looked good in those low-rider hip-hugging faded blue denims. Underneath her leather jacket she wore a black shiny T-shirt with a silver skyline image of San Francisco. Her perky nipples protruded, commanding his dick's attention.

"The shop is closed. But I can't leave a beautiful woman

like you in need. How can I help you?" Desmond remembered asking.

"Every time I turn off my car I have to get a jump to restart it." Her hair swayed to one side, releasing a fruity fragrance that lured him closer. Carlita had already lifted the hood and was bending over. Her booty formed cantaloupe-shaped imprints under her coat.

"Sounds like you may need a new battery. Let me check," Desmond had said.

Confirming his suspicions, he installed a used battery in Carlita's car. His tightwad boss would dock his pay if he'd given away a new heavy-duty battery. But he did give Carlita a used portable battery. "Keep this in your car at all times. That way if your battery ever dies again, you won't need to hook up to someone else's car. It's lightweight," he said, handing her the battery. "Hey, you wanna join me? I'm headed to the city for Dr. King's celebration in front of City Hall."

"Sure. Why not," Carlita said with the most alluring gaze and a kind of come-closer smile. He got in his Mustang, insisting she leave her sports utility vehicle at the shop. When he parked at MacArthur BART Station, Carlita waited for him to open her door. She swung her purse in one hand and his hand with the other. On the train, Carlita laid her head on his shoulder. Because they'd just met, Desmond resisted running his fingers through her hair, fearing she'd slap him upside the head or something.

In less than four hours Desmond had learned Carlita was off-the-chain funny. Sexy as hell. Had a big ole ass! Itty bitty titties. With a tiny waistline. Carlita was fine but she wasn't the one he wanted to marry or take home to his mama. Desmond had decided Carlita was just his friend.

Later he discovered Carlita could talk sports, shoot hoops, and cook! She had to cook for her four kids. Desmond didn't have anything against an older woman or a woman with children, but in this world of instant gratification and commercialization, Carlita needed to realize having a baby didn't guarantee she'd have a husband. Although she did come across as happy and content, Carlita had never been married. And Desmond didn't plan on adopting any woman's built-in family, so he knew she'd never become his wife. He wanted a family of his own. Maybe if Carlita had one kid, they could tie the knot. But four? Desmond couldn't get with that.

Carlita had her shit together, though. She didn't have to work because each of her almost grown and off to college kids' fathers paid four figures a month for child support. Carlita was in court so many times the judge knew her by her first name. She was quick to say, "I'm not looking for any handouts, I simply intend to give my children what they deserve. I didn't make 'em by myself and I'll be damned if I'm gon' raise 'em by myself."

Desmond went with Carlita to court a couple of times so he could learn what not to do whenever he did have kids. Carlita never lost a case and she gave her children all of what they needed and most of what they wanted. She owned her own home and she charged seventy-five dollars an hour, under the table, to help other females get paid for their kids and start their own businesses. Carlita prepared all the legal documents, and schooled her clients on what to wear. "Dress casual. Don't look too rich or too poor. And do not wear gaudy makeup or too much jewelry. Cry quietly but only if you think it'll help your case. Do not make a scene or curse out your baby's daddy in the courtroom."

One morning Carlita was on the docket four times. Took all them guys, lined them up, and got everything she wanted. So the lesson Desmond learned that day was women focused on the kids and men focused on the money and dumb stuff like what they thought the woman was doing with the child support. Well, that might not be dumb but it sure in the hell was insignificant. The judge didn't give a damn about those men complaining. In fact, the judge appeared annoyed whenever anyone didn't put the child's needs first.

When Desmond did marry, he wasn't getting a divorce. He was going to do it right the first time and take care of his wife and kid. Kids. Desmond would love for Fancy to have his son. Sons. And maybe one daughter. He wanted to fertilize three of her seeds. That's why he invested so much time in Fancy on New Year's Eve. New Year's Eve was all that until she cheated on him with dude. He had the finest woman up in that joint on his arm. It cost him, but hey, what was life if he couldn't splurge on his woman every once in a while?

He had a nice savings but was smart enough not to let Fancy or any other woman know. Desmond had saved one hundred dollars a week for several years without touching any of it. That money would help him get into law school one day. He shared a three-bedroom house in West Oakland that was always clean. Although Desmond barely saw his roommates, whether he was at home or away, he locked his bedroom door. And he kept his top shelf in the refrigerator stocked with the free sodas Tyronne gave him every weekend.

Desmond saved his money because he'd grown up poor. His mom and dad both worked hard to take care of him and his six siblings. Now that his folks were retired, they seldom went anywhere outside of Oakland. This year he'd planned to set aside extra cash so he could surprise his parents with a cruise to Alaska. He'd heard Alaska was beautiful and hoped one day to see for himself. Maybe he'd take Fancy to Alaska.

Desmond wondered whatever happened to the good old days. When a man was the king of his castle. Put food on the table. Kept a roof over his family's head. And his word was word. That's the kind of household he was raised in, back in Atlanta, Georgia. Moving to California was a shocker. California women weren't prettier than Georgia women, though. Georgia had some of the sweetest peaches he'd ever seen or tasted. Maybe he should consider moving back and hooking up with his high school sweetheart, Trina, since she still called him every week. California females had too many issues.

They hated the white girls, claiming they were taking all the black men. Desmond couldn't lie. White girls were more aggressive. But he liked them because they loved to have lots of fun and uninhibited sex. Desmond appreciated not having to impress white girls. They loved the real Desmond. They weren't trying to fix him up, hook him up, or tear him down. But sometimes, most of the times, he'd rather be with a sistah. They had a special kind of sexiness he couldn't explain, all their own. That was until the attitude kicked in, which was usually within the first five minutes. Maybe that was the appeal. Maybe sistahs' attitudes made them sexy.

If Desmond tried to holla at a sistah, she might holla back. As long as the white girl wasn't around. And as long as he wasn't in the faded blue cover-up jumpsuit he wore to work. Or wasn't riding his bike. Or wasn't on foot. Or if he wasn't standing at the bus stop. But that was okay with him because if she was at the bus stop, he didn't want to get with her either.

After Desmond told women where he worked, it never failed. They'd ask with disbelief, "If you're a mechanic, what are you doing riding the bus?" So a brotha can't help save the earth and conserve on gas? One sistah, seemed like her ass should've conserved gas and stopped eating so many beans or whatever the hell she'd eaten that caused her to pollute the air surrounding his three feet of space. Desmond could've played it off the way she did, rambling on, pretending her fart didn't stink, but why should he?

He said, "Damn, girl." She smiled and gave herself credit, thinking that was a compliment. Desmond wrote 1(800) exh-aust, the number Californians used to report automobiles polluting the air, on the back of his homemade business card and handed it to her. "Count to ten before you get on the bus!" She was pissed but he wasn't in the mood to put her emotions first. Women always expected that shit, too. Like a brotha didn't have needs above his waistline. It wasn't like he didn't have a ride. His car was clean. A custom-designed 1964 Mustang. Royal blue exterior. Light blue leather interior. Chrome rims. A real beauty. Just like Fancy.

CHAPTER 4

Fancy rolled over and stared at Desmond. Waking up with him was not what she'd planned, so Fancy eased out of bed, sat at her vanity, and began journaling a list of resolutions. First and foremost to lose the five pounds she'd gained munching at holiday parties, by the end of January. It was so easy for five pounds to turn into ten and ten to turn into twenty. Fancy knew firsthand because she was the chubbiest microwave-queen latchkey kid in her third grade class. And now that she was a perfect size seven, Fancy refused to be fat like her mother. When Caroline took a seat in a chair, her stomach took a seat in her lap. That grossed Fancy out so bad she did one thousand sit-ups every day: five hundred in the morning and the same before she went to sleep.

Fancy stood and tilted her chin. She scanned between her perky titties, past her pierced belly button, over her clipper-trimmed bush, down to her pedicure, and smiled.

Sitting back on the stool, Fancy penciled in goal number two: call Caroline once a week. For real this year. Most of the time, Fancy wrote with a pencil because she believed the only things that were certain and untimely were broke ugly men begging her for a date and death.

Third, was to find her a rich husband. Byron could become her new sponsor during their short-term engagement. Six months tops. Whew! Fancy tossed the gold lead-filled pen on the pad, then swiped her forehead with the back of her hand. That was enough commitments for the year.

Ding dong ding-dong. Ding dong ding-dong. The brass clock chimed, commanding her attention. Fancy glanced over, picking the sleep matter, mixed with leftover mascara, from the corners of her eyes. Seven o'clock. She glanced over her shoulder. Desmond drooled on her black silk pillowcase.

Fancy nudged his shoulder. "Dez, you need to get up, man. I've gotta go." That meant Desmond had to go, too. Fancy never allowed a man to stay in her apartment while she was away. Her appointment with Mandy, her psychologist, was in three hours and her New Year's lunch celebration with her girls, SaVoy and Tanya, was at noon.

"Damn, what time is it?" Desmond yawned and rolled onto his back while stretching his arms above his head.

Fancy squinted, then sang, "Hum, hum, hum, hum." She stared at Desmond without speaking a word.

Desmond's alluring eyes and broad smile softened her attitude, so Fancy gave him a half smile, kissed his dimple, and said, "Good morning, baby."

Desmond tossed back the covers. Fancy's eyes widened as Desmond's hard-on broke through the opening of his cotton boxers.

"Umm. Umm." Fancy cleared her throat, trying to conceal her approval. "Get up, Dez. For real. I gotta go." Fancy saw Desmond in a different light as the sun rays beamed through the vertical blinds, flickering across his slightly darker nipples that stood perfectly round atop his mushroomed muscular chest.

Last night Desmond nestled his head into her breasts, reciting his love poems: If You Only Knew, Mirage, and One Day.

> *One day*
> *In God's time*
> *I often pray*
> *This vision in my mind*
> *Will flourish within*
> *My lifetime*
> *Before I perish*
> *I cherish*
> *Each moment with you*
> *Old and new*
> *Funny and blue*
> *True I pray*
> *Every day*
> *You'll be mine*
> *One Day*
> *In God's time*

Desmond always ended each love poem with, "I love you, Fancy."

Fancy gazed out over the lake, remembering how good she felt stroking Desmond's hair until they fell asleep in one another's arms. She felt safe. Secure. She realized she was now lying beside Desmond, running her fingers through his untamed hair. Chestnut brown. Curly. Soft. Naturally soft. She swirled it around and around, creating a spiral loop.

"Happy New Year, Fancy. And happy birthday, too. This is going to be our year, girl. I can feel it!" Desmond wrapped his arm about her waist. New Year's Day had passed, right along with her birthday, but he was so upset about Byron. Fancy appreciated Desmond's acknowledgments and the fact that he'd never mentioned her slamming his car door.

She frowned, hoping Desmond wasn't about to break out into another one of his love poems. Fancy needed a strong, independent man. Not a man like Desmond who needed constant reassurance of her feelings. She stood, then grunted, "Umph! Umph! Umph!" Desmond's dick was pointed toward the ceiling. Fancy's toes dug into the carpet. As he stood and moved closer, her body trembled.

"I love you, Fancy."

Turning her head sideways to avoid getting a second whiff of his morning breath, Fancy casually responded, "I know, Dez."

The head of Desmond's stiff dick eased between the gap in her thighs, slid along her pubic hairs, down along her shaft, and pressed hard against her clit. Fancy took a deep breath.

"I want you," Desmond whispered in her ear, "to marry me. Be my wife."

The air inside Fancy's lungs escaped. She wasn't trying to start any bad habits or send Desmond any mixed signals. It was two days before her period and Desmond's dick was pulsating in synch with her throbbing pussy.

"Okay," Fancy lied, because she wanted to have sex. "I'll think about it *if* you apply *and* you are accepted into law school." Maybe she could help Desmond get serious about his resolution.

"For real. Damn! So you'll wear my ring." Desmond raced over and removed a small black velvet box from his denim pocket. The velvet wasn't rich and full. The sleek coating shone more than a pair of polyester pants that had been ironed on a cotton setting. Kneeling before her on one knee, he flipped the box open.

"Umph. Umph." Cupping her hand over her mouth, Fancy choked. That little bitty ass stone could hardly be considered a diamond. Some jeweler must have discovered a way to fuse two granules of sugar together and make them sparkle. Then that loser must have used the world's smallest tweezers to set it in sterling silver. Fancy turned and walked away, shaking her head in disbelief.

"I need to take a shower." Desmond had fucked up her hormones and he'd blown his first real chance to lick Miss Kitty. Fancy was all ready to wrap those lips men loved so much around Desmond's bulging head.

She removed a white washcloth and matching bath towel from the linen closet, sighed heavily, and said, "Just forget about it. I gotta go."

Fancy watched Desmond flop onto the bed, face-down. His ass sat higher than Tim Brown's of the Raiders. The silky dark hairs outlining the crack of Desmond's cheeks were so sexy Miss Kitty had become sad that she wasn't getting any dick. Fancy needed to cool off so she took a cold shower while listening to Jaheim's CD. What was Desmond thinking about when he bought that box of Cracker Jacks? Truly no reputable jeweler would make such a thing.

Fancy dried herself off. When she entered the bedroom, Desmond jumped up and said, "Some guy named Byron just called."

Shit! Why hadn't she turned off the ringer? Fancy bit her bottom lip, then asked, "What did you tell him?"

"That you were biz-zy." Desmond smiled, swinging his dick. Perhaps so Fancy could see what he insinuated was occupying her time or what she was missing. The definition in his abs leading down toward his crotch disappeared behind his dark pubic forest.

Fancy grabbed the handset, scrolled her caller ID, then sat on the foot of her bed and hit the dial button. "Hey, Byron. It's me, Fancy. You called?" She impatiently waited for a response. "Hello?"

"Yeah, who was that who answered your phone?" Byron questioned, then said, "I thought you lived alone."

"I do. That was just Dez," Fancy said, laughing. "He's just a friend. So, what's up?"

"I called to see if you're free next Friday night. Say around six," Byron said.

Available? Yes. Free? Never. Honey, Fancy worked to get paid. The only people who worked for free were volunteers. And Fancy Taylor wasn't volunteering Miss Kitty for no damn body. "Maybe I'm *available*. What'd you have in mind?" She casually responded, trying not to sound anxious.

"My company is hosting a fund-raiser. You looked so beautiful the other night when we met. I'd love to have you on my arm."

"Hold on. Let me check my calendar." Fancy moved the phone away from her ear and counted to fifteen. She watched Desmond disappear into the bathroom. "I did have a commitment but I can clear my calendar." That meant she'd have to reschedule her date with Steven, but Byron was an investment, so she'd squeeze him in.

"Great, I'll have my driver phone you on Monday to get your particulars. See you Friday. Oh, yeah. Wear something provocative. And don't bring any of your *friends*." Byron hung up the phone.

Obviously he didn't know Fancy very well. She always dressed provocative. When Fancy placed the handset on the base, Desmond walked out of the bathroom, then stood before her dripping wet. She couldn't determine which hung lower, his jaw or his now limp dick.

"Who was dude?" Desmond questioned, as if he were the man of her house.

"Oh, he's just a friend." Fancy shook her head and said, "You don't know him. Dez, where are your clothes? I told you—"

Desmond wedged his tongue between Fancy's lips, then said, "Better not be that loser from New Year's

Eve." Desmond picked up Fancy like she weighed thirty-five pounds instead of one hundred and thirty-five pounds and sat her on his lap as he took her seat on the edge of the bed. He hugged her waist, burying his face in her breasts. The heat exhaling from his nostrils warmed Fancy's breasts. They sat in silence as Desmond's chest rapidly rose and fell with each breath. Fancy positioned her hands on the side of his head, guiding his lips a short distance over to her protruding nipple.

Desmond bit, sucked, then mumbled with his mouth full, "Fancy, what do you want from me?"

Fancy's body shivered with anticipated pleasure. This was not the appropriate time for questioning. So she softly said, "Dez, you're the only true male friend I have. I don't want us to ruin our friendship by getting too serious." Desmond really was her only reliable male friend. "Besides, it's impolite to speak with your mouth full."

Before Desmond could say another word Fancy stuffed as much of her breast as she could into his warm mouth. First the right titty, then the left one. Fancy was so wet the moisture saturated her inner thighs.

Desmond must have felt it too because he picked her up and laid her atop the sheets and worked his mouth from her toes to her clit, up to her lips and back down to Miss Kitty. His tongue wiggled down her shaft. Fancy tried opening her legs but he immediately closed them. Desmond buried his face in Fancy's crotch, inhaled deeply, then began thrusting and flicking his tongue between her pubic hairs to the tip of her clit. Fancy trembled. Her entire body tingled. Just when she was about to cum, Desmond spread her legs and began fucking Fancy so good her eyes widened, then rolled backward and started watering. Her hips joined in his motion.

"Bring her all the way to me and don't move. Let me control this girl," Desmond whispered as he sat on his heels of his feet. The back of Fancy's head rested on the mattress like the bottom of a seesaw while Desmond leveled her hips with his.

Fancy shouted, "Damn you! Damn you! Please, Dez. Stop. Damn you. Stop! Please!" But Desmond ignored her pleas.

Fancy came again and again. Desmond switched positions, kissing, licking, and sucking Miss Kitty. Fancy's juices flowed continuously. After her fourth orgasm or so she started crying and couldn't stop.

Fancy wasn't sure she wanted Desmond to stop but she knew she couldn't take much more. Just when she thought he was through, he rolled her over flat onto her stomach and entered her from behind.

"Dammit! Dez." How did he know that was her favorite position?

First Desmond moved slow. Then fast. Then slow again. And then faster. Fancy came so hard she screamed, "Ooooooooooo!" in between yelling, "Yes! Fuck me, Daddy!" several times. If her neighbors weren't awake, they must have been now. After she tapered her yelling, Desmond French kissed the back of her neck, eased his hands underneath her body, and softly caressed her breasts. She felt his erection subsiding but he didn't pull out.

Fancy decided it was time for her to get on top when she heard, *Ding dong ding-dong. Ding dong ding-dong.*

"Shit!" Miss Kitty ejected Desmond's slippery dick. Fancy pushed him back and jumped out the bed, stumbling toward the clock. She had exactly forty-two minutes to shower, get dressed, and make it to Mandy's office in Berkeley. Desmond was the first man to really make love to every part of her body, and although she felt herself falling in love with him, Desmond would never know the truth.

CHAPTER 5

Barely making it to Mandy's in time for her morning appointment, Fancy parked at a meter on University Avenue. Jamming a plastic coin into the slot, she tied a Safeway grocery bag over the meter, pulled out her black marker, and wrote BROKEN in bold letters.

"Hi, Miss Diva," the receptionist said. "Go on in. Mandy's ready for you."

Fancy took her usual seat on the blue leather sofa and placed her mink coat beside her. Mandy swiveled in her high-back chair to face Fancy. Mandy's auburn hair was short and tapered to her head. The neatly trimmed edges reflected her orderly demeanor. Fancy wondered if Mandy had issues, too. Maybe she saw a psychologist on her day off. The tinted frameless eyeglasses which Mandy seldom looked through, always over, were classy but Fancy hated how her small round eyes pierced straight through her each time Mandy asked a question. She spoke soft and deliberate, pronouncing every syllable.

"So, what're your resolutions for this year? Prioritize them for me, Fancy." Mandy didn't waste any of Fancy's minutes with small talk or personal greetings.

Mandy remained silent. Before Fancy spoke, Mandy's Mont Blanc pen scrolled along the legal size pad.

Fancy quickly juggled the list in her head. She exhaled and began speaking. "Finding the right man is first. Since I already look good, I can make losing five pounds my second priority. . . . And last is Caroline 'cause she probably don't want me bothering her no way."

Mandy's slender hips hardly covered the leather seat. Her waist and breasts were disproportionately larger than her hips, but overall, Mandy was a small woman. Five foot one inch at best. Maybe one hundred pounds.

"I see," Mandy said, pressing the pen above her chocolate-painted lips. Then she rolled forward and handed Fancy a used sheet of loose-leaf paper. Before Fancy touched the paper she recognized it was her list of resolutions from last year with Caroline pulling up the rear.

"So. What's this for? Last year is history," Fancy said, dodging Mandy's reproaching brown eyes that sat deep below her neatly plucked brows. Fancy folded the paper and placed it on the sofa between her coat and thigh.

"Just thought it might help. So you think putting your mother last all the time will somehow help you to escape or forget how she's neglected you. Deserted you." Mandy paused and started writing.

Fancy picked a spot on the floral wallpaper and stared at a row of unaligned gardenias. Nervous energy stirred in the pit of her stomach whenever she talked about Caroline, so Fancy thought about Desmond. Fancy had no idea Desmond was such a great lover. Maybe she could change him. Help him to make more money. *Naw, forget that thought.* Desmond was happy working on cars. He wasn't serious about going to law school.

"Don't you see a pattern here?" Mandy asked, interrupting the one-on-none conversation in Fancy's head. "Do you love your mother?"

"Why do you keep asking me that!" Fancy crossed her legs and folded her arms. "Of course I love Caroline, but I hate her too! There's a part of me that wants to be her baby and another part that's sorry I'm her child. How come she can't see I need her? To hold me. Hug me." Fancy hugged herself and lowered her voice just above a whisper, "To tell me she loves me." Fancy closed her eyes to lock in the tears. Somehow they managed to escape down her cheeks into the corners of mouth.

Fancy helped herself to a Kleenex from a box on the end table beside her. "Why do I have to be her mother? I cleaned up her mess after she'd vomit all over her bed at night. She was always drunk! Sometimes I wish I was never born!" Fancy dried her tears only to make room for the fresh stream that immediately followed. She'd contemplated suicide several times but wouldn't dare tell Mandy. If Fancy killed herself, at least that would be the last time she'd suffer.

"I was the one who cooked for her. Made her bed. Washed her clothes. And literally washed her ass when she was hungover and couldn't get out the fucking bed to go buy groceries! I lived off frozen dinners and junk food! And I still can't cook!"

Fancy forced back the welling tears and said, "Mandy, I hate when you make me go down this road because you always leave me hanging! Now I'm supposed to find my own solution! To a problem I didn't even create! Bump that." Fancy uncrossed her legs and rocked back and forth because that's what she did when she was upset or nervous but didn't know what she was going to do or say next. Her stomach ached. Fancy wanted to break something. Hit something. Anything!

Mandy spoke softly again, "So getting married and having children of your own will help you to . . . what?" Mandy's perfectly set teeth, that almost looked too enormous for her mouth, were aligned with clear braces.

"Have somebody to love me!" Fancy said, jabbing her finger into her chest. Her throat started hurting so she lowered her voice. "And for me to love."

"You're twenty-two and you haven't taken time to love yourself. Is marriage what you really want?" Mandy's eyelids froze as she stared at Fancy.

"I thought we were discussing my goals not questioning my motive. Of course I want to get married."

"What about Desmond?" Mandy asked. "He seems to care about you."

Again Fancy avoided Mandy's eyes, this time gazing out the window only to see another window across the street. "What about him?" Fancy stopped rocking and folded her arms high across her chest.

"Based upon what you've told me, seems as though he cares a lot about you," Mandy said, then scribbled on her pad again.

"Desmond is just my friend. F-R-I-E-N-D," Fancy enunciated each letter.

Mandy stood and handed Fancy a rose from the blue vase. "Happy belated birthday, Fancy. Okay, well, that concludes our session for today."

Fancy felt the tension in Mandy's exhale but didn't hear a sigh. Sniffing the rose, Fancy gathered her coat and purse, and stood. "I'll call to schedule my next appoint."

Fancy strolled past the receptionist, out the door, and trotted across University. She slammed the rose on the concrete, then crushed the red petals beneath her tan suede knee-high boot. Removing the plastic bag from the meter, Fancy hopped in her car and headed to Café Zula in San Leandro. Maybe she'd stop coming to Mandy for a while like she had last year. She hadn't seen Mandy in almost four months and she was doing fine without her advice. *What advice?* Fancy thought.

Fancy parked at a meter behind SaVoy's platinum-colored sports utility vehicle and made her grand entrance, stepping into the restaurant like she was on time. A host Fancy hadn't seen before escorted her to the table. He glanced at SaVoy, then stared at Fancy and said, "You were definitely worth the wait if I must say so myself." Then he turned to SaVoy and said, "Miss, thank you for waiting."

SaVoy and Tanya were seated at their usual table in front of the huge Anthony Scott lifelike painting of a black woman in a white dress lounging on green pastures. Fancy always sat with her back toward the woman. The painting was beautiful but the woman felt so real Fancy wanted to order her something to eat.

"Girl, did you see how he was eyeing me like I was on his menu?" Fancy commented, not the least bit interested. He was just a host. Now the owner and chef, Leonard, if he didn't have a wife and kids, Fancy would've invited him over and given him a premier performance of a new dance. Leonard prepared the best Creole jambalaya, gumbo, and catfish. Not to mention the peach cobbler, bread pudding, and homemade pound cake. Leonard even served chitterlings but he wouldn't have to cook that at home for her because Fancy didn't eat pork.

Tanya laughed in agreement with Fancy, then said, "Yeah, yeah. I saw him staring at you, girl."

But not SaVoy. She probably liked him and thought Fancy wanted him. Fancy couldn't help it that men were drawn to her magnetic personality. Fancy decided SaVoy could have him. "SaVoy, you should get his number, girl. Want me to get it for you?"

"You can get it for me," Tanya said, laughing again.

Tanya was short and wide like a Weeble, and she wobbled when she walked. Her fingers were stubby and chunky. And that worn out ponytail she kept attaching to the back of her head was tacky and SaVoy knew it too but wouldn't admit it. Fancy didn't mind hanging out with Tanya because any man worth having would never show interest in Tanya. SaVoy was a different kind of competition, but Fancy's outspoken personality gave her an advantage over SaVoy.

Fancy shook her head in Tanya's direction. "Naw, he's not your type."

SaVoy casually asked, "How was your session with Mandy this morning?"

Fancy smiled because Leonard was greeting a guest at the table next to them. Whenever a man was interested in Fancy, SaVoy always changed the subject.

"It was cool," Fancy replied, then gave her girlfriends a synopsis of her New Year's resolutions.

"Why do you keep leaving out going to church?" SaVoy asked, but kept talking before Fancy could answer. "Come go with us"——she motioned toward Tanya, then continued——"and my dad this Sunday."

Fancy's eyes darted around the room like a bullet ricocheting off of the chandelier, to the long-stemmed flute in front of her, over to the stem of farm-grown cotton propped in a crystal vase on the adjacent table. Fancy could have looked at the cotton on their own table but it was too close. She wondered, if there truly was a God, why did He let those awful things happen to her as child? She used to pray when she was a child, but after she didn't get any answers, one night, over twelve years ago, Fancy stopped believing in God. The thought of going to church made Fancy feel the preacher would single her out. Fornication. *Fancy, that's a sin.* Adultery. *Fancy, that's a sin.* Coveting thy neighbor's ox or his ass . . . *Fancy, that's a sin, too.* Whew! "No thanks. I'll pass," Fancy said, because she was certain she'd committed every sex-related sin in the Bible and created a few new ones probably on a list awaiting entry into some revised New Testament.

"We ain't playin' Scrabble, girl. You'll end up in church sooner or later. God's only going to let you pass but so many times. Then——"

Tanya nodded in agreement with SaVoy, then blurted, "I'm hungry."

Tanya's mind always seemed to be off the subject but this time Fancy was glad. Plus, she knew SaVoy was telling the truth but she still didn't want to hear it. Tanya had recently started going to church with SaVoy.

Fancy looked at Tanya and said, "Girl, you need to start lifting weights with me and stop arm curling the silverware." Fancy curled the fork in one hand and the knife in the other and grunted, "Uuuhuh!"

SaVoy slapped Fancy's wrist. "Leave Tanya alone, Fancy. She's beautiful."

Tanya smiled at Fancy.

Yeah? Whatever. Not really. Tanya could look a lot better, but never as good as her. Fancy thought about giving them the lowdown on Desmond but opted not to because SaVoy would probably sprinkle her with the blessed Holy water she kept in her purse. Especially if Fancy had told them that after she slapped a non-spermicidal condom on Desmond's dick, she let him hit it in the rear. Fancy stopped using those spermicidal condoms after she'd read somewhere that they might promote the contraction of sexually transmitted diseases, including HIV and possibly interfere with her ability to have a baby.

Why couldn't Desmond have Byron's money and charisma? "I'll have my driver call and get your particulars." Fancy loved that shit!

"What particulars?" Tanya asked, interrupting Fancy's thoughts.

"Oh, I didn't realize I was talking out loud. But since you asked, I met a new man—Byron—at the gala the other night and he's having his driver pick me up Friday night."

SaVoy frowned and said, "You mean the gala Desmond spent all that money—"

The host walked over, handed SaVoy his business card and said, "Excuse me for interrupting, but I'm getting ready to leave. Call me. I'd love to take you out sometime."

Fancy looked at SaVoy and quickly changed the subject. "I told you I didn't want him. Girl, I can't cum off that income. And since you ain't seeing nobody and all, you should kick it with that brotha. Y'all were made for one another. Besides, what you savin' yourself for?"

"That's because I have something called *morals* and *standards*. And did you ever stop to think maybe he was *never* interested in you?"

"Oh, that's right. You're saving yourself for Tyronne. Girl, you can forget about him. Tyronne's allergic to virgins."

Miss wanna be perfect. SaVoy wasn't all that. Just because she looked damn near white with that straight ass hair, her daddy's was blacker than Wesley Snipes. Her 'papa' probably wasn't her real daddy. And SaVoy had issues, too, not knowing her mother at all.

Fancy tapped the knife and fork lying on the table. "Don't be jealous." She stood, twitched her hips, and said, "Don't hate. It's called 'pimp juice,' baby. I got that." Fancy winked at SaVoy as SaVoy shook her head.

On her way to the rest room, Fancy smiled, resenting SaVoy because her father spoiled her and Fancy had often heard him tell SaVoy, "I love you." Fancy longed for the day, any day, that she would hear Caroline speak those three words to her.

CHAPTER 6

Fancy scurried about her apartment trying to remember where she'd placed her ruby earring. Damn, she'd only removed it for a moment when she answered the phone. *Okay Fancy, backtrack. You were in your office on the computer when Adam phoned to confirm he'd be here at midnight, and then you raced to the bed. You sat on the love seat in the bedroom, and then lay across the bed. No, you shut down the computer, then went back and lay across the bed.* Thank goodness Fancy had found her earring next to her laptop.

Fastening her red leather swing coat, Fancy casually walked outside. A tall muscular Latino man stood next to a spotless Town Car sucking on a cigarette so hard that his lips caved into his mouth. Then he flicked the butt into the bushes and opened the rear door.

Fancy threw up her hand and yelled, "Hey! What are you doing? Trying to burn down my place!"

"Good evening, Ms. Taylor. You look lovely," he politely responded, waiting for her to settle into the backseat.

"Gracious! It's colder in here than it is outside!" Fancy complained, squirming on the cold leather seat.

She was still pissed about the cigarette but refused to mention it to his inconsiderate ass again.

"I've been instructed to drop you off at the restaurant. Mr. Van Lee would like to have an early dinner," the driver said as he adjusted the digital thermostat from sixty to seventy degrees.

"What restaurant?" Fancy asked, smiling.

The driver remained silent. He must have had selective hearing.

Whatever. "Sure, that's fine." Getting angry with the driver wasn't worth her time or energy. If Fancy didn't adjust her mood before she saw Byron, her face would become grimaced and make her look as though she were mad. That was definitely why whatever-his-name-was was a driver. Yeah, every day he probably calculated the number of days left before his retirement and where he'd have to work after he retired so he could continue living his low budget lifestyle.

Fancy grinned, then closed her eyes, trying to recall how Byron looked. Hopefully, he was as handsome as she remembered the night they met. What if she'd had too much to drink that night and Byron was ugly? Well, at least he had money and one of the most seductive voices she'd heard over the telephone. Fancy glanced in the driver's rearview mirror and smiled at herself. The weekly facial she received from De La Peau Day Spa on Park Boulevard kept her dark skin radiant.

An early dinner with Byron was fine but a late night out wasn't happening. Not tonight. Fancy tried keeping her mind occupied with anything except the fact that after her date with Byron she had to service her main sponsor. She'd have to make it home no later than eleven to prepare for Adam. Her rent was due Monday and the nosy landlady loved having a legitimate reason to eavesdrop outside Fancy's door. Working for Harry's property management firm was a benefit because prior to receiving Harry's signature, Fancy reviewed all of the late and eviction notices so she knew her legal rights as a tenant.

The driver picked up his cellular, pressed one button, and said, "Mr. Van Lee. We're right out front."

No way. The same place they'd met. She'd always wanted to dine at the Ritz Carlton's dining room. While shopping in the nearby area, she'd seen limousines line up outside the hotel. Fancy's smile grew wider and wider.

Byron greeted her at the entrance with white roses wrapped in cellophane. "Hey, you. You look marvelous. I hope you don't mind the detour. I'm famished." Byron's lips pressed against her cheek. Fancy's Chai-colored glossy lips puckered in the air.

"Not at all. I could stand to eat a little something myself," Fancy lied because she hadn't told Byron she didn't eat after six o'clock. Drinking unsweetened prune juice before noon and after six was how Fancy kept her system clean, her metabolism high, and her body fat low. Alcohol was her weakness, so if she drank the night before she had to work out an extra hour the next morning to burn off the extra calories.

"What? What are smiling about?" Byron asked, smiling back at her.

"You are even more handsome than I remembered. Thanks for the flowers."

The maître d' paraded by each table swiftly perusing each one. He seated them at a round linen-covered table with two high-backed old-fashioned chairs. "Your server will be with you shortly, Mr. Van Lee."

By the time the maître d' turned, a waiter dressed in a black tuxedo had arrived at their table. "Would you like the usual, Mr. Van Lee?"

Fancy frowned. That was rude. Why didn't he ask her first?

Byron looked at her and said, "Is everything okay? You look worried."

Raising her eyebrows to release the tension Fancy said, "No, I'm fine. I was just wondering where I'd seen a replica of the painting in the lobby before. That's all."

"The usual is fine," Byron replied. The waiter placed white linen napkins across their laps, then raced off.

The usual. Hum, Fancy thought, looking at Byron's diamond cufflinks. Obviously he'd recently had a facial, too. When Fancy visited her hair stylist, Raeshelle, at Top Notch, she noticed more men came in for services than women—in-grown hair treatments, facials, and manicures. Byron's thick eyebrows were no longer connected. Gazing at the back of his hairy hands, Fancy wondered if Byron had a hairy chest and thighs.

"You look beautiful," Byron said

Fancy certainly hoped so. She'd taken the day off. Had a massage. Manicure. Pedicure. And she'd had her weave tightened, all sponsored by Steven.

"So what did you do today besides miss me," Fancy crooned.

Byron tugged at his tie and stretched his neck. "Miss you? You must have me confused—"

"Come closer. Let me do that for you." Gently, Fancy placed her hand underneath his tie and loosened the knot until he exhaled. Then she unfastened his top button.

"Nice touch," Byron said, holding and kissing the back of her hand. "So tell me about Fancy. What type of work do you do? Are you in school? What are your hobbies?"

Fancy never disclosed more information than she received. He didn't need to know her life history but Fancy needed to know his. "I work here in the Financial District. I'm not in school but I'm always learning." Fancy smiled. "Oh, yeah. And I enjoy physical and mental challenges. How's that?"

Byron smiled while shaking his head.

Before he could ask another question, Fancy asked, "So, how about you? Are you married?"

"Actually, I'm happily single. Thirty going on thirty-one. *Never* married. Would love to have two kids, a boy and a girl, but I hardly have time for myself." His roaming brown eyes traveled from Fancy's face down to her cleavage and back to her luscious lips. Then he added, "And so far I like what I see, Ms. Taylor."

While Byron slowly traced the lifeline inside her palm with his manicured fingers, a different waiter in the same style tuxedo placed small salads before them.

"I always order roughage. I hope you don't mind." Byron immediately started eating the mixed leafy greens.

"Not at all." Hopefully Byron wasn't a control fanatic. One thing Fancy did not like was an inconsiderate man.

"So tonight I need you to greet my guests with a smile," he mumbled while chewing. "And charm them into making large donations. No man can resist your beauty. I know I can't." Byron swallowed, sipped his wine, then smiled.

She guessed that meant her breasts because that's exactly where his eyes were focused, again. "What exactly are these donations for?"

Munching on the freshly baked bread he said, "Lobbyist."

"Lobbyist?" Fancy reached for her half-full wineglass.

"Absolutely. Every major organization needs people willing to support their cause. I happen to own a company that dumps toxic waste. We have to have a place to dump *and* we need prior government approval. Unfortunately, there are activists who oppose every site we propose so my company pays lobbyists to represent us on Capitol Hill. Got it?"

"That's interesting. Yeah, I do get it." If lobbyists received all-expenses paid trips to D.C., Fancy wanted to represent Byron's company. Hopefully, being his wife wouldn't be a conflict of interest. Fancy didn't think Byron noticed or cared that she hadn't touched her food. She chose to sip on the merlot instead since she'd be sharpening her skills, pippin' rich men all night.

"So how's a woman like myself to benefit from such an ordeal?"

"Five percent," Byron said, right before swishing a gulp of wine inside his mouth.

Fancy felt her eyebrow raise a notch. "Of what?" she casually asked.

Byron swallowed, then said, "Everything *you* collect."

Shit, Adam could fuck himself tonight.

"After the checks clear, my accountant will send you a check. Usually within ten business days."

Damn, her rent was due in two days. Fancy didn't want to sound desperate so she chilled until it was time to head to the fund-raiser. Adam was off and back on her schedule in less than sixty seconds.

They finished eating, then rode less than a mile to another hotel. Byron educated Fancy on how to approach each potential donor.

"If he's shorter than you, the three-three rule applies. Compliment him three times in the first three minutes, then stop. Do not shake his hand. Now, if he's taller than you, shake his hand. Hold it for six seconds, then cover the top of his hand with your left hand and hold it there for nine seconds. That's the six-nine rule. Always get the pledge commitment within five minutes. Anyone who stalls longer than five minutes is only interested in you and the only thing he'll commit to if you keep talking is a date. Regardless if he's interested in contributing or not, fill out the form for him, then ask him to pledge an amount and sign the card. Always get the signature. A pledge is no good without a signature. If he keeps talking and never looks at the card, tell him you'll be back and move on. Got it?"

Fancy's smile widened. "Yeah. I've got it."

Fancy propositioned one guy so well he offered to take her to China. She wasn't interested in seeing China but she did take his business card. In fact, she collected quite a few cards. The next guy she met was taller.

"Hi, I'm Fancy Taylor." Fancy extended her hand. "And you are?"

He had the sexiest half smile Fancy had witnessed all night. "If you don't know who I am, you'd better ask somebody."

With locks covering the back of his neck, Fancy doubted he was anyone worth knowing.

A pale-complexioned female with hair flowing almost to her butt shook Fancy's hand and said, "Don't pay him any attention. He's always that way." Then she handed Fancy a check for seventy-five grand. The man started scanning the room when the woman who had just handed Fancy the check tapped him on the shoulder. "This is Darius Jones and my name is Ashlee Anderson."

Fancy looked at her and smiled, trying not to choke. Couldn't be. That couldn't possibly be him. Fancy quickly responded to Darius, "Excuse me. Do you have a card?"

He looked down at Fancy and replied, "I'm highly visible but hardly accessible. I don't even carry ID."

Darius walked over to Byron and a small group of men. The other men damn near bowed to Darius, greeting him with wide smiles, handshakes, and pats on the back. Ashlee gave a sort of toot-a-loo grin and walked over to a group of women who started kissing up to her.

Damn, his ass was arrogant and fine. Fancy's heart raced faster than her thoughts, wondering how she could get him to notice her the way she wanted him to. Fancy was amazed and perplexed at the same time. "Thanks for your generous contribution," she whispered.

Was that woman his wife? She wasn't wearing a ring.

Fancy walked over to a different group of men and listened to them ramble on about politics. Across the room she watched Darius closely, studying his confident mannerisms.

Byron eased beside her and whispered in Fancy's ear, "Don't even think about using those numbers. You're mine."

Fancy smiled as her heart throbbed, not for Byron, but she was no man's fool. Fancy always had backup. If Byron didn't screw up like all the rest, he had nothing to worry about. Except, Darius. Fancy decided at that moment, she would meet Mr. Jones again under more favorable circumstances.

At the end of the night, Fancy couldn't believe she'd collected almost five hundred thousand dollars. That meant she had earned nearly twenty-five thousand dollars in one night. Damn. A few gigs a year like that one and Adam, Tony, and Steven could fuck each other.

"You did well," Byron said. "So well, I want to take you to my place and celebrate."

"I'd love to but not tonight."

"Why not?"

"I have to get up early." Fancy lied, then said, "I promised my mother I'd go with her to Cache Creek. She loves that casino."

"Well, tell your mother I said gambling is wasting money on someone else's dream. Never gamble. Always invest. Remember that. Like you. You're an investment." Byron kissed Fancy on the cheek. "I'll have my driver take you home. I'll call you next week."

Yeah, hopefully about her check. Fancy smiled and kissed Byron on the cheek, close to his ear. She kissed square on the jaw when it was innocent. She kissed close to the ear or lips when she wanted to send sexual undertones. At the moment her clit was riding her thong like a jockey on a racehorse.

Darius walked by with Ashlee, patted Byron on the shoulder, and said, "See ya at the crib in a few, man."

Damn. She couldn't change her mind without being obvious. The ride back to her place was a blur.

Shaking her from her thoughts the driver announced, "You're home, Ms. Taylor." Fancy glanced around the neighborhood and noticed Adam's car parked across the street. She hurried to her door pretending she hadn't noticed him since the driver waited for her to get inside. Adam banged on the door.

She jumped like he'd startled her. "Damn! What's up with the banging?" Fancy asked, letting him in.

"Who was that? Why are you dressed up?" Adam asked.

Fancy wiggled her naked ring finger in front of his face, then unlocked the door. Adam proved having money didn't always make the man. Although he owned a construction company, Adam often spent more hours on his job sites than his employees.

Fancy laid out the bath towels. Adam knew the routine. He showered. She showered and lotioned her body and slipped into her lingerie.

Leaning back on the down-feather pillows, she ran her hands over her feet. Adam shifted his eyes to the corner of his sockets and eyed her silver pole. Not tonight. In fact, not ever again. This was a new year and Fancy wasn't starting any unwanted habits. She softly scratched her inner thighs. Her body tingled. She parted her legs. Inserted her finger into her vagina. Tasted herself. Imagining she was fucking Darius, Fancy repeated the motion several times. Before turning on her vibrator, she let Adam suck her fingers. Fancy inserted the humming tip at the mouth of her vagina as Adam sucked the juices from her clit. Adam took control of the vibrator and massaged her G spot.

Fancy rotated her hips and moaned, "Oh, Adam. I want you. I want you to fuck me. Fuck your pussy, Adam." For a moment, Fancy's mind was like a puppet performing for a ventriloquist. Empty. She performed his song, "Adam. Adam. Oh, Adam," as she ripped open Adam's pants. Sat on his lap. Straddled him. Moved up and down on his dick now mimicking a puppet on a string. She glanced over at her clock. Adam would finish in about fifteen more minutes but five minutes would be better so Fancy said, "I've been a bad girl, Daddy! Spank me! Spank me until I cum all over your big hard dick." Adam's dick wasn't nearly as big as his wallet. Each time Adam's hand landed on her ass Fancy jumped and yelled, "Yes, Daddy!"

Please hurry up and handle your business so I can go to sleep, Fancy thought, but her lips said, "Oh, baby, you feel so good I can't stop cumming. You're the best big daddy." Fancy moaned his name again. She grabbed the headboard and slammed her ass into Adam's pelvis. Fancy switched positions. She mounted Adam and rode him fast, pressing and curving her shoulders, waist, and hips into every movement. "What's my name!" she yelled, grinding harder. *Cum on! Hurry up!* Fancy bounced on his dick. *Hurry—the—fuck—up!* Fancy worked up a sweat. She worked Adam as fast as she could until he'd exhausted each of his three condoms. Pretending Adam had worn her out, Fancy collapsed on her bed.

Adam showered, then placed twenty one hundred dollar bills on her dresser. He kissed her forehead and said, "I love you, woman." Fancy didn't move, so Adam stumbled up several stairs into her foyer and out her front door.

Fancy grabbed the yellow Lysol can and began fumigating her room. She opened her patio window. Showered. Pampered herself with body oils and lotions. She sat on her vanity stool, tilted the mirror, and checked Miss Kitty. All was well—no irritations, redness, or swelling or abnormal discharge—so she snuggled under her covers, and gazed at the lake, fantasizing about Darius Jones until she fell asleep.

CHAPTER 7

SaVoy Edmonds best described herself in two words: Daddy's girl. For two reasons: one, unlike some people who didn't know their father, SaVoy never knew her mother. Secondly, she loved how her father spoiled her. Any man who wouldn't treat SaVoy equal to or better than the way her father did would never share her heart, her mind, or her body.

SaVoy worked part-time cashiering at her daddy's grocery store, and went to church every Sunday. Well, almost every Sunday. Most guys who knew she was a virgin practically auditioned to be her first lover, especially the ones at church. They couldn't figure out why she was so happy about celibacy. But SaVoy read straight through them. They weren't interested in her. They merely wanted bragging rights to pronounce their conquest.

Glad it was Wednesday and almost time for Tyronne to deliver her order, SaVoy smiled at the neighborhood regular customer when he walked up to her cash register with a bag of potato chips and an orange soda.

SaVoy opened her hand and said, "That'll be two dollars and ten cents."

He unfolded a roll of two twenties that covered about

forty one-dollar bills. As he placed three singles in her palm he held on to SaVoy's hand.

SaVoy frowned and pulled away. "Don't do that."

"Let a broth holla."

"Why should I?"

He licked his lips and replied, " 'Cause you look good. That's why."

"You think so?" SaVoy said, dropping his change in his hand.

He smiled and said, "Fo sho," chasing her hand's every move.

"Why?" SaVoy asked, knowing she wasn't interested but curious to hear what he'd say. James wasn't her type. He didn't have a job. Wasn't looking for a job. Always had lots of cash and he still lived at home with his mother.

He kept smiling and replied, " 'Cause you get it from your mama? Hell, I don't know, girl. So you gon' give me the digits or what?"

SaVoy drew a letter C followed by a down stroke and ended with a period. He walked away singing his usual tune. " 'I'm gonna make you love me. Oh, yes I am . . .' "

SaVoy didn't feel she was better than him or anyone else. She enjoyed trying to outthink everyone. Thinking was something SaVoy believed not enough people did. At least not very well.

Someday she'd meet a guy who was down to earth and down with her. SaVoy wanted to marry a black man who loved her. Not the facts that she looked white and was still a virgin. She loved black men. The way they sagged their pants. The way they dipped one hip lower than the other while walking. The way they articulated their words and wove slang throughout their sentences. She found most young black men were sharp. Intelligent. They could talk politics, sports, and play her favorite video games. SaVoy could beat any guy's butt when it came to playing Madden football. With the Rams as her team

she seldom lost a game. Papa had bought her the net-
work adapter and ordered DSL so she could whip her
opponents on-line from the convenience of their family
room big screen TV.

The hum of Tyronne's truck engine shutting off
commanded her attention. SaVoy leaned over her counter
and watched him unload six of the ten cases of sodas
she'd ordered. He'd have to make a second trip for the
remaining cases.

"Hey, you. What's up?" Tyronne asked, opening the
cooler.

SaVoy especially enjoyed whenever Tyronne stopped
by the store to "shoot the shit," as he said. If he agreed
with her he'd nod real slow and say, "Jeah," instead of
yeah. Or if he asked her a question, and she responded
incorrectly, Tyronne would say, "You're fired!" and then
he'd place his hand flat in front her face with his fingers spread wide apart. SaVoy intentionally got fired at
least once a week.

"Nothing much. Just studying." One more semester
at San Francisco State University and SaVoy would complete her bachelor of arts courses.

Tyronne would be gentle. SaVoy could tell by watching how meticulously he stocked each soda, rhythmi-
cally twisting all the labels face out. His head bobbed
like a song was playing inside. It didn't matter that
Tyronne hadn't been to college. Tyronne had dreams.
Big dreams! They sometimes dreamed together. He had
an honest job so SaVoy made sure every week she
placed an order with his company. And on his delivery
day she insisted on working alone at the store.

Tyronne closed the cooler, rolled his dolly over to
her register, and said, "You're fired!"

"Why?" SaVoy asked, not caring. "I didn't even do
anything." Tyronne had no idea how many times she'd
wanted to kiss his hand. His lips. Ears. Neck. Tyronne
aroused things inside her she'd never felt. Her nipples

tingled. Her stomach churned. Her heart palpitated at the sound of his deep penetrating voice. Although SaVoy didn't know much about sex, she felt like sexing Tyronne.

"Because your backpack is on the floor and it's closed. So you can't possibly be studying, woman."

As Tyronne walked away SaVoy thought, *Oh, yes I was. I was studying your muscular biceps, triceps, quads, hamstrings, and tight behind.*

Tyronne never tried to impress her with what he had or what he was going to get. He didn't seem to have much but he was thoughtful. Unlike her friend Fancy, the way SaVoy saw it, whatever material possessions Tyronne owned, belonged to him. She didn't want it. If he cared to share, that was cool but that was his choice.

SaVoy's dad always said, "If you can't put it in your pocket and take it with you, don't worry about it." Made a lot of sense once she was old enough to understand. So she thought about Tyronne often when he wasn't around but she didn't worry about him.

She didn't worry much about her mama, either. Daddy said, "You can't miss what you never had." SaVoy disagreed because she missed her mama. Especially when she saw other mothers and daughters holding hands. Laughing. Shopping. Dining. She missed her mama on Mother's Day. On their birthdays. So she said a special prayer every night hoping that God would someday answer. SaVoy didn't know her mother's birthday. Age. Nationality. She didn't know if her mom was dead. Alive. Sick. Well. She wondered if her mom thought about her at all.

SaVoy couldn't comprehend why her best friend Fancy disliked her mother so much. But she realized she wasn't in Fancy's position. Just seemed as though Fancy should've loved her mother while she could instead of hating her mother for what she didn't do.

"Love. Love. Love," SaVoy whispered as she wiped

water from the conveyor belt. "The cemetery is no place to start loving anybody." One day Fancy wouldn't have a mother to hate or to love.

Tyronne returned with a floral bouquet filled with tulips: white, lilac, deep red, and yellow. "You got a stapler?"

"Sure," SaVoy said, handing him the black stapler.

Tyronne took an Almond Joy, that he hadn't paid for, from the candy rack and stapled it to a card that read "2 Remember the Times." He handed her the flowers and said, "Peace. I'm out. See ya next week."

SaVoy placed the card and the candy bar inside her backpack. Tyronne had never asked her to be his lady. Maybe he already had one, but if he did he never talked about her. And if he did, he probably wouldn't have given her flowers.

SaVoy loved Papa. That's what she called her daddy, and he called her Baby Girl. Tyronne was the first man, other than Papa, to give her flowers. Papa gave her flowers all the time. SaVoy was his only girl but she had an older brother, Samuel. They were ten years apart. Samuel came home every Easter and SaVoy visited them every Christmas. Samuel lived in Chicago with his wife and two kids.

Papa also said, "People will only do what you allow them to do." He never said, "Baby Girl keep your panties up and your dress down." Or "Don't get pregnant." Sure, they talked about sex. He said the choice was hers. But to remember that there would only be one first of anything in life and seldom would she have control over choosing someone to be first. Daddy emphasized how losing her virginity was special. He said, "It's one of the most important decisions you'll ever make, Baby Girl."

Tyronne wasn't as tough as he pretended. Maybe she'd choose him to be her first. SaVoy knew what it felt like being first. In her senior year, she was voted the first

African-American female most likely to become a minister. Not because she lived a holy life, at least she didn't think so. She simply treated people the way she wanted to be treated. She briefly considered Theology school. Realizing choosing such a direction wasn't her duty, she practiced sitting quietly for thirty minutes every morning, waiting on God to give her an answer. And He did. And it wasn't ministry in the traditional sense. She also prayed about Tyronne and was pleased God hadn't said Tyronne wasn't the one.

So SaVoy continued to share love. Lots of love. From her heart. To children. Seniors. Family. Friends. SaVoy couldn't make anyone love her in return but she demanded respect. She spoke her mind, always seeking to bring out the best in others. Not condemn. Or gossip. But Fancy was her hardest challenge. She refused to give up on Fancy because there was hope. Fancy just didn't know how to love herself, so she had sex with all those different guys believing she was getting over on them because they gave her money. SaVoy didn't like her best friend's lifestyle so she tried teaching Fancy how to invest the money instead of throwing it all away on material things that could never increase her self-worth.

SaVoy remembered one day she'd told Fancy, "You may look like a runway model on the outside but your self-esteem needs a boost." She saw right through Fancy's hard exterior, always pretending she had it all together.

"You are not my second counselor. Mama. Whatever," Fancy had protested.

But SaVoy didn't feel she tried to be any of those things to Fancy. "I'm not. I'm your friend. Desmond is your friend, too. He cherishes the ground you walk on and all you ever do is trample all over him. One day you'll see, and one day he'll wise up, because the Lord giveth and the Lord taketh away. And that means people, too."

SaVoy smiled as she sniffed her flowers and watched Tyronne drive off in his truck.

CHAPTER 8

Desmond sat on the sofa beside his mother, placed a check for one thousand dollars in her hand, and curled her fingers over it. His sister had called yesterday to tell him his parents needed a lump sum of money to pay the special tax assessment on the house. His father was proud and would've worked a part-time job before asking any of his children for money. Mom really hadn't asked but she had a certain knack for mentioning things in a roundabout way.

When his sister called him yesterday she'd said, "Mama called me. Did she say anything to you?"

Desmond had replied, "No. About what? Is everything okay?" He was the youngest and his mother still spoiled him. Desmond ate at his parents' house every day except Saturday. Mama didn't cook on Saturdays but she insisted he drop off his dirty laundry Saturday mornings. She'd wash and fold his clothes, which he picked up on Sundays, usually after dinner.

"Yes, and no," his sister had replied. "They're fine. But Mama said, 'Suga Puddin', what you think the govament gon' do if we don't pay our three thousand dolla tax bill?' So I called to let you know between the six of us we've come up with the money so you don't have to worry. We want you to keep saving for law school."

That was considerate of his siblings but Desmond wanted to do his part. He refused to be the only one not contributing. Desmond appreciated how everyone in the family always catered to him.

The money he'd planned to spend on his parents' trip to Alaska, Mom and Dad could use whenever they wanted. Maybe take a trip to Las Vegas or something. Dad would like that.

Desmond tried to leave before his mother started planning his future again. As soon as he stood his mama said, "Whatever happened to dat nice girl Trina? You talk to her lately?"

"Yeah, Ma. I talked with Trina on the way over here." His mother had probably talked to Trina this morning too, since she called his mom every week.

"You not talkin' on dat cell phone and drivin' at the same time, I hope."

"Ma, I used my hands-free"—Desmond wiggled his fingers—"headset."

"Well, if you ask me, and I know you didn't, dat Trina girl is the one you should marry. Have some kids with. But whateva you do," Mama shook her finger then said, "don't marry dat fast Fanny girl and surely not dat Carlita. She's too old and she already done had her litter. Georgia ain't dat far away. Do like your father did with me and send for the girl."

Trina wanted to move to California, get married, and have his kids. Desmond wanted her to come to California but not just to be his wife. What if their relationship didn't work? Desmond didn't want to feel responsible for taking care of her. And if he didn't take care of Trina, his entire family and Trina's family would blame him for everything.

"I love you, lady." Desmond leaned over and kissed his mother's cheek. "I can't make it back for dinner but

I'll see you tomorrow. Going to the game with Tyronne. Bye, Ma."

"Okay, baby," his mother said, securing the check in her bosom.

Desmond tossed his laundry basket in the trunk. On the way to Tyronne's house he wondered what made some families close and others distant. Why some people were happy all the time and others angry for no reason. Why when a woman did something wrong it never seemed as serious as when a man did the same thing? Why did the black man carry the weight of America on his shoulders? Wondering when, not if, he'd have to deal with the law. Flagrant injustice motivated Desmond to become a criminal attorney.

Too many of his male friends, both in Georgia and California—if they weren't serving time—had unjustifiable probations. Not two or three months probation. More of them had three to five years probation. Just another way for the system to incarcerate the so-called free black man by limiting his freedom. And the new generation of male teenagers—Desmond's jaw clenched at the thought of how many of them were being killed. Especially in Oakland.

Bam! Bam! Bam! Tyronne banged on Desmond's window, then opened the car door. "Man, let's bump this Realizm, Ghetto Scriptures," Tyronne said, closing the door. Before Tyronne fastened his seat belt, he ejected Desmond's CD.

"How you gon' break the law. You can't just scratch the new Snoop for . . . *Realizm*."

Tyronne bounced his head to "Nothing to Lose." "Just chill and listen to the lyrics. This is part of the Hip Hop Elevation straight out of Oakland. You know dude, Darrin Hodges?"

"Yeah, and?"

"This is his shit. His artists. No shootin' up, no killin' up, no trashin' females, none of dat. Darrin's bringing back what hip-hop used to be all about. The music man," Tyronne said, dancing in his seat. "Check out Blayze. You ain't heard nothing till you've heard Blayze, and you know how I feel about felines on the mic. But she's one bad sistah spittin' 'Till We Reach the Top.' "

Desmond parked in the overflow lot at the Coliseum stadium. Dust hovered around his Mustang so he rolled up his window and motioned for Tyronne to do the same. The crunchy sound of gravel and dirt faded then stopped as he turned off his humming engine. Kickoff for the Raiders game was twenty minutes away.

"What'd you do last night?" Tyronne asked.

"Took Fancy to dinner and a movie," Desmond said, smiling.

"When you gon' learn? Man, forget Fancy. You need to be with SaVoy," Tyronne said, inhaling the smoke rising from an oversize barbecue grill at a tailgate party.

Desmond thought for a moment, then said, "Man, I can't. I already got with Fancy. Last night, too." Desmond smiled again.

"Read my lips, man. Forget Fancy! The only reason you been chasing that ho is because you know you can't have her. And if you ever got her, you could never keep her. You claim you want an intelligent woman. SaVoy walks across the stage to get her degree this summer. Man, just talk to her. I bet *she* can help you get into law school. Fancy chasin' that dollar, man. You can't catch no feline who's paper chasin'. Hell, I'd fuck Fancy but she ain't having that. Too uppity. I'm telling you. SaVoy is the one for you, Dez. And stop lyin', nigga. I didn't miss that comment about you 'got with Fancy.' "

Desmond peeped through the crowd trying to determine how much longer they'd have to wait before getting to the gate. SaVoy was nice and beautiful, but there was something missing. She wasn't fiery and freaky like Fancy. Desmond didn't have to prove anything to Tyronne. It was probably best Tyronne didn't believe he'd been intimate with Fancy. Desmond looked over at Tyronne and said, "That's funny. I thought SaVoy was the one for *you*." Desmond couldn't believe he'd told that lie. SaVoy was too good for Tyronne. If Desmond hadn't gotten with Fancy, he probably would've dated SaVoy. Desmond pulled out two tickets and handed them to the agent at the gate. The walk up the winding ramp was so crowded they'd missed the kickoff.

"Naw," Tyronne objected, "we just friends. SaVoy's cool and all but—"

"But what? She's too smart for you? Excuse me, intelligent. We might as well grab a couple of brews and something to eat before we settle in our seats." Tyronne looked at his ticket. Suite 17. "You the man today, Dez."

Desmond wanted a hot link but dismissed the thought, knowing his stomach would protest, so he ordered nachos, with extra cheese and a tap beer. Tyronne ordered the same with lots of jalapeño peppers on top.

"Hell no, she's not too intelligent for me," Tyronne said while paying for both orders.

"Then what?" Desmond hunched his shoulders.

"Okay, you can't repeat this shit," Tyronne whispered. "I do like her. A lot. But you know how I am. I've gots lots of pros jocking lé cheval. I'm not ready to settle down. But if I were . . . you're right. I think she's too deep for a brother. Plus, you really can't repeat this shit." Tyronne cupped his hand between his mouth and Desmond's ear and whispered, "She's a virgin."

Desmond stepped back. His eyes widened as he mouthed in slow motion, "You lyin'." Desmond's voice escalated. "Really!" and tapered off. "A virgin? At her age." Then Desmond tilted sideways and yelled, "Whoa!"

"So what. Now you interested?" Tyronne questioned, curling one corner of his lips.

"Man, if you're not—" Desmond said.

"Go for it, man. But don't let that be your only reason," Tyronne said.

"Man, you know I'm just kidding. SaVoy likes you."
Although Desmond wanted SaVoy to like him, he knew
she was seriously interested in Tyronne. Why? Desmond
had no idea because SaVoy and Tyronne were complete
opposites.

The crowd started roaring so they raced into the sky-
box. Beer splashed from both cups. They stood staring
at the field through the open window just in time to see
a black and silver jersey cross the field goal line. The
fans roared louder when the referee threw both hands
vertically in the air, signaling the extra point was good.
At halftime Desmond showed Tyronne the ticket stubs.

"Dawg, how'd you get these?" Tyronne asked, watching the woman place a red tag on his wrist for entry into
the members only club.

"My boss. You know he's well connected. He works on
half the Raiders' cars. In fact, those are the only cars he
personally works on."

"Man"—Tyronne tapped Desmond on the shoulder
and nodded to his left—"isn't that your girl?"

Frowning, Desmond asked, "Who? Carlita?"

"Naw, dawg. Fancy." Tyronne nodded again.

Desmond looked over and saw Fancy dressed in high-
heel shoes, black leather pants, and a silver fluffy sweater.
Desmond's jaw clenched. Fancy's hair flowed over her
back as she threw her head back with laughter. She
never let go of dude's arm. The same damn dude Fancy
met at the New Year's Eve gala. He was dressed in a button down black suit, with a collarless shirt buttoned up
to his neck.

"Let's go over and check ole girl out," Tyronne said,
heading in Fancy's direction.

"Naw, man." Desmond grabbed Tyronne's shoulder.
"I'm through with her."

"Desmond! Desmond!" Fancy yelled, waving and
walking in their direction. What the hell did she expect
him to say? *Thanks for letting me get your pussy wet for dude.*

Damn, Desmond had just had sex with Fancy last night. He guessed her tears were as phony as the way she was acting, grinning and shit in his face.

Desmond nodded, then casually said, "Hey, what's up?"

"Desmond, this is Byron. Byron, this here is my friend Desmond." Fancy smiled, holding Bryon's arm tighter.

Byron extended his hand. Desmond squeezed Byron's fingers extra tight. "What's up?"

Byron frowned.

"Dez, man, we gotta cut." Tyronne shook his head toward Fancy and said, "Trifflin' ho." Then Tyronne said, "Man, I see some fine-ass felines in the club. Let's go."

When Desmond glanced at the bar, he agreed. The club was packed with women in half tops and black spandex pants, dancing like they were Raiderettes.

"Don't trip, dawg. How many times I'mma hafta school you? Forget dat ho," Tyronne said.

Desmond refused to openly disagree with Tyronne this time. He couldn't blame Fancy for wanting more than he had to offer. He couldn't compete with dude. Byron. Whatever his name was. Desmond thought his name was Van. Or Stan. Or something like that.

After the game, Desmond dropped off Tyronne and went to Carlita's. Although she'd given him a key months ago, this was the first time he'd let himself in without ringing the doorbell. Carlita would give him a warm massage, make love to him, and take his mind off Fancy.

CHAPTER 9

Fancy twirled around her pole, slipped into her sheer stockings, winter-white wool pantsuit, and laced up her ivory ankle boots. Buttoning her double-breasted almond peacoat, she grabbed her designer purse and headed to her car. Fancy spent her entire week living for this day. Today was not a typical Friday. Tomorrow she'd take her first trip to Capitol Hill, with Byron. Fancy hurried to the Lake Merritt BART Station because if she arrived five minutes after nine-thirty she wouldn't have a space to park. Her friend, who worked the graveyard shift, glanced over his shoulder. The reverse lights on his truck shone. Fancy smiled, waved, and mouthed, *Thank you, baby,* as she blew him a kiss, knowing that was as close as he'd ever get to any of her lips. Stepping onto the escalator, Fancy shivered, recalling Byron's sweaty flesh sliding against hers.

Last night, Byron's passionate lovemaking brought tears to her eyes. Like playing a game of one-on-one basketball, Byron had predicted her every move. Fancy didn't have to tell Byron when to slow down, when not to switch positions, or when she was getting ready to cum. She didn't have to ask Byron to hold her afterward or call her before she left for work this morning. Although he hadn't paid her the twenty-five thousand dollars he said she'd earned, Byron promised she'd make some real money while they were in D.C.

The four-car train was slightly crowded. The few passengers that didn't have seats huddled in the doorway. Fancy swayed her hips and stood in front of the best-dressed man she'd noticed.

"Please, sit," he said, gesturing with a warm smile.

Fancy returned the smile and replied, "Why, thank you."

She sat, crossed her ankles, and thumbed through last July's issue of *Jet* magazine. Immediately she flipped to the "Beauty of the Week." The fabulous photo of her in a safari bikini leaning against her dance pole brought a smile to her face. The guy standing over her smiled too.

Exiting at Montgomery Street, Fancy chatted then exchanged cards with the gentleman that offered her his seat because this week she hadn't given anyone her number. Byron had no idea how he had her changing her diva ways simply to please him.

Selectively handing out three cards a week, Fancy never had a problem getting a date. The information on the card had her name, title, Real Estate Leasing Agent, E-mail address, and home number. After changing her cellular number three times, and being forced to enter into a new one-year plan each time, Fancy quit giving out her cell number. The few times she'd forwarded her cell phone calls, the cellular company charged ten cents per minute plus hidden fees that made her curse out the customer service representative. So now when Fancy left home she forwarded her home number to her cell because SBC charged one low monthly flat rate for call forwarding. The only people who now had her cellular number were SaVoy, Tanya, Caroline, and Desmond.

Fancy strolled into her private office at ten o'clock and closed the door. Two messages registered on her display so she checked the caller ID, hoping at least one of the calls was from Byron.

Tanya had called at nine. She must have forgotten Fancy worked ten to two and got paid from nine to five. Fancy deleted the message without listening to it. Tanya never had anything interesting to say. The next call was from Caroline. Fancy started to hit three for deletion, then stopped and listened.

"Hi, Fancy. This is your mother. I need you to call me. The doctor says I may need to have surgery and I was wondering if you could take me to my next—"

Fancy hit the delete button and sighed. She had promised to call Caroline once a week. It was already February and she hadn't called Caroline once this year. Byron had become her priority. Byron was more important than SaVoy, Tanya, Desmond, and Caroline. Whenever Fancy saw his name appear on her caller ID, butterflies fluttered inside her stomach. Fancy hadn't thought about Caroline since her last appointment with Mandy, which was over a month ago. Fancy tapped her pencil on the desk calendar pad, hit the speaker button, and dialed Tanya's number.

"Hello," a man's voice echoed through the receiver.

"Hi, this is Fancy. Let me speak with Tanya."

"Tanya's at work. And you woke me up so don't call us before five o'clock. P.M."

Us? Before five what? "Who in the hell are you?"

"This is Tanya's man, William. I don't want you single females makin' a bad impression on my woman. Tanya's got a real man now. She ain't goin' to no clubs, malls, or anywhere else without my permission. You got that?" William slammed the phone so hard Fancy grabbed her ear.

Oh, hell no! His ass done moved in and took over in less than eight weeks. Fancy hit her speaker button twice. Her second phone line rang. She hesitated before answering, "Good morning, Harry."

"Can I see you in my office?" Harry didn't wait for a response. Through her rectangular-shaped window, Fancy saw Harry smiling and closing his blinds. His office window was directly across from hers.

Fancy unbuttoned her coat and secured the loop over the brass hook behind her door. Her hips swayed as she entered Harry's office. "Good morning, baby." Fancy locked his door and unbuttoned her blouse with ease. It was their morning routine.

"Come here," Harry commanded, palming her breasts with his short stubby fingers.

Fancy rubbed his short wooly afro. Harry's lips suctioned over her nipple.

"Oh, I need some cream to go with my coffee this morning. I missed you this weekend. We're going to have to start taking weekend trips again. Unbutton your pants. I need to taste you."

Fancy pushed Harry's head away and buttoned her blouse. Now that she'd met Byron she was no longer interested in pleasing Harry. And since she had to wean Harry eventually, she might as well start now. Harry switched seats from his high-back office recliner to his armless computer chair. He rolled up close, tossed his tie over his shoulder, and eagerly fumbled to unfasten Fancy's belt.

Fancy moved his hands and refastened her belt. Harry's unwillingness to commit to marriage had demoted him to sponsor-only status. Soon he'd become a nonbeneficiary sponsor because after today she was permanently cutting Harry off from Miss Kitty. Fridays, Saturdays, and Sundays were now exclusively reserved for Byron. Fancy pushed Harry away again.

"I have work to do, Mr. Washington."

"Your job is to keep Harry happy," he said, looking at his erection.

"Do not pull him out," Fancy said, pointing at the bulge in Harry's gray slacks. "I'm warning you. I'm opening the door."

Fancy glanced at Harry's file cabinet. The key was seldom in the lock. It was now. For months she'd tried getting into his personal files. Harry's ten-thirty meeting was fifteen minutes away. Fancy relocked the door and pleased Harry so good he started panting, barely catching his breath before answering his phone.

"Whew," he exhaled, then picked up the receiver. "Yes, Allyanna," he paused, then said, "Oh, shit! Allyanna, I lost track of the time. Go ahead and start the meeting. I'll be there in two minutes," Harry said, buckling his belt. He motioned to Fancy to stand behind the door. "Get yourself together. And make sure you call Mrs. Lovely about her apartment repairs ASAP. Oh, yeah. And schedule a meeting for Monday afternoon with Ray Leon at the City of Oakland regarding my mixed-use development on Harrison Street."

Mixed use? Fancy knew if she was serious about learning the industry she had to understand the terminology. Mixed use. She repeated the words in her head several times.

"Sure. I'll clear my calendar and I can accompany you to City Hall."

"No, Allyanna will be there. Your job is to look pretty and, of course"—Harry fluttered his eyebrows and eyed his erection—"to keep Harry happy. And Harry is very happy this morning." He closed his jacket and then shut the door.

Harry needed to lay off the viagra. What was he going to do when he turned forty? Determined to learn the real estate business, even if she had to teach herself, Fancy locked the door and opened Harry's personal file drawer. Her fingertips glided across the tabs. Medical. She pulled out the folder and read his policy. Family coverage? "What the hell?" Fancy whispered, then retrieved the folder marked Taxes. She cursed as she read Harry's filing status. Joint? Exhaling she said, "Damn," and opened his Suspense file. A short "humph," was accompanied by a shot of hot air escaping her nostrils. Tuition? She thumbed through his personal budget. She was in the top five on his list, a one thousand dollar monthly bonus was allocated in addition to the fifteen hundred dollars Harry paid her every two weeks. The thousand dollars barely covered her tax, medical, and dental deductions.

Dental. Family? Liabilities. Assets. Condos. The place Harry called home where he'd taken her once was nowhere on his list of assets. Fancy took a deep breath and held it. Primary residence. Her lungs deflated as she whispered, "Sacramento? Not Marina Heights in San Francisco." Her eyes widened. She thought all Harry owned were six single-family homes and several apartment buildings.

Fancy scanned the prior months' budgets. Allyanna was on his list along with all the other women in the office. He must have been fucking them, too. She kicked the file cabinet and scuffed her new boots. "Aw, shit!" Fancy squinted. She rubbed her thumb over Harry Jr.'s tuition. Sarah's tuition. And Michael's day care? Fancy flopped in Harry's chair and waited for his return.

Why was Harry so secretive? Fancy heard Harry's keys jiggling inside the lock and raced behind the door. When he stepped inside Fancy slammed the door so hard it sprang back. She stood two inches from his face and asked, "What is your marital status! What are your living arrangements! And exactly how many kids do you have!"

Harry reared back, closed his door, and spoke low but firm, "What the hell are you talking about?" Harry glanced at the files scattered on his desk. "Please tell me you did not go through my files." He stared at Fancy, then grabbed her biceps, pulling her close. "Answer me, dammit. Did you go through my personal files?"

Peeling his fingers away, Fancy said, "You liar! How could you?" She forced fake tears that streamed down her cheeks. "I hate you! I hate you! Liar! Liar!"

"Stop yelling." Harry fanned the air in front of Fancy's face. "Let me explain. Okay. Yes, I do have a wife."

Fancy didn't realize she was frowning until he started frowning, too. Harry exhaled, then bit his bottom lip. Fancy remained silent and stared at Harry.

"Listen. I'm not in love with her anymore. But I can't afford to divorce her right now because we have too many investments. Finances. Children. Property"—then he shrugged, laughed and added, "and a dog. His name is Buster."

Fancy hysterically leaped from the chair, "Buster! Buster! Mutherfucka! That's not funny!" She wanted to let the real Fancy Taylor drop-kick his ass but she had to keep her psycho personality under wraps. Plus, Fancy had earned her monthly bonus and had every intention of getting paid with no intent of ever laying his lying ass again.

Harry responded between tight lips, "Don't curse me." Then he stepped toward her and said, "Look. Let's discuss this over lunch."

Fancy stepped back. "Why don't you invite the other women in the office, too? We can have an orgy."

Harry's lips curled upward. He cupped his hand over his mouth and said, "Hum," raising his eyebrows.

Fancy punched Harry on the shoulder.

"I'm kidding. Lighten up. I told you we can discuss this over lunch."

"There's nothing to discuss." When Fancy opened the door, everyone was huddled at Allyanna's desk.

"Get back to work before I fire all of you!" Harry yelled.

Fancy slammed her door and dialed the number she'd memorized from Harry's file. She pressed 9-1-6 . . . and waited.

"Hello?" A woman answered.

Fancy smiled to perk up her voice. "Hello, Mrs. Washington?"

"Yes, this is Mrs. Washington," she responded.

"I don't believe this shit. I've been fucking Harry for two years. Two. Years. Lying ass muthafucka."

"Excuse me," the woman said.

Fancy placed the receiver on the base and took the rest of the day off.

CHAPTER 10

Today was "Bring Your Child to Work" day and since Fancy didn't have any kids, she borrowed her neighbor's dog. Buddy was a perfectly groomed miniature schnauzer with a shiny black coat and a long beard. Glancing in the mirror, Fancy admired the pinstriped miniskirt suit Steven had bought. Her cinnamon open-toe sling-back shoes matched her stripes. Fancy placed Buddy in her workout bag, stored his container of chicken strips in the side pocket, and headed to the BART station.

Peeping inside the bag she said, "Promise me you'll be quiet so we don't get kicked off the train."

Instead of parking at Lake Merritt, Fancy drove to West Oakland. That way they only had to ride two train stops. Buddy squirmed around in the bag.

A masculine-looking woman with a deep voice asked, "You wanna sit down?"

"No, thanks," Fancy replied, avoiding eye contact.

Closing her book the woman asked with disbelief, "Is that a dog?"

"Yes!" Fancy eyed the woman's wedding band and

sarcastically commented, "I see you have one, too." Fancy smiled and teased Buddy's long eyebrows.

"Huh. What?" The woman silently faced the window. Since the train was traveling under the bay, there was nothing to see except concrete walls.

As soon as Fancy exited the station, she let Buddy trot several blocks uphill to the office. Harry had left for his early morning flight to New York, and he'd locked his door, so she made an about-face and slipped into her office. Fancy scrolled through the on-line yellow pages and dialed the florist. "Yes, I'd like to order the largest bleeding heart you have."

"Are you sure you want to order our largest? It's awfully big and very expensive. Four hundred and fifty dollars." The woman listened then said, "Okay. Which mortuary would you like us to deliver to?"

Fancy rattled off Harry's home address in Sacramento.

"Okay, what would you like on the banner?"

"Put R. I. P., Henrietta Washington." Fancy billed the expense to Harry's account.

Harry had promised to promote her to property supervisor as soon as a position became available. Fancy suddenly realized as long as she kept Harry happy, Harry would tell her whatever he thought she wanted to hear. His firm owned thirty-six apartment complexes in the Bay Area and managed another forty-eight properties across the country—not the few properties he'd led her to believe. Why would Harry lie about how many properties he owned? One day Fancy would own and manage properties, too. Harry made it seem easy. Always flying off somewhere every week. His flight to New York City was scheduled to leave in thirty minutes from San Francisco International Airport. Fancy loved New York and although Harry had invited her to go, he canceled her reservation after she went through his files. Byron had canceled her trip, too, but hadn't said why.

Fancy had bigger and better plans. Since Harry wouldn't teach her about property management, she decided she'd learn on her own. She looked at her E-mail task list, picked up the phone, and called her favorite tenant. Mrs. Lovely always had a complaint.

"Good morning, Mrs. Lovely. This is Fancy Taylor with Washington and Associates property management. How can I help you?"

"Baby. The man came out to fix my commode last week but it's leaking again. And there's a hole in the flo' next to the commode. Oh, yeah, and it's done come aloose. I practically fell in the waduh this morning."

"Yes, Mrs. Lovely. I'll have someone come out right away. Better yet, Mrs. Lovely, I'll be out to your apartment this afternoon."

Fancy had forgotten about Buddy until he ran past her office. Several kids chased him. One little girl scooped Buddy up and started carrying him around.

If she were serious about learning the business, Fancy needed to see Mrs. Lovely's place. The bathroom couldn't be that bad.

"Okay, baby. I'll be here all day. I'll cook suppa early. That ways you can join me if you like. I'll cook a little extra."

Fancy frowned. No matter how friendly Mrs. Lovely was, Fancy was not eating at a stranger's home. "I'll be there by three."

Fancy surfed the Internet and billed all her real estate salesperson and broker courses to Harry's credit card. She billed the real estate exam fees under miscellaneous, completed an expense report, and made the amount payable to herself. She contacted the Institute of Real Estate Management and prepaid for each course required to become a certified property manager. Fancy was most interested in commercial leasing and acquisition. Instead of owning apartment buildings she wanted to own commercial property. Skyscrapers. For the first time in her life, Fancy envisioned becoming one of the power players.

The telephone interrupted her thoughts. It was Harry so Fancy answered, "Hello."

"Hey, I missed my flight. Can't get out until six so I'm headed back to the office. Why don't you take care of me before my trip? We can do lunch. Reserve us a room at the usual," Harry said.

Fancy replied, "I can't. I promised I'd visit Mrs. Lovely." She was not canceling her appointment with Mrs. Lovely.

"Don't forget who cuts your check. It's not Mrs. Lovely. It's me."

No, he was not pulling rank. Bastard. "No, Harry. Not today." Fancy didn't offer an explanation nor an excuse.

"Okay, look, pack your things and move to cubicle two. I want you moved by the time I make it to the office."

"But Allyanna is in cubicle two. Besides, I'm not moving to a cubicle. I've earned my office."

"Yes, you have. But you haven't earned your keep. I have too many tenants calling me complaining about you."

Harry must have been crazy if he thought Fancy was moving out of her plush office. "Bye, Harry."

"Oh, yeah. Allyanna says she's allergic to dogs, so after you finish moving, take Buddy home immediately. Forward me to Allyanna."

Fancy hung up the phone and stomped over to Allyanna's desk. She kissed her lips inward twice, signaling for Buddy. He didn't respond so Fancy sat in Allyanna's visitor's chair, patted her thigh, then rolled her eyes at Allyanna. "Where's Buddy?"

"If we're lucky, he's dead. Why would anyone bring an animal to work? He's not a kid. By the way, Harry's wife says if you don't stop sleeping with her husband she's going to—"

Fancy politely picked up Allyanna's grand Starbuck's cup. The coffee was still warm. Fancy removed the lid and emptied the remaining contents on Allyanna's desk.

Allyanna screamed, "You witch!"

Fancy stood and stared at Allyanna. Allyanna pinched the wet papers and held them over the wastebasket.

"Yeah, I thought so," Fancy said, then walked away.

How did Allyanna know Harry was married? Fancy walked up and down each aisle searching for Buddy. The kids were huddled in an aisle, peeping at Allyanna.

Fancy walked over to the kids and asked, "Has anyone seen Buddy?"

The little girl who had been carrying him pointed at the boy next to her.

Fancy's eyes widened. "What did you do with Buddy?" She grabbed both the kids by the hands and dragged them into her office.

"Where's Buddy?"

The little boy scratched his head. Fancy placed her hands on his shoulders and rattled him back and forth. "You'd better tell me or—"

"Or what!" Allyanna interrupted, pushing open Fancy's door. "Get your hands off my kid."

Tears swelled in Fancy's eyes. "He's not my dog. I've got to find him. Where's Buddy?"

"My son don't play with no dogs. She had the dog. Ask her. You shouldn't have brought him here in the first place." Allyanna walked away, holding her son's hand.

The little girl whispered, "He's dead."

Fancy's head snapped in the little girl's direction. "Dead! Dead! What do you mean he's dead!"

The little girl pointed and said, "Check the rest room," and ran to her mother.

Fancy ran to the rest room. The door was locked.

"What's all this commotion?" Harry asked, walking into the office.

"Buddy is in the rest room and the door is locked."

Harry removed his spare key. He unlocked the door, opened it, and looked inside. "Nope he's not in here. I told you to take him home."

Fancy was relieved that Buddy wasn't in the rest room but worried because, now where was Buddy?

Allyanna brushed by Harry and entered the rest room. "Oh, my gosh!" Allyanna held her stomach and laughed.

Fancy rushed into the stall. When she saw Buddy, all Fancy saw were his innocent eyes. Buddy was stuck in the toilet bowl covered in white toilet tissue and chocolate candy bars. Peanuts floated around his sticky coat.

"Don't move." Fancy ran to her office, grabbed the workout bag, and raced back to the rest room. She waved a chicken strip in front of Buddy's nose until he hopped inside the bag. Fancy doubted Buddy would win any dog contest, especially the one her neighbor had entered him into this weekend.

"Bad ass kids." Maybe having children wasn't such a good idea after all because if Fancy were their mother, she surely would've beaten them.

CHAPTER 11

Fancy called in sick on Friday. She laced her jogging shoes, stretched her hamstrings, and then did a full split in both directions. Why had Harry lied about his situation? Not mentioning he had a wife was the same as lying. As long as Fancy kept promising to please Harry, he either didn't care or didn't know she was the one who'd sent the bleeding heart, causing Mrs. Washington to place herself under house arrest. Although Fancy no longer desired Harry sexually, she adamantly wanted Mrs. Washington to leave his cheating ass. Seeing Harry happy, taking Allyanna out to lunch every other day, tied Fancy's stomach in knots. Sending Harry's wife that floral arrangement marked the beginning of Harry's demise.

"Let's see, first I'll E-mail a copy of his list of clients to my personal E-mail address, then I'll forward all of his phone calls to my cell phone." Since Fancy had recorded Harry's outgoing message, she'd duplicate the message on her phone. What if Byron questioned her? Fancy would think about that after she changed her home phone number. Fancy stood on her balcony and gazed at the mid-afternoon sun rays hovering over the lake like a sheet of glass.

The telephone rang, interrupting her plot against Harry. Fancy hurried to answer. "Hello."

"Hey, this is Steven. What are you doing tonight?"

"Busy. Why? What's up?"

"I've got two tickets to the Golden Gate Theatre tonight. You can wear that sexy black number I bought you yesterday."

Fancy rolled her eyes and silently exhaled. "I'm getting ready to go run the lake." Steven was crazy if he thought she'd waste wearing one of her new party dresses on a date with him. The long black shawl wrapped around a sleeveless stretch-lace minidress. With that outfit she could go from amazingly gorgeous to I-know-you-wanna-fuck-me in less than five seconds.

Steven sang, "I have the money you asked for."

Fancy thought about it for a moment. "I gotta go. Good-bye."

When the phone rang again, Fancy answered, "I said, no!"

"But I haven't asked yet." Byron's voice was friendly.

"Oh, no. I'm sorry. I thought you were Tanya calling back. Hi, baby."

"Would you like to accompany me tonight?"

Fancy spoke softly, "Yes, I'd love to."

"I'll pick you up at five. Bye."

"Bye, baby."

Fancy hung up and immediately called the phone company. "Yes, I'd like to change my number. Someone is harassing me."

"Okay, hold please."

Fancy smiled as the operator gave her a private number. Steven was dismissed. Harry was about to be pissed. And Adam was the only sponsor worth servicing and soon he'd be history.

In less than an hour, Fancy jogged three laps—almost ten miles—around Lake Merritt. She soaked in a tub of black cherry salt water then wrapped hot steamy towels around her legs for five minutes. Generously smoothing virgin olive oil on her legs, Fancy shaved. Byron had all the qualities she wanted in a man. Wealthy. Intelligent. Handsome. Masculine. Attentive. No wife or kids. And he cared about her. Fancy dried off, tossed the towel in its hamper, and sifted through her wardrobe. Tonight she would dress extra provocative for her man. Steven's investment was the perfect outfit for the occasion.

Red sling-back open-toe shoes displayed her African pedicure. Her body tingled from the peppermint body lotion. The softest after-five dress, that she'd just removed the tag from, caressed her body and her naked booty. The hemline rested six inches above her knees. Her nipples stood firm, highlighting her cleavage.

Fancy waited in the lobby because if Byron came up to get her, they'd end up having sex on the balcony again. But this time it was five o'clock in the evening not late at night or early morning.

When Byron entered the lobby, Fancy twirled and floated into his arms.

"Hi, baby. Um, you smell good," Fancy said. She lovingly smoothed her hand over the back of Byron's head and massaged his neck.

"You know what that does to me. Remember last weekend." Byron nodded at the doorman, and then smiled at Fancy. "You look absolutely beautiful."

"Thanks," Fancy said, easing into his Jaguar.

"I have a surprise." Byron eased his hand up Fancy's thigh. "Whoa, I see you have one too." His smile widened.

"Oh, I love surprises." Fancy closed her eyes.

"Not so fast this time," Byron said. "I'll tell you later."

Byron had already given her a diamond tennis bracelet, the platinum anklet she was wearing, and several rings. Maybe tonight he'd give her the ring she'd earned.

Byron pulled into a long driveway high in the Oakland Hills.

Fancy laughed. "Okay, whose house are we christening tonight?"

"Honey, this brother is strictly business. He is the man. This might as well be his vacation home because he's never here."

Large white pillars separated the house and driveway. Walking up two flights of stairs into the mansion, Fancy imagined herself living there with Byron. What if that was their new home and Byron was proposing to her tonight?

Fancy's eye's widened as she stepped inside. Oh, hell no! No way. This couldn't be her new home. Gorgeous women in tuxedo bikinis pranced around in stilettos serving smiles. Before one of them got too close to Byron, Fancy frowned at her, then tightly hugged Byron's arm.

"Who did you say lives here?" Fancy asked Byron, entering a crowded room. Everyone was standing because there were no chairs in the room.

"Here he comes now," Byron said, then whispered, "You have to watch him. He loves pretty women."

"Hey, Byron. Glad you could make it, man."

Fancy could never forget those perfect locks.

Byron's friend eyed Fancy. "All-star?" He looked at Byron and raised an eyebrow.

Byron nodded and said, "For sho. This is my lady, Fancy Taylor. Fancy, this is my boy, Darius Jones."

Lady? Fancy thought. Byron hadn't introduced her like that before. Damn, Darius was fine as hell. Tall as heaven. And had Miss Kitty singing his praises.

"Look, man"—Darius patted Byron on the back— "enjoy yourselves." Darius smiled, winked at Byron, and kissed two of the models as they passed.

"He's who did you say?" Fancy needed more information on this arrogant Darius guy. Her first encounter with him at Byron's fund-raiser was counterproductive, but Fancy had a plan.

"You've heard of Black Diamonds, right?" Byron asked.

"I believe so," Fancy replied. Who hadn't heard of Black Diamonds?

"Well, Jada Diamond, the owner of Black Diamonds, is his mother and she's standing over there next to her new husband." Byron pointed, then added, "Wellington Jones is Darius's father." Byron escorted Fancy upstairs. She listened intently. As Byron volunteered information, Fancy stored the data in her memory bank.

Fancy's eyes widened. "Are you serious? He is *the* Darius Jones? Darius Jones of Somebody's Gotta Be On Top Enterprises?" Fancy stood at the top of the staircase observing Darius. At this point she was more interested in touring her new home than marrying Byron. Byron had created unimaginable opportunities for Fancy.

"That's him." Byron grabbed Fancy's hand. "Let's check out his guest rooms," Byron said with a horny, devilish grin.

"I'm hungry," Fancy lied. "Can we get something to eat first?" She led Byron down the stairs so she could get closer to Darius. Watching the models, Fancy wondered if they were live-in servants. Those anorexic, breast-implanted hoochies would be the first ones fired after Fancy moved in.

"What's an all-star?" Fancy asked Byron, holding a china saucer of hors d'oeuvres she had no intention of eating.

"Oh, that's just a term we use for . . . hum . . . how can I say this." Byron shook his head. "On second thought, you don't wanna know. But it is a compliment."

"Okay, if you insist. So how do you know Darius?" Fancy asked.

"We played ball together at Georgetown U in D.C. His real father, Darryl Williams, is a retired NBA player, who was also our head coach. That's enough questions about Darius. You wanna know what your surprise is?" Byron hugged Fancy.

"I sure do," Fancy said, hugging Byron and gazing over his shoulder at Darius. Darius winked and smiled at her so Fancy smiled too.

Byron led Fancy to the front porch. He removed a small box from his pocket and handed it to Fancy.

"What's this?"

"Open it."

Fancy delicately peeled away the wrapping. Frowning, she questioned, "A key?" It was a tiny little gold key that resembled one that would fit an old-fashioned padlock. She smiled at Byron. "To what?"

"You'll see. Let's go."

This was the best evening Fancy had had in long time. Marrying Darius was her destiny. Why else would she keep running into him? When Byron parked in front of her apartment building, there was a new metallic white two-seater Benz wrapped in a red ribbon.

"This key doesn't fit a car."

"You're right. I'll trade you," Byron said, handing her the key to the car.

Fancy switched the keys and gave Byron a huge kiss. Lipstick was all over his mouth. She tore the ribbon and sat behind the wheel of her new car. Fancy inhaled. This was the first time someone had given her a new car. The car Desmond gave her was pre-owned, but the Benz! That was fancy! And Fancy. Sixty-nine miles registered on the odometer.

"I gotta get going," Byron said, walking away. "I'll call you in the morning."

Fancy kissed Byron long and soft. "Why don't you come upstairs so I can thank you properly?"

"No, I really have to get going."

"So what was the other key to?" Fancy asked.

Byron glimpsed at Fancy and replied, "For starters, my heart. I'm not so sure it's me you want. Enjoy the ride." Then he walked away.

CHAPTER 12

Vigorously SaVoy brushed her teeth, rinsed with a blue-mint mouthwash, smiled in the mirror, and said, "I love you. Choose the words you speak today very carefully. Lord, if my words influence anyone, I pray that I make a positive difference in their life."

Every morning SaVoy was happy because sunrise represented a new beginning. Each night she prayed, and whatever troubles she encountered throughout the day, SaVoy left them with the Lord and slept peacefully. With her affirmation in mind, SaVoy went into the family room, gathered her books, and checked her backpack, hoping she hadn't forgotten anything this time. "Bye, Papa. I'm going to the library, then to class. I'll relieve Tanya at three. Have a wonderful day, Papa."

Not quite forty, barely five-foot-four inches, her dad was a handsome man. A no-nonsense man. A loving and caring man. His mustache slightly curved at the corners and tickled her jaw when he kissed her good-bye. Papa had dark brown eyes, broad shoulders, and the same long slender nose she had. When SaVoy hugged her father, a shadow crossed the kitchen doorway commanding her attention.

SaVoy's eyes widened as she smiled. "Hi, Vanessa."

For as long as SaVoy remembered, Vanessa was the only woman Papa had dated. But why hadn't Papa married Vanessa? Maybe because she was always out of town on business. Or perhaps Papa wouldn't marry Vanessa because she placed her career ahead of having his baby and had aborted his child. Last year when she turned forty—despite Papa's protest—Vanessa had a tubal ligation.

"Hi. I'm in here trying to decide what to cook with these eggs. How's college coming along?"

Vanessa's personality was a lot like Papa's. Straightforward. Kind. But unlike Papa, Vanessa didn't censor her words. Before SaVoy began her menstrual cycle, Vanessa had told SaVoy the truth about menstruation, where babies came from, and how a woman conceived. Vanessa introduced SaVoy to plays at the Black Repertory Theatre, the ballet, and musicals at the Paramount. The last time Vanessa stayed the night at their house, she had shared information—about sex and relationships—that left SaVoy with unanswered questions.

SaVoy raised her voice and replied, "Fine. Glad it's almost over though so I can take a break."

Vanessa stood in the kitchen doorway waving a green plastic spatula. "Forget about a break, honey. Keep going until you get your PhD. Then you can take a break."

The highest degree Vanessa had was a Master's so SaVoy imagined Vanessa, like Papa, wanted her education to exceed theirs.

"Well, actually, I could use your opinion on something—that is, if you have time," SaVoy said slowly, walking down the narrow hallway to her bedroom. Vanessa followed her into the room and closed the door.

SaVoy sat on the edge of her bed, gazed up at Vanessa, and said, "Remember when you told me I could have sex and remain a virgin?"

Vanessa swiveled the computer chair around. "And

so that's what you want to know so early in the morning?" Vanessa sat, then propped her long legs across the bed, dangling Papa's house slippers over the side.

"Yeah, I do. 'Cause there's this guy I like. A lot. But he doesn't know that I like him. But every time I'm around him, I get butterflies. I get nervous and excited at the same time. Sometimes I want to kiss him. And even though I've never had sex, something inside me wants to have sex with him. I've prayed those feelings would go away, but they haven't. I mean, I've had feelings of attraction before. But I've never felt, you know, like this."

Vanessa sat beside SaVoy and said, "Well, I know you have to get to class but, here's what you should think about. Have a sexual relationship with yourself, first."

SaVoy shook her head and frowned. "I don't understand."

"Just listen to me, SaVoy. How long have you known this guy?"

"Seventeen months."

"That's good. So you know his people? Family? Friends?"

"Just one of his friends, but mainly I know Tyronne because he delivers beverages to the store."

"Okay." Vanessa nodded. "That's a start. But you need to ask him questions about his family and his upbringing. You learn a lot about a person when you know who they really are."

How could SaVoy ask Tyronne personal questions without having him ask questions about her mother?

"Now, back to your hormones. Get to know your body. And one way you can do that is through experimenting with masturbation. Then on your first sexual encounter with your partner, explore his body, with the lights on, and allow him to do the same with yours. Make certain he has excellent hygiene. No penetration.

Wait to have intercourse because the first time is painful. Actually, honey, the first few times might be painful. Take it slow." Then Vanessa emphatically said, "And no matter how experienced he is, make him wear a condom."

Masturbation? Before intercourse? SaVoy wanted and needed to know how and why but she didn't want to interrupt Vanessa so she'd ask for details later.

"Look, honey, boys are taught at an early age that masturbation is acceptable. For them, looking at naked women in *Playboy, Hustler,* and *Penthouse* magazines is normal. But most women never talk to or teach young girls that masturbation is safe. One, you can't contract any diseases. Two, it's safe because you definitely won't get pregnant. And three, it's necessary because you need to learn your body before sharing yourself with someone else."

SaVoy appreciated how Vanessa took time explaining sex. Vanessa's casual approach and honesty helped to lighten the subject. For a moment, SaVoy thought about Tyronne. And how Tyronne brightened her day and brought a smile to her face without speaking a word.

Vanessa said, "You know, my niece is graduating from high school this year. Well, she has X-rated magazines but she doesn't have to hide them. She has male and female condoms and she knows how to use them properly. And I told her, like I'm telling you: always carry your own condoms and you"—Vanessa pointed at SaVoy—"always check the expiration date before opening the condom. And even though my niece hasn't had intercourse, she knows a lot more about sex than her peers. Now that she's no longer curious about what an orgasm feels like, she's confident and in no rush to lose her virginity. And she has no problem telling guys no.

"If you don't remember anything else I've said, SaVoy, never forget that abstinence is abnormal. You are supposed to have desires. Honey, the laws of nature dictate reproduction in every living organism and you are no exception. I just want you to make healthy choices."

SaVoy glanced at the clock on her wall. She could wait another twenty minutes but then she had to leave or she'd be late for class. SaVoy wished she didn't have to go to class today because she was learning so much from Vanessa.

Vanessa threw her head back in laughter and said, "Don't wear out your clit fingers." She held up her middle fingers, rotated them in the air, and said, "You know why these are called clit fingers?"

SaVoy shook her head and stared at Vanessa.

"Honey, because they're the longest! Nobody masturbates with a pinky . . . unless it's a dick in disguise." Vanessa tossed her head back again, then patted SaVoy's leg. "Honey, a dick the size of a pinky can only be used for masturbation but if you know how to masturbate, you can love that man and wear his dick out! Once you learn your body, you'll know there's no such thing as a dick that's too big or too small. But I must admit, a big dick is a beautiful thing because it can hit the G spot and the clit at the same time. Now the smaller dick, let it focus on the clit and you work your own G spot from the inside. Vanessa will explain that one to you later. You just need to learn how to get your orgasm on because believe me, he will get his, with or without you."

Vanessa unbuttoned her blouse, stood in front of SaVoy, and unfastened her bra. Vanessa breasts were firm and plump. Her erect nipples were a much darker shade of chocolate than the rest of her body.

SaVoy frowned, then looked away.

"Honey, you'd better pay attention 'cause Vanessa's only going to show you this once."

SaVoy hesitantly watched Vanessa.

"When you take a shower you probably wash your breasts without thinking about them."

SaVoy remained silent but agreed and continued to listen.

"Next time you wash your breasts, hold them in your hands. Squeeze them. Stroke them. Pinch your nipples. Your nipples are loaded with nerve endings. Never let a man make love to you without caressing your breasts. And once a month check them like this." Vanessa placed her left hand behind her right shoulder. Her elbow pointed toward the ceiling. Then she moved her three middle fingers in small circular motions. Massaging around her breast, Vanessa started at the outermost part and worked her way in a slow spiral pattern and stopped at the nipple.

"Once you learn your body, you'll know when something doesn't feel right. Honey, you need to do this the rest of your life but only once a month. Doctors suggest right after your period but, baby, you may not have a period every month so I say pick the same date as your birthday and examine yourself."

Vanessa shook her titties from side to side. Then she fastened her bra and buttoned her blouse. "And don't be afraid to move your titties, hips, whatever. Sex is like dancing." Vanessa's body gyrated. "The more you move the better it feels."

Papa knocked on the door and said, "Breakfast is ready."

Whew! SaVoy had begun questioning whether Vanessa was giving too much information. "Thanks, Vanessa. I've got to hurry to class but I really appreciate your advice."

"Honey, don't mention it. Anytime you have a question, let Vanessa know."

On her way to San Francisco, SaVoy shifted her thoughts from Tyronne and wondered how she could help Tanya get rid of that strange guy William who practically held Tanya hostage in her own home. After

William moved in, the only place SaVoy saw Tanya was at work.

SaVoy parked one block away from the campus and prayed the professor didn't call on her in class. She quickly entered the room, sat in the back of the class, booted up her laptop, and E-mailed the professor her assignment. As soon as class was over, SaVoy stopped at the main library across from San Francisco's City Hall. After hours of studying and transcribing the tape recorded lecture notes, SaVoy drove to the store thinking how she could help her daddy buy the building at the end of his ten-year lease, which expired next year.

SaVoy entered the store and said, "Hey, Tanya. How's it going?" then tossed her backpack on the floor behind the counter.

"Fine. Tyronne came by. Said he might come back later."

SaVoy stood in front of the cooler, opened the door, and stuck her head in. She closed the freezer and smiled at Tanya. "Oh, that man is so fine."

"Who? Tyronne? Where'd that come from? He's not your type." Tanya locked the front door, pulled her cash drawer, and carried the money into the office.

SaVoy followed Tanya. "That's what's so exciting about him. He's not my type at all." She watched Tanya count her drawer.

She counted her ones, scribbled on her close-out report form, and then did the same with the fives, tens, twenties, and coins.

"Oh, yeah. I accepted a job offer this morning cashiering at the new retail store opening in Emeryville. They don't open for another month so I can work here until then," Tanya said, handing SaVoy the piece of paper.

Tanya's drawer always balanced perfectly. Although SaVoy trusted Tanya, she had to remain professional and keep track of Papa's inventory and his money. SaVoy wondered how much Tanya knew about sex.

"I wish there was something I could do to keep you here. Look, if you still want a few hours, we can work something out." SaVoy locked the money in a safe and left fifty dollars in small bills and change in the drawer. SaVoy looked at Tanya and asked, "How does a woman know when she's had an orgasm?"

Tanya's forehead wrinkled. "I'm not sure it's automatic for women like it is for men." Tanya scratched her head. "Why? Are you—"

"No. I'm just curious, that's all." SaVoy carried her cash drawer to the register.

"I gotta run. William gets upset if I keep him waiting too long. He's taking me to see *Brown Sugar* but I'm going to secretly feast my eyes on Boris." Tanya smiled.

Undoubtedly William was paying with Tanya's money because William didn't have a job. And he didn't want a job. He'd convinced Tanya her car was his car and because he was the man of the house she should let him manage her money. Whenever SaVoy tried to tell Tanya to always handle her own money, Tanya became defensive and sided with William. So SaVoy stopped giving Tanya advice.

"Oh, yeah. Before I forget," Tanya said, "I've been meaning to ask, have you heard from Fancy?"

Now that was someone who knew everything there was to know about sex. "You know how Fancy is. She's probably met a new sponsor for her horseback excursions or something." SaVoy laughed. "I'll call her in a few. Have fun and tell William I said hello." There was no reason for SaVoy to be upset with William. He hadn't mistreated Tanya.

SaVoy placed her psychology textbook on the counter. She picked up the phone and dialed Fancy's number. SaVoy's eyes widened. The corners of her mouth spread to opposite ends. Before the first ring, SaVoy quickly hung up.

"Hey, you," Tyronne said, then licked his lips. "How's

your little college course coming along?" Tyronne stood in front of the counter, spread his legs apart, and folded his arms across his well-defined chest. He was her superhero. His biceps protruded perfectly under his loose-fitting short-sleeve uniform. Tyronne's upper body was shaped like a cobra. His back was muscular. Strong. Wide. His incredible waist was small and flat.

SaVoy didn't care that Tyronne had dropped out of college, but why did he minimize her efforts? Fortunately she'd learned in psychology not to take things personally.

"I heard you stopped by earlier. I was surprised because it's Monday. But I'm always happy to see you." SaVoy smiled again.

"Wow. Is that what you learned in college today? It's Monday."

SaVoy became quiet and looked at Tyronne.

"Aw, I'm sorry. I didn't mean to offend your three point eight GPA. But you do look cute when you're upset." Tyronne walked behind the counter and opened his arms, offering a hug.

Tyronne's hug was tighter and lasted longer than usual. SaVoy's heartbeat quickened as her hands gently rubbed his back. Did Tyronne intentionally thrust his pelvis deep into her abdomen? His unbelievably huge bulge pressed against her belly button. Quickly SaVoy stepped back.

Tyronne laughed and asked, "You okay?"

Noticing the imprint of Tyronne's penis was larger than she'd imagined, SaVoy looked away. Were her eyes deceiving her? Or did that outline extend from between Tyronne's legs up to his belt buckle? Tyronne's head bobbed. He licked his lips and smiled. A customer entered the store so Tyronne walked back to the other side of the counter.

"How much for the AAA batteries? Four pack," the customer asked.

SaVoy wanted a second look at Tyronne's privates for verification but didn't want to appear obvious. Focusing on the customer, she answered, "Four ninety-nine plus tax," and removed a pack from the wall behind her and handed them to the customer.

"Damn, that's highway robbery." The customer flipped the package over and stared at the price.

Tyronne said, "That's why it's called a convenience store, my brother. By the time you drive to the super-market or drugstore, park your car, stand in line—and hope they have them on sale . . ." Tyronne raised his hand. "But. If they don't, you still gon' spend four dollars. You might as well go on and get the batteries now."

"Yeah, that's true. But she need to lower the price."

SaVoy placed his receipt and batteries in the bag. "Thanks. Come back again."

"I can't stand cheap ass niggas," Tyronne said after the guy left the store.

SaVoy stared at Tyronne, wondering why she was so attracted to him.

"I'm sorry, I mean cheap ass men."

SaVoy chose her words carefully and acknowledged Tyronne's efforts. "Thank you, Tyronne. That's better." SaVoy wasn't trying to change Tyronne but she realized if she encouraged his poor choice of words, Tyronne might start using profanity. Even worse, one day he might decide to use a few of those nasty words on her.

"I need your female perspective. Um, umm." Tyronne covered his mouth and cleared his throat. "Do you think a brother like myself should take a woman to see Michael Baisden's *Men Cry in the Dark?*"

"Yeah, of course. Why not?" SaVoy grinned. She'd been so busy, all she had time to do was talk about going to the play. Fancy was going with Byron. Tanya was going with William. Desmond was taking Carlita. Seemingly she was the only one who didn't have tickets or a date.

"It's not one of those mushy type plays with men in

tights dancing across the stage? Or women puttin' brothas down, is it?" Tyronne struck a familiar heroic pose with his arms folded high across his chest.

"No, Tyronne. You'll like it. So, who are you taking?" Vanessa once told her never to assume anything when dealing with men.

Casually, Tyronne said, "A friend. You don't know her."

SaVoy's smile faded. "Oh, I see." SaVoy's voice was flat. "Well, I'm sure she'll enjoy the play."

"She's just a friend. Always complaining I don't take her anywhere. Thanks for the tip. Now, if I don't like the play you know I'm gon' fire you on Wednesday. Peace. I'm out." Tyronne slapped the counter and left.

Why did it even matter that he was taking someone else? He wasn't her man. Tyronne was her friend. A friend she liked a lot but didn't know how to express her feelings to. Didn't he know she liked him? Couldn't he tell by her actions and reactions toward him? SaVoy swallowed the emotional lump in her throat and fluttered her eyelids, washing back the spate of salty water clouding her vision. She flipped open her psychology book but couldn't concentrate on any of the words. Then she remembered she was supposed to call Fancy.

SaVoy dialed Fancy's work number. Fancy answered on the first ring.

"Washington and Associates. This is Fancy Taylor." Fancy's voice became softer, then she said, "Speak to me."

"Hey, I see you're still seducing all your callers. How are you? Haven't heard from you in a couple of days," SaVoy responded.

"Only the wealthy ones," Fancy responded. Her tone instantly lost its seductiveness. "I'm fine. Just dealing with this jerk-off of a boss. He's upset because I quit letting him lick Miss Kitty." Fancy's voice perked up. "But I'm into Byron. I love me some Byron. He's the one.

He's going to be my husband. I bought a bridal catalog yesterday and I want you to help me plan our wedding."

"Has Byron mentioned marriage? Bought you a ring? Or proposed?" SaVoy asked, because this wasn't the first time Fancy had met "the one."

"No, but he did buy me a new Benz. The ring will automatically follow. You know how men are. They expect us to take the lead. That's why you haven't gotten a date with Tyronne. You keep waiting for him to ask you out first. Tyronne has a big dick just like my Byron. Girl, I have a built-in dickarometer. They can't conceal those luscious weapons. And, girl, you can't wait for a man that's hung and gifted to ask you out. You gotta jump on that with your legs wide open and ride that shit till it collapses." Fancy gasped. "My bad. You still a virgin. On second thought, you'd better not fuck with that big dick. It'll just ruin you into a heavenly ho and have you speakin' in tongues. At least wait until after you graduate, 'cause once you've sucked and fucked a big one, you won't be able to think straight. Let me pull out my calendar. What are you doing Sunday morning? I'll bring the catalog. This one just came out. It's for African-American brides and it is the bomb!"

SaVoy exhaled, then said, "The same thing you should be doing—"

Before SaVoy could finish Fancy said, "My bad. Church. How about Saturday morning?"

"Saturday is fine, Fancy."

"Good. I'll change my horseback riding appointment with Byron from Saturday to Sunday and I'll go rollerblading early Saturday morning. I'll pick you up around nine. I know this fabulous breakfast spot secluded up in the hills. White people mainly eat there so you'll fit right in." Fancy laughed.

SaVoy asked, "Should I call and invite Tanya?"

"If you must. But I doubt she can get a weekend pass from the warden."

SaVoy couldn't disagree with Fancy, this time. "Fancy can I ask you a question about sex?"

"Oh, oh. Okay, go ahead."

"How does a woman know when she's experienced an orgasm?"

Fancy started breathing heavy into the phone. "Haaaa. Haaaaa. Damn, you! Damn, you! Yes! Fuck me! Harder! Harder! Ooooooooo! But for you, you'll probably find yourself screaming praises and calling God's name."

SaVoy shook her head and said, "I knew I shouldn't have asked you."

"Suit yourself. But I've got go. Here comes horny Harry licking his damn lips again."

SaVoy hung up the phone wondering if Fancy was right about Tyronne. Did she really need to make the first move to get Tyronne's attention? Would making an advance alter their relationship? Maybe the girl Tyronne said was just his friend was really his girlfriend. SaVoy needed to talk with Vanessa. She picked up the phone and dialed Vanessa's number.

"We're sorry. The person you are calling does not accept calls from unidentified callers . . ."

SaVoy knew that. She dialed star-eight-two, then quietly hung up the phone as several customers entered the store.

CHAPTER 13

Desmond stood outside Carlita's door debating whether to ring the bell or go to Fancy's apartment. Fancy had left several messages, each one saying she needed him. Not the way he preferred. The brakes on her new car were squeaking, again. If she was so happy with dude, why did she keep calling him? How could Fancy just have sex with him and then act as if they never consummated their friendship? A voice inside his head whispered, *Just leave. Go over to Fancy's. Come back to Carlita's later or tomorrow.*

How could Desmond compete with the wealthy men who generously gave Fancy everything she wanted, including a fifty thousand dollar car? After dude gave Fancy the Benz, Fancy gave Desmond back his old car and said, "If you don't want it, Dez, get rid of it." Desmond sat on the bench by Carlita's door and gnawed his fingernail. Why did he keep revisiting the same issues? Something inside him just wouldn't let go of Fancy. Was it his pride? Or was it the fact that despite all of Fancy's flaws, Desmond was still in love with her?

All Desmond wanted was to love Fancy, be true to her, and he wouldn't hurt her like most of the insensitive guys she dated. If being rich also meant he had to become insensitive and arrogant, Desmond would rather remain a mechanic. But that wasn't his future plan. Becoming a famous attorney was his destiny. If Fancy would support him now, he'd stay with her forever. If she waited until after he became rich and famous, it would hurt him because at best she would be just a friend.

Shaking his head he reached for the door knocker. Maybe if no one heard him he could honestly tell Carlita he came by but no one answered the door. Yeah, right, a household of five, at ten o'clock at night, and everyone was gone. Desmond stopped debating with himself and pressed the lit rectangle.

Ding-dong.

A silhouette of beauty emerged before his eyes. Carlita opened the door wearing an ankle-length black sheer robe with nothing—*nothing*—underneath.

"Hi, baby. You can use your key, you know."

"And miss out on seeing my woman open the door looking all sexy? I'm glad I didn't."

Desmond smiled and followed Carlita into the living room. As Carlita jiggled her butt, the belt tied around her waist seemed determined not to let the smooth material covering her voluptuous ass become buried between Carlita's cheeks. Her hair was loose and swayed, releasing the sweet freshness he'd come to love. A dab of vanilla aromatherapy oil rubbed in her palms, lightly run through her hair then brushed throughout was one of Carlita's secrets. Desmond loved Carlita. But he wasn't in love with her like she was with him. Barry White's "I'm Gonna Love You Just a Little More, Baby" resonated throughout the house.

Carlita pointed toward the couch and sang, " 'I'm gonna love you, love you, love you.' "

A tray of freshly sliced mangos arranged in the shape of a heart decorated a simple black platter, which sat centered on the glass-top coffee table. A bottle of champagne rested in an ice bucket next to two extra-long-stemmed wineglasses. The familiar scent of strawberry candles burned along with several jasmine incense sticks. The house was pleasantly quiet.

"Where the kids?" Desmond asked, looking around.

Kids. Desmond shouldn't call them kids because he was only six years older than Carlita's oldest. The minute they would hear his voice they'd rush into the living room and challenge him to a game of Madden or chess. Carlita didn't condone wrestling in her house so pillow fighting was out of the question, at least when she was home. Carlita would say, "I don't have money to throw away on carelessness. You break something in this house, you will pay for it with cash or I will beat your ass." Most of Carlita's promises were fulfilled so when they broke the lamp in her son's bedroom, Desmond rushed to IKEA and bought a new one.

"At my sister's. I asked her to keep them for me this weekend. I needed a Carlita weekend." She leaned over and softly kissed his lips, slipping a slice of mango in the corners of their now interlocked jaws.

"Umm." Sucking and slurping, Desmond couldn't tell which was sweeter—Carlita's tongue or the sugary fruit.

It was Friday night so Desmond should have been excited he had thirty-six to forty-eight hours to have Carlita all to himself. Instead he was already thinking of an excuse not to be available Saturday or Sunday.

Carlita rubbed her hand through his hair, then massaged the back of his neck. Desmond's eyes automatically closed, his head instantly fell, causing his chin to hit his collarbone. Desmond remembered how his mother used to rub the back of his head when he was a little boy. The relaxing sensation immediately cleared his mind.

"So, how was your day?" Carlita asked, working her fingers into his pressure points.

"Fine," Desmond mumbled, "fine."

Fancy was the woman of his dreams, but Carlita was a real woman. Fancy never offered nor gave him a massage. Maybe that's why Desmond preferred dating older women. They cooked, cleaned, and still had time to please their man.

Desmond muttered, "And yours?"

"Oh, I had a fabulous day. I spent my day at the Orinda spa. I started with a manicure and pedicure. Then I had a ninety-minute body massage. Ooh that felt so good." Carlita moaned like she was having an orgasm. "Have you ever had a hot-stone massage?" Carlita asked, tasting the tip of his fingers.

"No, but from the way you're turning me on with those noises, sounds like I need to."

"Yeeesssss," Carlita hissed, then softly kissed his neck. "Next time I'll make us an appointment." Kneading the joints in his hand she continued, "After the massage, I had a wonderful peppermint body scrub. Then I lounged in the eucalyptus steam sauna for twenty minutes and I ended with a shampoo and blow dry at Top Notch."

Carlita made blow-dry sound like blow job when she whispered in Desmond's ear. His dick pressed harder against his pants. Top Notch. Where had he heard that before? Aw, shit! That was where Fancy went to get her hair done.

"Well, whoever does your hair, she does a great job. It's beautiful," Desmond said, running his fingers through Carlita's hair.

After talking for about an hour, Carlita kissed from his lips to his Adam's apple and slid his shirt down his arms, leaving it underneath his back. Carlita pressed a button and the black leather sofa vibrated. Then she began licking his nipples, biting his chest, and grazing her lips all over his body. Lightly scratching her nails over his chest, abs, and back, Carlita maneuvered her red fingernails and unbuttoned his pants. Cautiously she lowered his zipper and peeped inside. Slipping her soft hand underneath the elastic band of his boxer briefs, she massaged his dick, then caressed the head.

"Oh, baby. Look what I've found." Carlita's eyes beamed with excitement, then she whispered, "Get up for a moment."

Desmond sprang from the sofa and watched Carlita as she spread a beach size towel on the sofa. "Lay back and open your legs."

Desmond sprawled like a frog on his back with his legs open as wide as he could stretch them.

Carlita enjoyed every inch of his now mango flavored dick as she took her time. Syrupy juices oozed between his cheeks. Occasionally Carlita flicked the tip of her tongue over his rectal opening. Desmond closed his eyes when Carlita gently French kissed the sensitive spot right below his balls. Desmond threw one leg over the back of the couch and suspended the other in the air so Carlita could get closer.

Semen seeped from his head. "Oh—my—god," Desmond whispered repeatedly. "I love you, woman."

Carlita eased his left ball into her mouth and slowly stroked his shaft. When she started humming, his nut vibrated in her mouth. Desmond grabbed the back of her head and gripped her hair. Carlita never complained about him messing up her hair. Easing his right nut into her mouth, Carlita hummed again. His dick throbbed. Carlita's tongue wiggled from the base of his penis, up his shaft.

She stopped at the spot that connected the shaft and head, and gently rubbed the crevice with a slice of mango. When his fluids oozed from the opening and spilled over the top, Carlita savored his juices. Her lips surrounded his head as she sucked his cum, taking all of him into her warm mouth. Carlita was such a woman. His woman. She began rotating his head in her mouth like it was her favorite lollipop.

"Damn, that feels good. Suck your dick, woman. Do the damn thing. Oh, yeah, baby. Do dat shit," Desmond said as he watched Carlita.

Carlita had taught him a man should only suck five places on a woman's body: lips, tits, clit, fingers, and toes. "Bite and lick everywhere else." She'd added, "Amateurs suck. Pros bite. Sucking leaves passion marks. Bites marks are gone by the time you're finished making love. Passion marks stay for days and generate more trouble than they're worth."

Desmond's fluids escaped once more but a lot more of his juices were ready to explode in Carlita's mouth. He was on the verge of cumming. Carlita had him going. Going. Going. Insane. Skin tingling. Toes curling. Back arching. Carlita removed her robe, then coaxed him to the reclining chair. She pressed a button and the chair started vibrating. She pressed another button and the leather got warmer. Carlita held his dick and spanked his head against her clit until she came. She straddled him, placing one leg at a time over each of his shoulders and rested her feet at the top of the recliner. With his dick deep inside, Carlita took her time rocking back and forth to the melodic groove of Sade. She rocked. And rocked. And rocked, until the recliner fully extended.

Desmond palmed as much as he could of Carlita's ass and pulled her hips into his each time theirs met. He plucked her nipples with his teeth while she held him close.

Carlita deliciously whispered, "This is the best dick I have ever had," right before she French kissed his ear.

"Your pussy is so tight, so juicy, hot, and so, so wet. I just want to explode deep inside you. Say my name, baby. What's my name?"

Carlita seductively said, "Desmond." Then she moaned, "Desmond. Ooh, Desmond, I love you," Carlita purred in the sexiest voice he'd ever heard.

Desmond pulled her hips closer and thrust his deeper. "I'm cumming, baby. Daddy is cumming all up in his pussy. This is all for you, woman. Hold me. Tighter." His fluids flowed hard. Carlita's ass churned up and down, converting his cum into cream.

Carlita moaned louder. "I'm cumming with you."

She pressed harder, forcing the recliner to unexpectedly lean back another notch. This time Desmond felt the head of his dick slip into Carlita's vaginal cul-de-sac. Her legs folded underneath her thighs as Carlita rode him like she was cumming across a finish line.

Desmond felt his dick slipping out. Carlita turned off the vibrator and rocked until she was satisfied. Then she coaxed him to her bed, rubbed his entire body down with a nice hot towel, dried him off, and tucked him in. Desmond slept for what seemed like hours until his cellular phone woke him up.

He fumbled in the dark, following the tune to the living room. It was Fancy.

Desmond whispered, "What's up?"

"Desmond, I'm stranded."

Trying not to wake Carlita he retreated to the kitchen still whispering, "Stranded? Where are you?"

"I have a flat tire. I'm stuck in San Francisco. I need you to come and get me. Now, Dez! I'm scared. I need you!"

Moving the phone away from his ear and peeping into the living room, Desmond said, "Okay, I'm on my way. I'll call you back in five minutes."

Desmond dressed quietly. He went into the bedroom. Carlita was sitting up in the bed. "Where are you going?" she asked calmly.

"Tyronne's car broke down. I gotta go help him out. I'll call you tomorrow."

Carlita rolled over and pulled the covers up to her neck.

As soon as Desmond closed his car door, he speed dialed Fancy's number. "Where are you?"

"You've gotta hurry, Dez, it's dark out here," Fancy cried.

"Calm down. Where are you?" Desmond had run the last two lights before getting on the freeway. "I'm in my car right now crossing the Bay Bridge. Tell me where you are."

"I'm off the Caesar Chavez exit at the gas station near The Clam House."

The Clam House was a nice affordable seafood restaurant. Desmond had taken Fancy to lunch there a few months ago.

"What in hell are you doing over there at one o'clock in the morning? I'll be there in five minutes." Desmond tossed his cell phone on the passenger seat and plunged his accelerator to the floor. When he pulled into the gas station, he saw Fancy but he didn't see her car.

"Oh thank you, Dez, for coming to get me." Fancy hugged his neck so tight he couldn't move.

Desmond looked around. "Where is your car?"

"Byron had it towed to your shop. That's why I needed you to hurry."

Frowning at Fancy he asked, "Then why didn't you have dude give you a ride?"

Fancy threw her arms around Desmond, again. "I'm so happy to see you. I'll tell you all about this crazy night when I get home. Right now I'm just tired, cold, and a little tipsy."

Turning on the heater, Desmond drove in silence, occasionally watching Fancy stretch her red dress down to her knees.

"I hope I didn't wake you," she said, reaching for his hand.

Desmond gazed over at Fancy. "It's okay. How long you gon' keep lettin' these guys use you?"

Fancy laughed. "Stop trying to be psychic. It's not your strong suit."

Sighing heavily, Desmond parked in front of Fancy's

building, turned off the engine, and escorted Fancy to her front door.

"Come in. Keep me company."

That meant she wanted him to play psychologist until she could get to Mandy's couch. As long as he didn't comment, everything would go well. Carlita had worn him out so Desmond wasn't interested in making love to Fancy tonight. But he would enjoy holding her in his arms.

"Cool," Desmond responded.

Fancy drew a warm bath. Desmond washed her back and listened to her.

"I was on my way home from a date with Byron and all of sudden my tire blew out. At the same time, Byron had gotten an emergency call. Otherwise he would have brought me home. So he called his tow company and left as soon the guys arrived. After the two guys placed my Benz on the flatbed, 'cause you know they can't drag an expensive car around like they do the cheap ones, the driver said he was not instructed to give me a ride home and he had no seat belt for me to wear. Then they took my Benz and left me at the station and advised me to call someone to pick me up. Just wait until I tell Byron. He's going to fire those losers.

"So, you see, I would've been stranded if you hadn't come to my rescue," Fancy said, reaching her finger deep inside her vagina, then splashing her hand around in the water.

The story didn't sound legitimate but Desmond had already heard enough. "You need to stop seeing dude. Any man that leaves you stranded doesn't give a damn about you," Desmond said. He clenched his jaw and handed Fancy a bath towel.

"Have you ever been in love, Desmond?"

Twice. Trina and Fancy. "Just with you." Desmond followed Fancy into her bedroom and watched as she sat on the vanity stool, lowered the magnifying mirror, and spread her legs.

Desmond felt an erection stirring in his pants. "What are you doing?"

"Before I turn out the lights, I have to make sure Miss Kitty is all right."

Desmond doubted the extra massage of Fancy's clit was part of the checkup. Then again, maybe it was.

"Stay with me tonight, Dez. I don't wanna be alone."

Desmond removed his clothes and eased under the down-feather comforter. The lights around the lake reflected off of the still water. Peaceful. Serene. The crescent moon floated above the hillside. Fancy snuggled her butt and back into his pubic hairs and his chest. Fancy's naked body was silky soft. She reached behind, grasping his hand, then tucked his arm underneath hers. Desmond whispered:

> *"Is this a mirage*
> *As I massage your breasts*
> *She's nibbling upon my chest*
> *And she's willing to do*
> *For me*
> *All the things I want*
> *To do for you*
>
> *Is this a mirage*
> *As I contemplate*
> *Whether to wipe this slate*
> *Clean or to cling*
> *To your being*
> *Even though you are constant fleeing*
>
> *So maybe it is a mirage*
> *That won't disappear*
> *Or eradicate my fears*
> *That one day*
> *You won't be near*
> *To hear*

Me say
I love you
Because someone else will appear

Again and again
Each time with a different name
This is insane
Because I can touch you
And I can smell you
And I can taste you
And I can make love to you
But I cannot have you

So what do
I do
When this mirage
Becomes clear
And someone else
Is lying here
With you"

"I love you, Fancy."

"Yeah, I know, Dez." Fancy paused, then said, "Good night."

CHAPTER 14

"Why? Why? Why? Why? Why are wealthy men so heartless?" Fancy tried to find an answer before speaking with Mandy. She parked in a familiar space on University Avenue, watching time go by on the digital clock. Ten more minutes before her appointment. Seemed as though their last meeting was weeks ago but nearly three months had passed since she'd spoken with Mandy. Fancy needed yet dreaded participating in yet another counseling session because her prior problems were unresolved and new troubles had developed. The only resolution she'd fulfilled was losing weight. As long as Fancy was fabulous on the outside, no one could tell she was less than perfect on the inside.

Don't cry, Fancy. Don't you dare cry, you hear me. Fancy wasn't sure if her thoughts provoked the emotions that brought tears to her eyes. Maybe today she'd tell Mandy what really happened to her as a child. That her obsession with working out was her way of running away from the truth. But Fancy couldn't outrun the demons that stole her breath away in the middle of the night while she slept. Nor could she outwrestle the evil spirits that held her down, preventing her from moving, screaming, kicking, or crying out for help the past three nights when Desmond held her in his arms. "Forget about it," Fancy said, patting a tissue below her eyes and underneath her nose. "It's over. It's done. It's history."

Fancy lowered her sun visor, flipped open the mirror, and gazed deep into her pupils until her image faded. A vision of Desmond's friend Carlita popped into her mind. Yesterday when she and Desmond had breakfast at Lynn & Lu's, the waiter had just brought their food when Carlita entered wearing a pair of faded blue jeans. The top she'd worn was cute. Open back. Brown suede spaghetti straps crisscrossed about her back. That wasn't the first time Fancy had seen her but she was shocked that Carlita was Desmond's friend. Carlita, the only other woman their hair stylist called *Ms. Diva,* was beautiful and seemed so secure every time Fancy saw her at Top Notch. The one thing they had in common was when they walked into the salon, their hair looked so good, they should've been walking out. Fancy was calling their stylist Raeshelle early tomorrow morning to get the details on Carlita. How could a woman like Carlita be seriously interested in her Desmond?

Fancy was surprised when Carlita had stopped in front of Desmond, holding her to-go Styrofoam container, and said, "Hey, baby. Tyronne get his car taken care of Friday night? Oh, how rude of me," she said, switching the Styrofoam to the other hand, "I'm Carlita. And you are?"

Staring at Carlita's hand, Fancy recalled saying, "Desmond's friend." Desmond must have truly cared for her if he'd left Carlita's house at one in the morning to rescue her.

Fancy pictured Desmond's mouth hanging open for thirty seconds before the words, "Uh, yeah. I was going to call you," escaped in response to Carlita's question. Had Desmond just told Carlita a lie or not the truth? Was there a difference?

Carlita politely said, "Call me later. Enjoy your breakfast. Nice meeting you, Fancy." With her Styrofoam container level with her waistline, Carlita left, hauling the biggest ass Fancy had ever seen.

Fancy wasn't surprised Carlita knew her name. But how much did Carlita know about her? When she looked at Desmond, Fancy remembered saying, "So that's Carlita."

"Yeeessss. *Carrrliita.*" The way Desmond rolled her name off of his tongue like Carlita was the banana walnut waffle with warm maple syrup that he'd eased into his mouth made Fancy conceal her jealousy. That was history. She needed to focus on the present.

Now, Fancy speed dialed Adam's number. His automated voice mail answered immediately. "Adam, baby. This is Fancy. Call me." When she ended the call, her digital clock displayed ten-o-three. Fancy closed her visor, retrieved her white plastic grocery bag, covered the meter, and dashed across the street into Mandy's office.

The receptionist continued typing and said, "Hi, Fancy. Go on in and have a seat. Mandy is waiting for you."

Fancy sat on the sofa, crossed her legs, and sat in silence.

"I detect we are not in a good mood today. Why?" Mandy asked, placing the yellow legal size pad in her lap.

"There's so much to say, I don't know where to start." Fancy sighed heavily and became quiet. She forced back her tears then said, "One moment Harry adored me, bought me expensive gifts, and took me out. On a day like today, normally I wouldn't have to go into the office at all. I know it's just a matter of time before Harry expects me to work eight hours a day. But that's okay because I'm going to quit and start my own business soon."

Fancy avoided eye contact with Mandy. "Then there's my fiancé, Byron. We don't go out much. He claims he's busy but I believe he's afraid to make a commitment. Once I showed him the wedding colors, the cake, and the three possible locations for our ceremony, Byron doesn't call me as much as he used to."

Not waiting for Mandy to respond, Fancy exhaled and continued, "You don't understand. I gave up *all* of my sponsors for Byron. Well, actually Adam stopped calling and he won't return my calls, so basically I had to pay my own rent for March. And a single paycheck doesn't cover my rent, because Harry cut off my bonuses, because I stopped having sex with him, so now I'm going to be late paying for April." Fancy didn't tell Mandy she also didn't have enough money to pay for the session. Fancy wondered if Desmond was happy with Carlita. That was silly. Of course he wasn't. He spent the entire weekend at her place.

"Byron? You mean the one who hasn't paid you for all those fund-raisers Byron? Or is this someone new?" Mandy peered over her glasses.

"My future husband, Byron. He spends lots of money on me. He bought me a car, so I know he loves me. Our wedding colors are platinum and white. SaVoy will be my maid of honor. Tanya is a bridesmaid. I've created a diet plan to help Tanya lose weight. Trying to fit a size sixteen into a size twelve won't work. I'm going to start taking her hiking with me. I told her to put William out. Let's see, where was I? Oh, yeah. Two women from my Thursday night spin class will also be bridesmaids. I still have to find a flower girl, though. And since Desmond is my best friend, he can give me away."

Raising her hand barely above her note pad, Mandy shook her head and said, "Wait a minute. You need to slow down. We can't discuss everything in thirty minutes."

"No, actually I need to hurry up. I have a date with Byron tonight. And I have to figure out how I'm going to get my hair and nails done before seven. And I mentioned to Desmond yesterday over breakfast that I'm in love with Byron."

"Okay, Fancy. Forget about Byron and Desmond and all of your sponsors. Don't you see the pattern? When you have sex with them, they're happy with you. When you don't, with the exception of Desmond, the others move on to someone else who will have sex with them. Now, Fancy. What about you? Is this what you honestly want?"

"Why do you keep spending my dime asking me about myself? I live with me every second of every day. I need you to help solve my problems." Maybe this was a good time for Fancy to open up to Mandy about her past. Trying to find the right words, Fancy sat quietly, constructing sentences in her head.

Mandy stared for a long time over the top of her glasses. Softly she asked, "How's Caroline?"

Fancy sighed heavily and said, "Sick."

"Sick? Or sickening?" Mandy questioned.

"Both."

"She's sick. What's wrong?" Mandy slid her glasses up her nose. "How long?"

"Caroline exaggerates. It's not that serious. She left me a message saying something about how she was bleeding all over herself for almost three weeks straight. Messing up her clothes and stuff, and her car seat. Afraid to go to work 'cause she was soaking through maxi pads like crazy. I think she said the doctor told her she has fibroids. Since she said there was no rush to have surgery, I don't know why she tied up my voice mail with that long drawn out monologue. It's not like I'm going to take care of her again, even if she does have to have a hysterectomy."

"Oh, Fancy. That's not good. Despite what you think of Caroline, she is your mother." Mandy was starting to sound like SaVoy.

"Yeah, yeah. But she still doesn't have time for me. La, la, la, la, la . . . it's the same old song." Fancy bowed in her seat. "Can we change the subject?"

Mandy's eyes shifted to the left. She bit her bottom lip, and then tilted her head, letting her frames travel to the tip of her nose. Fancy felt the tension in Mandy's exhale but didn't hear a sigh.

Fancy stood and said, "I know that look. This concludes our session."

"No, wait." Mandy opened her bottom drawer, pulled out a book, and handed it to Fancy. "Give this to your mother. For me. Please."

Fancy looked at the cover. Flipped the book over, then back to the cover. "*It's a Sistah Thing: A Guide to Understanding and Dealing with Fibroids for Black Women* by Monique R. Brown. These women don't look like Caroline. The one in the middle looks like me."

"Good point," Mandy said. "If your mother has fibroids, you need to know her history. Take care of yourself, Fancy."

Fancy started her engine and speed dialed Raeshelle's number. When the answering machine beeped, Fancy said, "Raeshelle! I know it's Monday and you always close the shop to braid hair but could you please pick up the phone." Fancy paused. "Raeshelle! I know you're there. Pick up the phone, it's me Fancy." Fancy waited a few seconds, then hung up. She merged before the Eighteenth Street exit and drove toward the tollbooths. Traffic to the city at ten in the morning was a breeze. Fancy was surprised Harry wasn't in his office, so she whisked into hers and closed the door.

Four messages registered on her display. "Hi, Fancy. This is Tanya. I—" Delete. "Hey, girl. Haven't heard from you in—" Fancy deleted SaVoy's message. "Hi, this is Adam." Fancy smiled. "I didn't want to disturb you so I called your work number. But listen. I've enjoyed the time we've spent together but I got married in February. That's why I haven't returned your calls. My wife changed our home number, I'm changing my cell number, and please don't disturb me at work. Take care of my kitty. After the newness of this marriage thing wears off, I'll call you. Bye." Fancy hit four to replay the message, then deleted it. "Hey, this is Byron." Fancy smiled again. "I have to cancel our date tonight. I'll call you when I'm back in town."

Fancy deleted the last message and stared at her computer. *Fuck Adam. Who did he think he was? His kitty. Not hardly.* Fancy logged on to the real estate Web site but couldn't concentrate on the real estate principles. She could use her key and wait for Byron at his place. When the phone rang, Fancy stared at the receiver, then pressed the speaker button and said, "Yes, Harry."

"I need to see you in my office," Harry said, then hung up.

What would Harry do if she didn't go to his office? Fancy thought about the lies she'd told her girlfriends. Not all, but most of the clothes and jewelry she owned, she'd bought cash, or charged to her Mastercard, Visa, or Discover, which were all over the limit. Soon she'd have to change her home phone number again to avoid the bill collectors.

Fancy stood in the full-length mirror behind her door. Her short tan leather skirt showed off her shapely thighs. The tapered long-sleeve tan sweater outlined her breasts. Her high heels accentuated her toned calves. Her French manicure, African pedicure, and hair weave looked good but not great. Since Byron canceled, she could keep her standing Tuesday appointments. With the exception of the two hundred dollars she had in her purse, Fancy was broke. She stared at her radiant image trying to see what men saw in her besides her beauty. Fancy opened her door, walked into Harry's office, closed his door, and smiled.

CHAPTER 15

SaVoy accepted Vanessa's advice and explored her womanhood. Several times she'd come close to climaxing, but stopped before having an orgasm. SaVoy teased her sudsy nipples. They tingled. She watched the tips harden. Her soapy hands caressed her breasts. SaVoy leaned back in the tub, took a deep breath, and then exhaled. She closed her eyes. SaVoy stroked her clit, trying to prevent the questions stirring in her head from diminishing the strange sensation.

"Feel. Don't think. Feel. Don't think." Vanessa's words resounded in her mind.

SaVoy breathed deeply and exhaled through her mouth. This time she inserted the tip of her longest finger into her vagina. Then she slid it out and over her clitoris. She repeated the movement again and again. Each stroke aroused her a little bit more than the one before. Her body trembled. Chill bumps covered her arms. SaVoy wanted to experience her first orgasm alone. The strokes to her clitoris and shaft were more pleasurable than the mild penetration of her fingertip into her vagina, so SaVoy massaged the outside and squeezed her muscles on the inside.

SaVoy inhaled. This time she held her breath for a few seconds in order to heighten the feeling. Vanessa had explained how a woman had two orgasmic secretion points and a man had only one. When SaVoy really learned her body, Vanessa said she could have an hour-long orgasm from her clitoris, really powerful ones inside her vagina after she became sexually active, and sometimes both at the same time. If she, or her partner, played with her clit during penetration she could score a triple-double orgasm: one direct score by massaging her clit while being on top of her partner, one assist from her partner teasing her clit in a doggie-style position, and one rebound; right after her partner had an orgasm she could have two more.

"Ah, this does feel good," SaVoy whispered.

"The more you move, the better it feels." Vanessa's words surfaced again.

SaVoy's bath water wavered and splashed. "Oh. Oh. Oh. Oh, my God." SaVoy squeezed her thighs together as her hips rose above the water. Rapidly she inhaled and exhaled with shallow breaths. "Oooo. My God." Her hips were now under the water in a race against her fingers. SaVoy muffled the pitch in her voice. "Ahh. Ahh." SaVoy collapsed in the tub and said, "Wow!" So that's what sex is all about. Fancy was right. But why was an orgasm so powerful she called God's name aloud? Was that supposed to happen? She could ask Vanessa when she returned from her business trip next week.

Overwhelming joy stirred inside SaVoy as she dried herself off. The last time she remembered being that happy was when Papa bought her a car for her sixteenth birthday. SaVoy sang and danced as she prepared for her graduation party. This day signified two major accomplishments, education and womanhood.

SaVoy knelt beside her bed to pray, "Dear Lord, Thank you for blessing me with the strength and intelligence to earn this degree. Let Thy will be done as I move forward doing your will and giving back to my community. And Lord, you know in my heart I wasn't lusting. I was experimenting. Amen." SaVoy's prayers didn't have to be long. Just sincere.

SaVoy slipped into a black after-five dress. She found Papa sitting in the family room working the crossword puzzle.

"You ready, Baby Girl?" her father asked, looking up with a huge grin.

Why was he grinning? He couldn't have heard her because her bathroom was inside her bedroom, her music was turned up loud, and she'd locked both doors.

"Yes, Papa. I'm ready." SaVoy extended her arms, warmly embracing her father.

"Sit down for a minute. Let me talk to you." Papa patted the empty space beside him.

SaVoy nervously sat beside her father on the sofa.

"I apologize for keeping your mother away from you. I was wrong. You know I've always protected you thinking what I was doing was best for you. Vanessa helped me to realize what I was doing was what was best for me. My not allowing you to grow up with your mother was wrong."

"Oh, Papa. You've sacrificed so much for me. I don't fault you. It's okay." Why was he discussing this before her party?

"No, it's not, Baby Girl. It's not okay. I've decided to tell you all about your mother. But that can wait until after the party. I'm not sure how you'll handle it. But it's time for you to know."

"Thank you, Papa. I've prayed every night for my mama."

"I know, Baby Girl. I know. We'll talk again later tonight. Now let's get to the party and celebrate! My baby has a college degree!" Papa smiled, then said, "I have a surprise for you. Vanessa you can come out now!"

"Oh, my goodness!" SaVoy hugged her father, then hugged Vanessa. A wide smile covered SaVoy's face.

"Honey, I cut that meeting short. Told them I'd be back on Tuesday. When you're the boss, you're in control. Remember that."

SaVoy's stomach tied in knots. The happy knots intertwined with the sad ones. She didn't know what to think or feel about her mother so she prayed silently in the car while Papa drove and Vanessa talked about her trip. The parking lot was half full. She didn't have a lot of friends but she was popular in her class so the upstairs banquet room at H's Lordship was large enough to comfortably seat two hundred people.

SaVoy greeted each of her guests personally. Fancy and Byron had arrived. "Hi. Thanks for coming." SaVoy was already regretting having sat Fancy and Desmond at the same table.

"Hey, girl. Congratulations!" Fancy handed SaVoy a neatly wrapped package inside a Tiffany bag. "This is my Byron. Byron Van Lee. SaVoy Edmonds, one of my very best friends."

"Pleased to meet you." Byron smiled. "So what's next on your agenda?"

Fancy turned her head and said, "Oh, look who just walked in. Desmond, Tyronne, and Carlita."

"I have so many plans. First, I have ten months to figure out how to buy the building my father is leasing for his grocery store. I want to surprise him. He's sacrificed so much for me. And I'm thinking about applying to grad school at Stanford."

"Here's my card. Maybe I can assist you with helping your father and getting into Stanford. Call me." Byron handed SaVoy his card and said, "You are absolutely beautiful." Byron stared at her. Not in a lustful way but nevertheless he made SaVoy uncomfortable.

"Who invited Caroline?" Fancy said, eyeing SaVoy.

SaVoy shook her head and replied, "Fancy, she's your

mother. It's my party. I invited her. Thanks, Byron. I'll call you next week." SaVoy was pleased to see Tyronne hadn't brought a date. Tanya and William entered behind Caroline.

SaVoy greeted them, then searched the room until she found Vanessa. "Can I talk to you? Privately. For a minute," SaVoy asked, grabbing Vanessa's hand.

"Of course, honey. Let's step outside on the balcony."

SaVoy looked at Vanessa and said, "Guess what?"

"Honey, Vanessa doesn't need to guess. A glow like that can only mean one thing."

"Yes. I did. This morning. Thank you for telling me about pleasing myself. Now I just have to figure out how to get Tyronne's attention." SaVoy glanced through the glass doors at Tyronne. "Tyronne makes me so nervous. To make my celebration special, I want to slow dance with him tonight. What should I do?"

"When you dance with him, don't think. Feel. Feel Tyronne's body next to yours. Feel his heart beat against your heart. Don't think. Feel. Move with him. Remember, the more you move, the better it feels. But this time you need to move slow and follow his lead."

"What if he doesn't ask me to dance?"

"Honey, this is your party. Ask him."

"But what will everyone think of me? If I ask him, I might look desperate."

"Who cares what other people think? It's not about them. It's about you. And how you feel about Tyronne." Vanessa winked. "You'll be fine. Come on, let's go back inside."

"Desmond, you are not my man!" SaVoy recognized Fancy's voice and hurried over to Fancy and Desmond.

SaVoy whispered between clenched teeth, "Fancy what are you doing?"

"That's okay, we're leaving," Desmond said, tugging the back of Carlita's chair. Carlita didn't move.

SaVoy looked around the room for Byron so he could help calm Fancy. "Where's Byron?"

Fancy snapped at SaVoy. "Why? Why are you concerned about where Byron is?"

SaVoy bowed her head and silently said a short prayer.

Tyronne pulled Desmond aside. When they returned, Desmond sat between beside Carlita and away from Fancy.

SaVoy was relieved when Byron sat between Carlita and Fancy.

"So, how have you been?" Byron asked Carlita.

Carlita calmly nodded. "Fine, and you?"

"I've been good. How are the kids? I imagine they're almost grown by now," Byron answered. His eyes softened as though he and Carlita were more than friends.

When Desmond opened his mouth, Tyronne's eyes narrowed. Desmond clenched his jaw.

SaVoy looked across the table and could not believe that Fancy was unusually quiet. Caroline must have left because SaVoy hadn't seen her since the party started. Fancy probably said something ugly to Caroline.

Vanessa disrupted the private conversations and said, "Round table discussion. Not to sound sexist, I'll generalize and say people who date a lot of different people are compensating for their inadequacies. It's not because they want multiple partners. It's just that multiple partners feed their egos and compensate for their lack of imagination. Really, if a person has a great imagination, they can always find new ways to stimulate their partner. Because when they're with different people they're usually not doing anything new or different. It's just that the partner is different."

SaVoy frowned. She thought Vanessa was going to say something about her accomplishments. After all, this was her graduation party.

Byron responded. "See, that's where I disagree. Having multiple partners is healthy. That's the only way a person can find out what they really like. Or don't like. What I'd like to know is why do women place materialistic values over a man's character?"

Everyone at the table stared or glanced at Fancy.

Papa looked at Tyronne and said, "Let me ask you a question. How many women are you dating?"

"Who? Me?" Tyronne asked, pointing at himself.

"Yes. You, young man," Papa said.

"Papa. Don't. You're embarrassing me. Don't answer that Tyronne. Let's dance," SaVoy said, pulling Tyronne away from his seat.

Tyronne stood, then said, "I'll take the fifth on answering that question, Mr. Edmonds. But I will say this. When I was engaged, I was faithful."

While they danced, SaVoy listened to Tyronne talk about Lisa. "When I think back, the signs were there. Next time, if there is a next time, I won't hide anything. I'll lay my cell phone on the table right along with my wallet or whatever and tell her I have nothing to hide. Nothing. Then I'll let her know how I feel about her. Now if she contacts any of those people, I'll know I have an insecure woman and fire her on the spot."

Wow. That was one condition under which SaVoy did not want Tyronne to fire her.

SaVoy swayed, following Tyronne's lead.

"You really are smart. How come you don't have a man?"

SaVoy softly answered, "You haven't asked."

Tyronne stepped back. "For real. Don't play. You'd date someone like me?"

"For real. Unless there's something about you I should know," SaVoy said.

Tyronne didn't speak another word. When their dance was over he didn't return to the table. He went outside on the balcony. After almost all the guests had left, SaVoy joined Tyronne on the balcony.

"Why are you still out here?"

"Enjoying the peacefulness. It's nice and quiet. Sometimes I enjoy being alone. Especially on a night like tonight when the peeps inside were so out of control."

SaVoy stood quietly next to Tyronne.

"Can a brother have a kiss?"

"Okay." SaVoy closed her eyes. She felt Tyronne's moist lips touch hers. This wasn't her first kiss but it was their first kiss and she'd never forget the moment. SaVoy felt Tyronne's hands travel through her hair down to her shoulders. He massaged her back, then embraced her. She held him close, sucking his tongue in and out of her mouth. She opened her eyes. His were still closed. She looked at Tyronne, hoping that wouldn't be their last kiss. Then SaVoy closed her eyes and listened to the waves washing upon the boulders, praying that this was the beginning of a beautiful relationship.

SaVoy's special day was complete when Papa told her about her mother. They sat in the family room. Vanessa went into Papa's room and closed the door.

Papa sat quietly for a while, then said, "Your mother abandoned you when you were six months old. She claimed she wouldn't make a good mother. She was afraid. Said she was depressed. Too young to be a mother. Something about postpartum blues. I told her 'if you leave us, don't come back.' I thought that would be enough to make her stay. Since she didn't, I figured she was seeing someone else or her family had disowned you because I was black. What kind of woman would leave her child?"

"Oh, Papa." SaVoy held her father's hand. "I don't know. But don't hate Mama." SaVoy squeezed her dad's hand. "I have so many questions."

"She's alive and doing well from what I hear. Last I heard she was living in Sacramento. I think she still lives there. I hope you forgive me. If you want to meet her, I'll find her."

"Do you have any pictures of her?" SaVoy wanted to see the woman she prayed for every night.

Papa left and came back with one four-by-six photo.

The pregnant white girl in the picture looked to be about fifteen. She was beautiful and SaVoy felt as though she was looking at a picture of herself when she was that age. She cried uncontrollably. Papa held her close.

SaVoy couldn't imagine how a child could raise a child. No high school degree. No steady income. That must have been hard. Especially for Papa. Papa was seventeen when SaVoy was born and they lived with his parents until she graduated from the sixth grade. That's when Papa had finally saved enough money to buy the store. The store. SaVoy thought about her first kiss with Tyronne. Now she understood how young girls could become lost in the fantasy. SaVoy was thankful she had the Lord, Papa, Vanessa, and her virginity. And soon, her mother and Tyronne.

CHAPTER 16

Fancy sat in Byron's living room waiting for him to come home. Where was he? Who was he with? Who in hell did Byron think he was, standing up Fancy Taylor? Sure he'd canceled dates with her on several occasions, but never had he not shown or called.

All dressed up, Fancy had sat in her lobby talking to the doorman for almost an hour. No way was she going back upstairs to her apartment after all she'd gone through to get ready. Manicure. Pedicure. Body scrub. She'd personally done all three. When Fancy arrived at Byron's, several cars blocked the driveway so she'd found the closest space available, two blocks away, that didn't have a street cleaning sign posted. Usually when she used her keys, she left the outside light on to let Byron know she was inside. Not tonight. She had to see or know whoever or whatever was more important than her.

Nine o'clock. Ten. Eleven. Fancy heard a noise outside. She tiptoed from the sofa to the door—trying not to bump into any objects in the dark room—and peeped out the window. Those got damn black-eyed raccoons were ransacking the neighbors' garbage cans. Fancy opened the door and yelled, "Get away from here!"

One raccoon covered his eyes; another ignored her and continued searching for food; while the third raced toward her. *Bam!* Fancy slammed the door. The last thing she needed was to contract rabies from an oversize rodent. She ignored the raccoon furiously scratching on the door. If she were lucky, the crazy raccoon might bite Byron in the ass and give him rabies. Then, right before Byron died, she could marry him, claim his inheritance, and live happily ever after.

Twelve o'clock. No Byron. Fancy scrolled Byron's caller ID, then dialed star seventy-two and forwarded his calls to her cell phone. *Don't be irrational.* That would definitely piss Byron off enough for him to end the relationship. Fancy dialed star seventy-three, listened for the interrupted dial tone, then hung up.

The black wool blanket they usually cuddled under to watch movies covered her body as Fancy curled into a fetal position on the sofa. Two of the three cushions shifted forward. Her shoulder, side, and butt bridged the gap. Instead of relaxing, uncurling her body, and repositioning the cushions, Fancy tucked her knees closer to her naked breasts and dozed off.

When she awakened, the lit digital clock on Byron's stereo displayed three, zero, zero. No Byron. Fancy sat, wondering if she shouldn't just go home. Four, zero, zero. The more she thought about leaving the angrier she'd become. Where in the hell was he? Daylight had beaten Byron to his doorstep. "Forget this. I'm out." Fancy gathered her thong, shoes, dress, and purse from the bedroom and tossed them on the edge of the sofa.

Her heart thumped in her throat as she heard laughter outside the door. Fancy's eyes tightened when the melodic laughter of a woman's voice penetrated the solid oak wood. Fancy stood behind the door anxiously waiting for it to open. Where were those damn raccoons when she needed them?

"You are so wonderful. I enjoyed myself immensely but I enjoyed you even more, baby," the woman said.

Fancy backed farther into the empty corner.

"You haven't seen anything yet. I've warned you. I'm single. Never married. No kids. You sure you don't want to work on conceiving Byron Junior tonight?"

"Oh, hell no!" Fancy yelled as she forcefully opened the door, prying the knob from Byron's grip. When Fancy saw the woman, her mouth fell open. Fancy froze.

Byron calmly said, "Why did I know you'd be here? Maybe because you parked *my* Benz down the street from *my* house."

The woman extended her hand to Fancy, "Hi, I'm Byron's friend, and you are?"

That shit was not funny. Fancy thought about breaking Byron's expensive vase over the woman's head. Then she stared at a more expensive painting hanging on the wall.

Byron said, "I wouldn't do that, Fancy, if I were you. Carlita, make yourself comfortable. I'll be right back." Byron picked up Fancy's shoes, handed them to her, and exited the room.

Carlita sat on the sofa beside Fancy's clothes and said, "So how does it feel?"

Fancy opened the door and said, "You are not welcome here. You need to leave our home." Fancy stomped her foot, then said, "Now!"

Carlita didn't flinch, twitch, or budge. "Having someone take your man doesn't feel good, now, does it? Don't worry. You'll get him back. Tomorrow. But tonight I'm going to teach him a few new techniques, then he can try them on you. Tomorrow."

Fancy aimed her magenta spiked heel at Carlita.

Byron walked in the room with a bottle of wine and two glasses. "Fancy, why are you still here? Either you leave on your own, or I will have you escorted out. You have exactly five minutes to decide."

Who in the hell did he think he was talking to?

Byron sat beside Carlita, poured two half glasses of merlot, and said, "So where were we?"

"Umm, I'm going to have my baby's baby, remember?"

Snatching the painting from the wall, Fancy raised the mahogany- framed Darryl Thompson original print in the air. The heaviness weighing on her shoulders rattled her body.

"Wake up. Wake up! Are you okay?" Desmond asked. "You must have had another bad dream."

Fancy closed her eyes real tight, then opened them. She looked at Desmond but saw the vivid scenes from her dream. Fancy's breasts heaved against Desmond's chest. Damn. Thoughts about Carlita had seeped into her subconscious. Watching Carlita and Byron interact at SaVoy's party was awkward for Fancy and she'd noticed the same uneasiness in Desmond's reactions. Byron and Carlita barely spoke to one another five minutes but it was apparent they were very well acquainted. Was it equally obvious to Byron and Carlita that Fancy and Desmond were intimate?

"Just hold me, Dez," Fancy said, grasping his back.

"I love you, Fancy. But I've gotta go." Desmond paused, then said, "Make that *we've* gotta go, to work. But if you need me to stay, you know I will."

"Go. I'll be fine." Fancy turned her back to Desmond and said, "Call me later."

Fancy gazed out her patio window. The sun was rising and seagulls were flying in front of the blinding orange ball creeping above Oakland's east hillside. The cloudless sky carried warm sun rays into her patio but Fancy knew although it was June, it was fifty degrees or below outside. A mirage. Just like her life. Just like Desmond had said. Fancy was not looking forward to leaving for work at eight o'clock. There was no parking place reserved for her at BART. The direct deposit pay wouldn't credit to her account until midnight. She could use her last few dollars to get to and from work or Fancy could roll over and go back to sleep and tomorrow, pretend this day never happened. Sleep. Dream. Fancy decided she needed to stop exclusively dating Byron. The more men she had in her life, the more money and options she had. Okay, the decision was final. Ride BART. And find a new sponsor.

Sitting at her desk, Fancy gazed at Byron's five-by-seven framed photo. He was especially handsome in his olive-colored slacks and black crew neck sweater. Byron was the first and only man she'd allowed herself to fall deeply in love with. Fancy tried to recall at what point she had fallen in love with Byron. Was it after their first date? First kiss? Before he bought her the car? Whatever happened to Darius Jones? He was the sponsor, husband, man she needed. Byron hadn't mentioned Darius lately. Was she really in love with Byron? What about Desmond? How did she honestly feel about Dez?

Of the two prospects she'd met on her way to work, neither was worthy of having her card. Byron hadn't proposed or agreed to a commitment so why did she feel as though she were cheating on him while talking to the other men? Her emotions were truly out of synch. Mandy could help. Oh, that's right. Fancy had forgotten she owed Mandy for their last session. Oh, well.

The telephone rang several times before Fancy realized it was ringing. Hoping the blocked number was Byron's, Fancy slowly said, "Speak to me."

"Hey, girl. It's five after five. I wasn't expecting you to answer the phone this late in the evening. How are you?" SaVoy's voice was perky.

"I'm fine. Waiting for Byron to call. We're going out

to dinner. What's up with you?" Fancy asked, lusting at Byron's image while clenching Miss Kitty between her thighs.

"Have you spoken with Desmond lately?"

"If this morning qualifies, yes. Why?"

"I was just wondering if he had mentioned Tyronne because I haven't seen or heard from him since my party." The perkiness in SaVoy's voice subsided into a light quiver.

Fancy imitated the seriousness in SaVoy's tone and said, "You haven't seen or heard from me either."

"Oh, Fancy. That's different."

"I could understand if a month had passed, but, girl-friend, it's only been, what, a week or so since your party."

"Never mind, Fancy."

"If you must know, no. Desmond has not mentioned Tyronne, so Tyronne must be okay. I warned you about those big dicks. You'd better stay away from Tyronne."

"It's not like that. Look, can I have Desmond's phone number?" SaVoy asked.

"Did I tell you where Byron is taking me tonight?"

"Fancy. I know you heard me."

"Girl, you've got it bad and you haven't even had any yet. Desmond's cell number is five, ten . . . Bye." Fancy hung up the phone because if SaVoy was that impatient, she wasn't interested in chatting.

Fancy stared in the mirror wondering how much longer she could hide the new growth under her tracks. This morning she'd spent an extra thirty minutes press-ing the edges. She had one more hour before Byron ar-rived so Fancy logged on to the real estate Web site and studied for her exam.

When the phone rang, Fancy answered, "Speak to me."

"Fancy, I need to see you in my office," Harry said, then hung up.

"Uh." Fancy sighed heavily. She smoothed her cream-colored skirt over her garter and stockings. Running her hands over her breasts, she straightened her waist-length long-sleeve jacket and left her door open in case Byron called. Fancy strolled into Harry's office.

Harry closed the door, then instructed, "Have a seat in my chair."

Fancy sat in Harry's chair and crossed her legs, intentionally exposing her garter. "What's up? I'm surprised you're working so late on Friday. No plans with the wife tonight?" Despite Fancy's attempts, Mrs. Washington hadn't divorced Harry.

Harry propped one leg on the edge of his desk and leaned toward Fancy. He removed his jacket and laid it on the desk beside him. "You look nice. You always look nice, Fancy. How about we go out someplace *nice* tonight. Would you like that? I'd like that." Harry loosened his tie. His eyes were glazed.

Fancy casually answered, "Oh, I can't. I already have plans."

"Well, I hope those plans include working off the twelve thousand dollars you charged to my business account." One of Harry's hands hoisted his belt. *Zip.* Fancy watched in disbelief as Harry stroked his dick. Her heart pounded as she uncrossed her legs, regretting all the times they'd had sex in his office.

"That's Mrs. Washington's job. Not mine," Fancy said, squinting at Harry.

"Well, I've just added it to your job description. If you don't get him back down, I'm gonna have to write you up for insubordination. Maybe even fire you."

Fancy stood. Lifted her skirt so Harry could get a good visual of the red thong. "Write this up, Harry," Fancy said, slapping her own ass.

Harry stood. Grabbed the back of Fancy's weave and slammed her against his desk. "You think I'm some kind of a joke?"

"What the fuck are you doing!" Fancy yelled. Each time she lifted herself off the desk, Harry forced her body flush against the large black-and-white calendar pad.

She felt his pants slide against her thighs, legs, then they dropped behind her ankles. "Harry, please. Don't do this. I'll pay you back. I promise," Fancy pleaded as his dick moved her thong aside and slid inside her vagina.

"You know you want me. And you know I don't care about the money. So let's stop playing games. You screw me. I screw you. And everybody's happy." Harry pressed both hands into her shoulder blades. His dick glided back and forth like he was enjoying every stroke. "I love you, Fancy." His rhythm increased. "Oh, how my heart bleeds for you." Harry started breathing hard. "I'm cumming baby. Daddy's cumming. Ow. Ah. Here it comes." Harry thrust deep and held himself inside. "Uuhhh!" The pulsation of his release came in waves as Harry jammed himself farther inside. He collapsed on top of Fancy, kissing the side of her lips as the opposite side of her face pressed against the desk. "I really do love you," he said, standing straight and reclaiming his limp dick.

Fancy didn't move. Her eyes fluttered as the box of wet wipes landed next to her head.

"Clean yourself up. I've gotta go."

Fancy's eyes squinted as she heard her telephone ring. Her fingers curled around the crystal paperweight. She picked it up and shouted, "Muthafucka!" then slammed the pointed edge against the side of Harry's head. "Muthafucka! I hate you! You gon' pay for this shit, Harry Washington!" Fancy's arm reared back. She wanted to hit Harry again and again until he felt her pain. Harry grabbed her hand. Fancy watched the blood stream down his face. The collar of his shirt changed from white to red.

"You're fired! If you show your trifling ass up here

Monday morning, I'll have you arrested. You hear me! Arrested! You know, you can go to jail for this shit!" Harry touched the blood streaming down his temple.

Fancy straightened her G-string, pulled down her skirt, and said, "Harry Washington, you are going to wish you never met Fancy Taylor." Running into her office, she locked the door. Fancy wanted to cry. What made Harry treat her that way? What had she done to deserve this? What gave Harry the right to rape her? Fancy laid her head on her desk and cried.

Her phone rang several times. Fancy sniffled, then answered, "Hello."

"Hello? What happened to my special greeting?" Byron asked.

"I have to cancel. Call me tomorrow." Fancy dried her tears.

"What's wrong, baby? I can hear it in your voice. What's wrong?"

"My mother. She's sick." Fancy hadn't lied because Caroline's condition had gotten worse. "I've got to go. I'll call you tomorrow."

Fancy stopped in the rest room and locked the door. She combed her hair, replenished her lipstick, removed her stockings, and put them in her purse. She removed her soiled thong, wrapped it in white paper napkins, and placed it beside her stockings. She brushed a dry paper towel over her clothes. The dark marks streaked across the front of her jacket and silk blouse. Fancy smiled in the mirror. "Don't walk out looking like a victim. Compose yourself. Hold your head high. No one knows what just happened to you." Unlocking the door, the only footsteps Fancy heard until she reached the lobby were her own.

Honk. Honk.

Fancy kept walking.

Honk. Honk. Honk.

"Fancy, it's me, Byron."

Fancy had bypassed Byron's black Benz without noticing. She walked over to him.

"Hey," Byron said, hugging her. "How you doin'? I was worried about you. Are you okay?"

"I'll be fine. Just had a rough day. I just want to go home."

"Sure. That's fine. But what were you doing? Cleaning out your file cabinet or something?" Byron said.

Fancy sat quietly. If she ignored Byron, maybe he'd shut the hell up or at least stop asking so many damn questions. Byron turned on his commercial free classical jazz station. "You sure you're okay?" he asked, caressing her thighs.

Fancy bit her the corner of her bottom lip. *Please stop asking questions.*

Byron parked by the lake, escorted her upstairs, and invited himself in. He sat on the bed and said, "Your mom will be fine, baby. I do understand because my mom has been sick for a while."

Fancy prepared two glasses of merlot, and handed one to Byron along with the television remote. "I'm going to take a bath."

"Whatever you want to do tonight is all right with me." Byron removed his shoes and stretched across her comforter.

Climbing the ladder in her converted closet, brown suede shoes in hand, Fancy placed them in the box. She loved Byron and hated Harry. She wanted to be alone but not really.

Fancy sprinkled black cherry and Epsom salts in her bath water. She twisted the plastic caps off of four douche bottles, tossed them into a plastic bag, and then sat on the toilet. Slipping into the hot water, Fancy cried. She inserted her finger into her vagina and squished it around. Harry was not getting off that easy.

Fancy was thankful Byron stayed with her. His company helped her to maintain her sanity. As much as she enjoyed sex, she'd never been raped. And she wasn't quite sure how to handle the situation. SaVoy often told her, "Prayer will get you through anything. Take your burdens to the Lord, and leave them there."

God probably didn't want to hear from Fancy Taylor. Not right now, anyway. Maybe she didn't want to hear from Him, either. Where was He when Harry raped her? Where was He when she was a child? And where was He when she was almost convicted of a hit and run? It wasn't her fault she'd shifted into first gear, plunged her accelerator, and watched her ex-boyfriend's eyes widen right before he landed on the hood of her car. His body fell into the street. Right in front of her car. He'd think twice before kicking her, or any other woman, in the ass again. Maybe there was a God up there somewhere because something had kept her from shifting into reverse and backing over her ex when he was behind the car.

"Ooohh," Fancy jumped, splashing water onto the rug.

"Sorry, I didn't mean to startle you," Byron said, closing the lid on the toilet as he took a seat. "You look so beautiful."

Fortunately she'd followed her first thought and hid the plastic bag of used Massengils. Byron toweled her off, undressed himself, slipped into the shower, and joined her in bed. His big dick grew larger as he embraced her from behind. When he kissed her neck, Fancy jumped. Obviously Byron thought it was his foreplay but Fancy couldn't shake the feeling of what had happened with Harry.

She closed her eyes as Byron penetrated her from behind.

Byron whispered in her ear, "I love you, Fancy."

Fancy longed to hear *I love you* from someone who cared, but all of a sudden she realized "I love you" had many different meanings and was only as sincere as the person who said it. That was the first time Byron had verbally expressed his feelings. Her vagina contracted several times, joining his deep pulsation. Fancy wrapped Byron's arms around her waist. "I love you, too, Byron," Fancy whispered. "Tell me something."

Byron scooted back. His hand pressed against her shoulder until her back lay flat against the mattress. He gently stroked the side of her face, tucking her hair behind her ear, which reminded Fancy she needed to retie her silk scarf.

"What's really on your mind?" Byron asked.

"Byron, what do you want from me?"

"That's easy. Friendship." Byron kissed her lips, then said, "Companionship." He kissed her again, then added, "Being on the road all the time gets lonely. I don't want to ruin what we have. Lots of women say they can deal with me being gone all the time but I know they really can't. But I do love you." Byron's lips pressed against hers.

"I love you, too," Fancy said, turning back onto her side. Fancy gazed at her pole that hadn't been used all year.

With Byron, *I love you* was a good place to start. When the sunlight peeped through the blinds awakening her, Fancy rolled over. The space where Byron had lain was warm. Running her fingers between her legs, she was moist. There was no morning horseback riding appointment so Fancy rolled back over. Maybe if she just slept a little longer, her life would become a little clearer, or speed by a lot quicker.

CHAPTER 17

Next Friday morning arrived with bittersweet memories of Harry and Byron. After soaking in depression—and locking herself in her apartment—for a week, yesterday Byron surprised Fancy with a deluxe spa-and-dinner package at the Claremont Resort. Then he'd given her a gift certificate to Top Notch Hair Salon so all Fancy had to do was schedule an appointment with Raeshelle. When Fancy asked, "Why haven't you paid me?" Byron replied, "Why did you wait so long to tell me you haven't been paid? I'll call my accountant first thing Monday morning."

Promises. Promises. Until Fancy had a check in her hand, she had no choice; she had to return to work. The eight-thirty train was overcrowded. An attractive well-dressed guy smiled down at her. Fancy avoided eye contact and stared out the window as the train zoomed through the tunnel. Fancy worried what would happen when Harry saw her walk into his office.

"Montgomery Street Station. Please watch your step as you exit the train," the conductor seductively said. His voice was deep yet soft.

"Oh," Fancy said, shaking her head, "this is my stop."

She slowly maneuvered uphill, stepping aside for anyone walking too close behind her. *Forget Harry.* Even if
Fancy were late, Harry couldn't fire her after forcing
himself upon her. By the time Fancy finished suing
Harry, she'd be his boss. Fancy and Associates was all
right, but Fancy Ass sounded better. If Whoopi could
name her company One Ho Productions, Fancy would
name her business whatever she wanted.

Fancy sashayed into Washington and Associates wearing a red mid-thigh oriental dress. Thick spiral curls
covered her gelled hairline. Thank goodness Raeshelle
agreed to redo her weave right after work. Quickly,
Fancy entered her office, locked the door, and closed
the blinds. Picking up the phone Fancy immediately
called the building's security office.

"Yes, I'd like to report a rape."

"A rape? This time of the morning? In this building?
Did you say a rape?" the man questioned.

"Yes, a rape. I'm on the fifth floor, suite 701. And my
name is Fancy Taylor." Fancy hung up, still not certain
that she'd done the right thing, but she had to do something. Moments later her phone rang.

"Washington and Associates property management,
speak to me."

"Is this Fancy Taylor?" The southern accent was un-
mistakable.

Fancy smiled, "Yes, Mrs. Lovely. How may I help you?"

"Honey, did you forget about me? I waited up until
late that night for you. You never showed up. You don't
return my calls. It's been months and I need some help
with this place. I can't afford to move else I'dda been
done gone way from here."

Fancy's eyes narrowed at the thought of Harry. She
couldn't ask Mrs. Lovely to repeat herself. Fancy was so
preoccupied with her problems that she hadn't heard
enough of what Mrs. Lovely said to respond appropri-
ately. "I apologize Mrs. Lovely. I promise—"

Knock. Knock. Knock.

"Excuse me, Mrs. Lovely, but may I call you back?" Fancy was in the process of hanging up the phone while Mrs. Lovely protested. Fancy cracked the door. Two men in blue uniforms stood outside.

"Good. You're here. Come, in," Fancy said, opening the door wider.

The short round guard continued standing outside and said, "Ms. Taylor?" in an authoritative manner. He knew who she was. All of the men and most of the women in the building knew of Fancy.

"Yes, come in." Fancy replied, stepping aside to clear his path.

The guard stood erect, clasped his hands behind his back, and said, "We've been instructed to escort you from the building. Would you please get your things and come with us?" His stout chubby fingers reached for her wrist.

Pulling her hand back, Fancy said, "I think you've got things twisted. I'm the one who called you."

Harry stood by looking on with Allyanna. The rest of his employees gathered in small separate groups within ear range. Two more security personnel walked up to Harry.

"Harry Washington. We've been instructed to escort you to our office for an investigation. Would you please come with us?" The taller security guard was kind of handsome but with his blue-collar job and the three kids out of wedlock, a thought of stroking his ego would be a waste of Fancy's time.

Harry removed his hand from his pocket and laughed nervously. Adding extra bass to his voice he said, "I think you gentlemen have made a mistake. I'm the one who requested my *former* employee, Ms. Taylor, be escorted from the building."

Fuck you, Harry Washington! I hate you!

When the taller guard tugged on his handcuffs, Fancy shivered. A flashback of Byron snapping red fur-lined cuffs on her ankles crossed Fancy's mind. She hoped they'd take Harry to jail and that the inmates would rape him. Maybe then he'd understand how she felt. Fancy had sex with Harry countless times—in his office, lunchtime nooners, even in the basement garage—but that did not give Harry the right to force himself upon her.

"Sir, I'm just doing my job. You can come willingly or I can use these." He jiggled the silver metal hoops, then he looked at Fancy and said, "Ma'am you're going to have to come with us, too."

The employees mumbled and whispered as the four guards escorted Fancy and Harry out the office. During their questioning, Harry did what any other rapist would have done. He lied. Laughing. Joking. As though no crime had been committed.

"Anyone in the office can verify we've openly had an affair since Ms. Taylor has worked for me. I won't deny that. But I did not rape her." Harry leaned back in the chair.

"That's a lie! I did not consent to him ramming his dick inside me that night! He's lying! Here's the evidence!" Fancy pulled a plastic bag out of her purse and shook it in Harry's face. "Semen and blood! I fought him. That's how he got that scar on his face! Ask him! Ask him!"

Harry's eyes widened as he stared at her red thong without blinking. He sat up. His bottom lip was moving up and down but no words came out of his mouth.

"Ma'am. We can call San Francisco PD and you can file charges if you'd like. But at this point it's up to you because he can file assault charges against you. I've seen far too many cases where nobody wins, both parties press charges, and both parties end up doing time. Maybe you two can work this out without involving the police."

Fancy yelled, "They can't arrest me for self-defense! Call the cops!"

Harry's shoulders stiffened. Fancy didn't give a damn about Harry. But she did care about Byron. What would Byron think of her? Would pressing charges against Harry ruin her chances of marrying Byron? Byron had just confessed his love for her.

"Wait." Fancy wrapped her fingers around the phone cradled in the guard's hand. She looked at her acrylic nails and was thankful the edges were now flush against her cuticles. "On second thought, don't call the cops. I'll handle this."

Harry followed Fancy to the elevator bank. When the doors closed, he lamented, "I can't believe you're serious." He leaned closer, then stepped back when the doors opened.

Fancy didn't respond; she disregarded his gossiping staff, casually walked into Harry's office, and sat in his chair. "Okay, rapist. Here's the deal. One hundred thousand dollars and I'll go away quietly."

Harry closed the door and said, "What? You must be kidding. You're not worth a hundred grand. Get your ungrateful ass out of my office."

"Oh, so now all of a sudden I'm ungrateful. Whateva." Fancy picked up Harry's phone and dialed nine, one . . . "You sure about this? 'Cause I don't care if your ass do time or you lose your business."

Harry took the receiver from Fancy. "Let me think about this. I'll call you next week. But *whateva* you do, do not"—he pointed at her wide-heeled black baby doll shoes—"do not step foot in my office. Ever!"

"Next week, by Friday, or I will call the cops," Fancy said, rolling her eyes away from Harry.

Fancy went into her office. She gathered her purse, her photo, and left. She was more upset because Harry wouldn't admit what he'd done was wrong. He honestly believed everything was her fault. The sexual act alone was nothing Fancy wasn't accustomed to. The violence, that was unacceptable. Unforgettable. Did she do something to deserve Harry's horrible treatment?

Naw, Fancy thought, shaking her head, *no way.* If her phone did not ring by five o'clock Friday, she was going to have Harry arrested, on his job, early Monday morning where everyone could see. She might even call "Seven on Your Side" news. And if Byron left her for standing up for her rights, he could kiss her ass, too. When Fancy arrived home, she called Byron but he was unavailable so she called Desmond.

"What's up? You wanna come over? I haven't seen my best friend in a while," Fancy said, thinking about all the unanswered messages Desmond had left on her home and cellular voice mail.

"Let me call you right back," Desmond replied.

"Okay." Fancy hung up her home phone and answered her cell phone.

"Hey, you."

Fancy smiled. "Hey, I just called you!"

"You wanna go out? I'll be by in a half hour to pick you up. I have fantastic news!" Byron said.

"Sure! I'll be ready." Fancy hung up the phone, showered, and was ready in twenty minutes. She sat at her vanity applying her lipstick. The tan designer minidress was perfect for a Friday night outing. Life was too short for Fancy to be miserable. Besides, Harry was probably somewhere screwing Allyanna or some other ungrateful female.

The buzzer rang from the outside call box so instead of letting Byron in, Fancy happily raced downstairs. When the elevator doors opened, Desmond was in the lobby talking to the doorman.

"You leaving? You just called me. I've been worried about you. But I see I shouldn't have," Desmond said, staring at the dress he'd bought her months ago for her birthday.

"Oh, I thought you were going to call me back. But then my friend called so I made plans. Go home. I'll call you when I get in." Fancy kissed Desmond on the cheek.

Desmond's jaw clenched, then he did a half nod upward. "You a trip."

Fancy hugged Desmond. "I need to talk to you, baby. I'mma call you. Later. I promise."

Byron was double-parked. When he opened the door, Desmond walked away and said, "I don't believe this shit."

Fancy leaned toward Byron, then tilted her chin sideways. Byron kissed her cheek. "So, where are we going?"

"It's a surprise!" Byron ran his hand over her silky smooth legs. "I really like how you take such great care of your body."

Fancy's July rent was due next week. Maybe it was time to move in with Byron, that way every day would be payday, and Byron could feel her legs anytime he wanted. But if Harry paid her as promised, Fancy could relax. If not, she'd have to think of asking Desmond or SaVoy for a loan. Or, despite her feelings for Byron, she'd have to find a sponsor.

Byron parked on a hilltop overlooking the Pacific Ocean and escorted her inside an unmarked building. The hallways were dimly lit, with muscular men in dark suits and sunglasses standing at each of the three doors.

Byron flashed a key—the small gold key she'd rejected in exchange for the Benz—and the man in the suit stepped aside. When the door opened, another one opened, then a third double-automatic sliding glass door parted.

Oh, my gosh. Fancy could smell the millionaires in the air. A woman walked up to Byron, handed him a drink and said, "What would your guest like, Mr. Van Lee?"

Fancy answered, "Cristal."

The woman left and returned so quickly Fancy blinked twice.

"A toast," Byron said, "to friendship and more."

Fancy smiled, then repeated Byron's words.

"You know you're special when I bring you here. In seven years, I've only brought two other women here."

Well, there wasn't anything wrong with Bryon's ability to remember. Fancy glanced around the room.

"Let me introduce you to some of my friends." Byron walked ahead of her, then stopped at the bar near the biggest big screen television Fancy had ever seen. "Excuse me fellas, I'd like to introduce my lady, Fancy Taylor."

When the heads turned in unison, Fancy smiled and softly said, "Hello."

A voice from behind them said, "What's up? Where you been?"

Casually, Fancy turned around.

"Man, where've *you* been?" Byron asked Darius.

"Brazil. Okinawa. Amsterdam. Paris. Spain. Trinidad. London. Speaking of London, man, did you see that?" Darius shook his head, then said, "That all-star, all-pro, first-round draft honey from England in the platinum lounge?"

All the men nodded as Byron shook his head.

How rude. Did Darius not see Fancy standing next to Byron?

Darius said, "She's freaky man. Her girlfriends look okay, but they're willing to tag." Darius's eyebrows shifted upward. As he smiled, all but two of the men left the room.

"Give me a minute. Don't go nowhere. Let me take this call."

What call? Byron's phone hadn't rung.

"Hello." Byron paused. He nodded and said, "Yeah, okay. I'm on my way."

Byron kissed Fancy and said, "Sorry, baby. I've gotta go." Then he asked Darius, "How long you in town?"

"Until tomorrow. But I'll be here for a minute."

Byron nodded, then walked ahead of Fancy. "I promise. I'll make it up to you, baby."

Make up what? Fancy thought as he drove toward the San Rafael Bridge.

Byron's hand roamed inside her dress and cupped her breast. "Why don't you take care of me, baby?"

Fancy leaned over Byron's lap and eased her lips over his head. She released just enough saliva to lubricate her strokes. Fancy stroked and stroked and sucked and stroked, hoping Byron would stay the night at her place or take her to his.

Byron's cellular phone vibrated. When he lowered his hand, Fancy noticed the caller ID. Home? What the fuck did that mean? Quickly she repeated the number in her mind several times as she deposited Byron's semen into a napkin.

"Hello." Byron paused. "Yes. Okay, I'll be there as fast as I can." Byron hung up and plunged his accelerator. The speedometer moved from seventy miles per hour to ninety.

Fancy repeated the number over and over in her mind. There was no need to ask Byron if everything was okay because she knew him well enough to know he wouldn't answer. Fancy scratched her head and said, "Damn, my hair. I completely forgot about my appointment."

Byron remained silent until they arrived at her apartment, then he said, "Good night, baby. I'll call you."

Before the doorman closed the door, Byron's tires left clouds of white smoke in the circular driveway. *What the hell just happened?* Fancy thought as she entered her apartment.

"How could you be so stupid?!" Fancy yelled in the mirror at her reflection. *Swish. Swish. Swish!* Her fists chased the July summer night's breeze blowing through the patio screen into her lonely bedroom.

CHAPTER 18

SaVoy was especially happy because it was Wednesday and she was finally going to see Tyronne. More than a month had passed since her party and since she'd last seen him. After Fancy had given her Desmond's number and Desmond had given SaVoy Tyronne's number, the first time she called him at home, Tyronne had said, "I'm busy. Let me hit you back." SaVoy remembered thinking, *back when?* But had replied, "Okay."

Vanessa had told her, "let me hit you, call you, back," meant whenever, and that she should wait until Tyronne called. Vanessa had said, "Honey, I don't mean wait as in sit by the phone. I mean don't you constantly call him. When a man is seriously interested in a woman, trust me, he'll call. However, there are the TC females out there. Those are the time consumers. Vanessa will tell you how to handle them later. Their strategy is if they can consume all of the man's leisure time, it doesn't matter if he's interested in another woman, he won't have time for her."

Tyronne had returned SaVoy's call three weeks later.

Vanessa had said, "That's okay, honey, because you're not his woman, so you're not his priority. Don't act like his woman until you are his woman. Don't buy him gifts—birthday, Valentine's, or Christmas—thinking that's going to make him more interested in you. Be yourself, SaVoy. That's always enough."

SaVoy put on her blue jeans and an orange sweatshirt. She didn't like the look so she changed into a large Raiders T-shirt. Too boyish. SaVoy changed again. The pile of clothes on her bed grew rapidly. Settling on a plain white tapered T-shirt, she kissed her father. "Bye, Papa."

Why hadn't Tyronne called after the party? Did she do something wrong? If that's how Tyronne was going to treat her, she shouldn't invest so much energy into thinking about him. Maybe SaVoy should forget about Tyronne. But her life needed excitement. Now that school was over, all she did was work and go to church. William still had Tanya on lockdown and Fancy . . . Who knew what she was up to? Maybe SaVoy should start a social club for her church peers in their twenties. Yeah, that was an idea she was sure Pastor Tellings would support. She'd invite the group to her house and organize a planning committee. They could plan a summer trip to Los Angeles or Hawaii.

Time between assisting customers at the grocery store passed slowly. SaVoy still had another hour before Tyronne's scheduled delivery. SaVoy organized her shelves, then glanced at the clock again. Fifteen minutes.

"Hey, what's up?" Desmond said, walking up to the counter.

"I'm surprised but glad to see you here. Thanks for giving me Tyronne's number." SaVoy smiled.

"You look nice," Desmond said. "I like the pink frost lip gloss. Nice eyebrows. I see you arched them."

Oh, good. If Desmond noticed her new look, surely Tyronne would notice the changes she'd made for him.

"Nice French manicure, too. Look, I need a favor. Can you help me apply to law school?" Desmond asked.

"Seriously! That's great. Of course I'll help you." Finally! Desmond was pursuing his dream. SaVoy felt blessed he'd ask her to help him. "Which schools?"

"I'm not sure. I wanna stay local."

"Don't limit your options. You're single with no kids. I think you should pursue the Ivy League schools. Have you registered to take the LSAT?"

"I did," Desmond said, nodding. "I'm scheduled for October."

"Good. I can assist you with your applications and if you want, I can help you study for the test. Vanessa has a lot of contacts so I'll ask her to help you. And there're lots of lawyers at my church who can give you recommendations."

"Man, seems like I should've asked sooner. Cool. Look, I gotta run. Can I get your number?"

SaVoy scribbled on the back of a register receipt and handed it to Desmond. She was happy Desmond had stopped by and that he'd helped take her mind off Tyronne. SaVoy picked up the phone and dialed Fancy's work number.

"Thank you for calling Washington and Associates. How may I help you?"

"Hi, may I speak with Fancy Taylor please?" SaVoy gazed out the storefront double glass doors.

"I'm sorry. Ms. Taylor is no longer with the company."

"What? As of when?"

"Ms. Taylor no longer works here. May I be of assistance?"

"No. Thank you." SaVoy hung up the phone.

She heard the familiar churning of Tyronne's truck and looked up. He was unloading her inventory. SaVoy pressed her hand against her aching stomach. She removed an *Essence* magazine from under the counter and flipped it open.

"Hey, you. Stop pretending you reading that six-month-old magazine," Tyronne said, standing with his hand truck in front of the counter.

"Hi." SaVoy felt her smile widen. She shifted her eyes to the side and took a deep breath. "Guess who stopped by today?"

"If it wasn't me, it doesn't matter."

SaVoy smiled. "Desmond. He asked me to help him get into law school."

"It's about time. I been tellin' my boy to do dat for a long time. So can a brother get a hug or what?" Tyronne walked behind the counter and spread his arms wide. He held her close and squeezed her shoulders.

SaVoy laid her head on Tyronne's chest. She was glad, this time, he hadn't thrust his pelvis into her hips. Tyronne held her as though he actually missed her.

"I'm on a tight schedule today. So I'mma stock and run."

SaVoy watched Tyronne load and unload his cart.

"You wanna go see Antoine Fisher this weekend?" Tyronne asked, heading toward the door.

SaVoy smiled and said, "Sure. I'd like that."

SaVoy wanted to tell Tyronne she'd met her mother. Her mom was nice and very soft-spoken and had said, "I can't quite explain why I left. I didn't understand it then, and I don't understand it now." After her mother had abandoned her, she'd decided not to have any more kids. "I feel like a failure. I was a child running away from my child. My baby. At least I picked the right father for you, sweetie."

SaVoy was glad she'd finally met her mom but didn't feel a special bond. Not like the one between her and Papa. She was grateful her prayers had been answered. SaVoy and her mom agreed to see one another again but her mom wouldn't commit to a date and SaVoy was at peace with her mother's decision, knowing that might be their first and last time seeing one another.

CHAPTER 19

Harry's initial offer was ridiculous. Ten thousand dollars. Fancy countered at one hundred. Harry had said, "Fifty thousand. Final offer. Take it or leave it." If Fancy weren't broke she would've said, "Kiss my ass Harry Washington. I'll see you in court!" But since most rape victims seldom found justice in the courtroom, Fancy agreed to accept the fifty grand. Harry said his attorney would prepare the contract but the money wouldn't be available for another two weeks. Fancy was so thrilled she invited Desmond over to celebrate because after calling Byron's home, Fancy needed time to figure out how to get rid of Mrs. Lee.

"Oh, hell yeah!" Fancy screamed loud enough to distract the early morning joggers across the street.

Falling in love with Desmond was not part of her plan. Whenever she needed him, he was there. With the exception of his family, nothing and no one in his life seemed more important than her, including Carlita.

Beep. Beep. Beep.

Desmond was pumping so hard Fancy forgot she'd accidentally turned on the microwave.

"Oh, yes. Yes, baby. That's my spot. Don't stop. Right

there." Fancy's voice escalated. "Right there, baby. Mama's getting ready to—"

"Aw, damn," Desmond said, as he pulled out and ejaculated all over Fancy's butt.

"Dez!" Fancy slapped his shoulder. "You didn't wait for me. That's selfish." Fancy led Desmond into her bedroom, lay on the bed, spread her legs, and parted her lips. "Dez, I'm not finished."

Desmond shook his head, plopped on the love seat, picked up the television remote and replied, "I am."

"Fine," Fancy said, heading for the bathroom, wondering who would quench the lustful burn spreading throughout her body like wildfire. For now, she would, in the shower. Although she didn't hear anything unusual, her sixth sense detected a presence that tingled the nerves along her neck, shoulders, and back. Fancy frowned, then turned.

"Damn, Dez. Make some noise or something so I can hear you."

"You know I'm here. Even when you don't see me." Desmond's hands guided her hips toward the counter, then gently leaned her body forward. An expensive bottle of perfume twirled inside the porcelain sink as Desmond gave an extra thrust to assist entry of his partially erect penis. Fancy's nipples grazed the cold marbled countertop. With each stroke Desmond grew harder and longer.

"Oh, yes," Fancy said, shifting her hips side to side.

You think I'm some kind of a joke? Harry's voice echoed between her ears.

What the fuck are you doing!

Each time Fancy lifted herself off the counter, Desmond pressed her body flush against the cold marble. Fancy stared in the mirror at Desmond, then closed her eyes.

Harry, please. Don't do this. I'll pay you back. I promise. You know you want me. And you know I don't care about the

*money. So let's stop playing games. You screw me. I screw you.
And everybody's happy.*

Desmond held her waist as his dick glided back and forth. "Aw, damn. You feel so good. I love you Fancy."

Fancy's arms and legs trembled.

"I'm cumming baby," Desmond said, stroking faster. "Cum with me this time, baby. Cum with me."

You think I'm some kind of a joke?

When Fancy opened her eyes, she saw Harry standing behind her. Stroking. Humping. Pumping. Sweating. Breathing hard.

"Get off me! Get off me!" Fancy's fists pounded on Desmond's chest. "I hate you, Harry! I hate you!" Fancy screamed, "Get off me!" Desmond's body landed against the wall as Fancy ran out of the bathroom.

Desmond chased her into the hallway, down the stairs, into the bedroom, and out onto the balcony, grabbing her waist as Fancy almost tumbled headfirst over the rail.

"Let me go! Let me go! Please, just let me go!"

"My God. What happened to you? This is Desmond. Fancy, this is Dez. It'll be okay, baby. I'm so sorry." Tears welled in Desmond's eyes. "Whatever he did to you, I'm sorry I wasn't there to protect you."

Fancy sat on the concrete. Desmond placed his arms under her folded knees and behind her back. Pressing Fancy's naked body to his, Desmond carried her inside to her bed. "What happened to you?"

The details of how Harry had raped her were so graphic, Fancy cried while telling Desmond the story. She explained why she wasn't pressing charges, but she didn't confess about the money Harry had agreed to pay.

"What's wrong with me, Dez? Am I a bad person?"

"Of course not. But I think you should call Mandy." Desmond hugged Fancy. "Fancy, you need help. You just tried to kill yourself."

"I did not try to kill myself. I was running so fast I

couldn't stop. There's a difference. I'm all right. And promise me you won't tell anyone. Especially Tyronne."

"I wouldn't do that. But even if you weren't trying to kill yourself, you almost did so I seriously think you need to talk to Mandy right away."

"I can't. I have no money. No job. I owe Mandy two hundred dollars and my landlord two thousand."

Desmond rocked Fancy in his arms and said, "What about your mom? Can she help you?"

"You're kidding. Right?"

"No, I wasn't." Desmond paused, then said, "Look, I'll give you two thousand dollars."

Fancy eyes widened. "Where are you going to get two thousand dollars to give me?"

"Don't worry about that." Desmond dug deep into his pants pocket and handed Fancy a Benjamin. "Here, I'll give you the rest later."

"Oh, thank you, Dez!" Fancy hugged and kissed Desmond.

If she had known Desmond would freely give her that much money, she would've asked a long time ago. Fancy removed the cordless from the base and dialed SaVoy's number. Until she could schedule an appointment with Mandy, Fancy needed someone to listen to her problems so she could sort things out in her mind. She wanted to call Tanya because Tanya was her perfect listener, but ninety percent of the time when William answered the phone, even if Tanya was home, Tanya wasn't available. SaVoy would give constructive feedback—probably too constructive—along with a few biblical quotes sprinkled throughout the conversation.

"Hey," SaVoy answered, sounding happy. "How are you? Where've you been? I called your job and they said you no longer work there."

"If that's what they said, it must be true." Fancy laughed. "That's part of the reason I'm calling, to see if you want to do breakfast."

"Breakfast sounds good. Where you wanna go?"

"Let me find something on-line." With all the places to eat in the Bay Area, Fancy seldom dined at the same restaurant twice. "I'll pick you up in about an hour. Bye."

"Who was that?" Desmond questioned.

"SaVoy." Fancy frowned when the corners of Desmond's lips damn near touched his ears. What was that about? "I just need someone to talk to other than myself."

Desmond's voice became perky. "SaVoy's really good at listening. And helping. Me, I listen but I still don't know what I can or should do to help."

"You've helped more than you know." Fancy kissed Desmond and went into the bathroom. She stared in the mirror and slid the dental floss between each space twice. *Girl, you almost killed yourself. So you've made a few mistakes. Who hasn't? Look at yourself.* The toothpaste fell off the toothbrush and washed down the drain with the running water. *You're beautiful. You're intelligent. Not very smart 'cause you do the same stupid shit over and over but you are intelligent because you know better. It's time you start doing better. Most women wish they had your beauty and brains.*

Fancy squirted more paste on the brush. *When you gon' tell Mandy about your childhood? You know he comes up for parole next year. And if he gets out, you know he's going to find you.* Fancy shivered, brushing her front teeth in a circular motion. *Forget him. He's not serious about harming me. It's Caroline he really wants. Besides, I'll be married with a new name by the time he's released.*

Selecting a pair of black fitted slacks, a beige cashmere sweater, and her ankle boots, Fancy dressed quickly. Then she sat at her vanity, parted her fresh weave one inch down the center, laid it flat, and bumped the ends. She patted her nose with a powder sponge. Eyebrows penciled. Lips lined. Chai lipstick. Fancy grabbed her gym bag and packed hiking boots, a sweatsuit, undergarments, and three towels: hand, face, and bath.

"Okay, Dez. Wake up. I'm ready to go."

"Can't a brother get some rest? Plus, I need to shower. I'll lock up before I leave."

Fancy hesitated, then said, "Okay, but don't answer my phone." After Desmond rolled over, Fancy went to the garage, got in her Benz, and headed over to SaVoy's.

The parking space next to SaVoy's car was taken so Fancy parked in SaVoy's driveway. The forest green hedges bordering the front lawn were immaculate. SaVoy stood in the doorway wearing a burnt-orange headwrap, hoop earrings, a light blue sweater, and jeans.

Opening her hand, Fancy wiggled her fingers. "Let's take your car. You know I've wanted to drive this baby ever since your dad bought it for you." That was partially true but the main reason was Fancy preferred saving her hundred dollars and using SaVoy's gas. Fuel prices were outrageously high. Two dollars and thirty cents a gallon. "I almost forgot. Go back inside and grab a pair of hiking boots."

Fancy sat behind SaVoy's steering wheel, removed a sheet of paper from her purse, and laid it upon the dashboard.

SaVoy climbed into the passenger seat of her SUV. "So where are we going?"

"I think we'll like it." From what Fancy had researched on-line, the quaint, affordable restaurant with a fantastic view and award-winning food was worth the trip. It was twelve miles north of the Golden Gate Bridge off Highway 1 near the hiking trails at Muir Woods. Not too close yet not too far from Mrs. Lee's house.

"So, what's going on with you?" SaVoy asked, turning off the radio.

"Let's start with you. How's Tyronne?"

SaVoy beamed. "He's fine. We went out the other night. Had a wonderful time."

Fancy glimpsed at SaVoy. "Does that mean you're no longer—"

"Oh, I'm not that easy. He has to go to church with me first."

"What's up with that?"

"Because going to church together helps to build a solid foundation for a relationship. That's why. But enough about me. What's going on with you?"

Fancy exhaled and said, "Issues. Love. Job. You name it. Family issues, too. That's if I include Caroline." An icebreaker would be better than starting off telling SaVoy her real problems, but where should Fancy start?

Fancy occasionally looked out over the water as she drove across the San Rafael Bridge. The same bridge she crossed while giving Byron a blow job. Now she hadn't heard from him since his so-called emergency. But that was all right. Mrs. Lee would soon meet Fancy Taylor. Fancy bounced to the tune of Missy Elliot playing in her head.

"Okay, and? I know something is bothering you."

"You're right. There's no way I'm going to end up a single old maid like Caroline. This year is my year to get married, settle down, and start having crumb-snatchers, in that order. I love men, and although I am discriminating, I don't discriminate. As long as the dick is permanently attached at birth—none of that 'I was born a woman now I wanna be a man' bullshit—it doesn't matter. Girl, he can even be bisexual. I really don't care as long as his ass is rich."

Fancy merged onto Highway 101.

SaVoy shook her head. "Now you're not making any sense."

Fancy held the directions, periodically glancing down, then focusing on the road signs.

"I'm trying to give you the history first. After profiling over two dozen men, I figured one package of testosterone was suitable for marriage."

Pleased that she'd found the Sunday Morning restaurant, Fancy pulled into the paved parking lot. The building sat isolated on its own cliff overlooking the ocean.

"Whoa, the view is gorgeous," SaVoy said, admiring the hillside.

With two people ahead of them, Fancy turned her back toward them and whispered, "Girl, I'm in my prime and my stuff is so good no man can whiff just once. Which is exactly why I need to find a husband while I'm ripe, right, tender, and tight."

The couple turned around. Fancy stared at them.

"I'm not sure what you're looking for in a man. What are you looking for?"

Fancy sang, "That's because you're not listening. I want a rich, handsome husband. But all the rich men are either married or gay. Trust me, I've done my own survey and my report shows the broke ones are readily available and expect to get laid every time they spend a dime. Like Tyronne. Bump that 'cause as fine and as intelligent as I am I know I deserve better."

"Now *that* I do agree with," SaVoy said. "But why should a rich man be interested in you? And please, let me do the talking when it comes to Tyronne."

Oh, no she didn't. Fancy raised her eyebrows and said, "You're kidding. Right?"

SaVoy set the menu aside and ordered a short stack of hotcakes with potatoes and sausage while Fancy ordered a vegetarian omelet with egg whites. "You'd better start eating less and exercising more or you're gonna end up like Tanya."

Conversation during breakfast excluded Byron and Harry. Fancy no longer wanted to discuss her personal issues with Miss Perfect.

After they'd finished eating, Fancy drove along the winding road, twisting and turning for miles until she reached Muir Woods. They had changed clothes in the rest room and locked their bags in the car. Fancy flashed her park pass and said, "Follow me."

Overlooking the redwood trees in the forest, Fancy stood quietly listening to the steam trickling between the boulders. She smiled thinking about Desmond. She stopped at the top of the mountain wondering in which direction Mrs. Lee lived.

"What happened with your job?"

"I quit," Fancy said, descending the trail. "I've decided to work for myself."

"Wow, that's a brave move. Doing what?"

"Commercial real estate sales and purchases."

"Oh, that reminds me, I'm having dinner with Byron next Friday."

"Byron who? My Byron?" Fancy continued hiking the narrow trail. The distance between the mountain and the cliff safely accommodated one person.

"Yes, he's helping me secure financing to buy the building Papa's leasing. Maybe, if you get a license, you can be my agent."

"When did all this take place?" Fancy thought SaVoy was her confidante. Having dinner with Byron behind her back was scandalous. It was good that Fancy hadn't told SaVoy about the rape.

"It's not like that, Fancy. It's strictly business. I'm not that kind of friend," SaVoy said, hiking behind Fancy.

"When did you get his number? How did he get your number?"

"Well, not the same way you did. He gave me his card at my party in front of you. But you were so busy keeping up with Desmond, Caroline, and Carlita, I guess you missed it. Fancy, I don't want Byron, and I didn't ask for his help. He offered."

"Whateva." Fancy stopped and motioned for SaVoy to stop too. "There's a yellow jacket nest along the wall." A dozen fat and yellow wasps were swarming the area. With less than three feet between the nest and cliff, Fancy said, "Don't panic. When you start walking, keep moving and don't stop. Just follow my pace." Fancy stepped briskly between the redwood roots protruding from the ground.

Once they made it beyond the nest, they were silent until SaVoy said, "Isn't it great Desmond's finally going to take the law exam?"

"Yeah, that's great," Fancy said. When in the hell did Desmond decide to take the test and why hadn't he told her?

When they exited the park, Fancy leaned over a trash can and heaved several times. Her undigested omelet landed on top of a Sunday newspaper and reminded her of Mrs. Lee.

"Are you okay?" SaVoy said, patting her back. "Give me the keys. I'll drive."

"No. I'm fine. I can drive." Fancy rinsed her mouth with bottled water, started the engine, and said, "We have one more stop to make."

CHAPTER 20

Life had a way of showing up with or without Fancy. The child growing inside her would now make her responsible or irresponsible for two lives. This kind of situation was supposed to happen to other women. Fancy had spent so much time trying to get her own life in order that she'd skipped a pill here and missed one there, but when she did remember she doubled her dosage like the nurse suggested. Maybe having a child would help her get serious about her goals instead of talking about them. Here she was, trying to tell Desmond to set his resolutions while most of her resolutions had become a delusion. A mirage. Hidden behind a façade.

"Okay, Fancy. Get serious." Fancy sat in her car on University Avenue. She was too young to have so many issues. Why was her life so difficult? Why couldn't she have fun like the U.C. Berkeley students, who were laughing and joking as they traveled in groups toward the campus?

Fancy slipped on her stilettos, grabbed her plastic bag and marker, then strolled across the street.

Beep. Beep. "Hey, Fancy!"

Who was shouting her name in the middle of the street? Fancy kept walking.

"It's me! Adam!"

Adam? Fancy stood on the embankment and glanced back to the side of the street she'd just crossed. "Hey!" Fancy smiled to conceal her damper emotions. "Call me!"

"Let me make the block. Wait for me."

Should she wait for Adam when she was five minutes late for her appointment with Mandy? Fancy stood in front of the coffee shop next door to Mandy's office. Adam parked in the red zone.

"How are you? Girl, you still lookin' good."

"I've been better. How's the married life treating you?"

"Not good. She's always complaining I'm not home enough. I can't sit at home and make money. A man like me has got to go where his business is. I can't build a house sitting in my own house. I'm trying very hard to keep her happy. But when that woman gets upset, she cuts me off." Adam drew an imaginary line across his waist.

Fancy couldn't lie and say it was good seeing him. She could tell him she was pregnant and that the baby was his. "Adam, it was meant for us to see one another. How else could I tell you that I'm pregnant with your child?"

"Hey, hold on a minute. You don't look pregnant to me and we haven't been together for"—Adam counted on his fingers—"four months."

"Bye, Adam." Fancy entered the coffee shop.

"Wait! Let me park my car! I'll have a cup of coffee with you!"

As soon as Adam drove around the corner, Fancy dashed into Mandy's office. The receptionist looked at the clock. "You're late and Mandy has another appointment in ten minutes. You're going to have to reschedule."

Fancy bypassed the receptionist and entered Mandy's office.

Mandy swiveled in her direction. "Fancy, I have another client in a few minutes so you'll have to reschedule. Or you can wait. If my ten o'clock doesn't show by ten after, I can see you then."

"Why don't you see me now, and if your ten o'clock shows up, at ten after, I'll leave."

Mandy motioned for Fancy to have a seat.

Fancy's dry eyes looked directly at Mandy. "Harry raped me. Byron won't return my calls, and I'm pregnant," Fancy said, holding her flat stomach. She kicked off her shoes and curled her heels underneath her butt.

"Raped? Pregnant? Oh, my gosh, Fancy, no. Did you report this to the police? Is it Harry's baby? Have you seen a doctor?" Mandy asked.

Mandy had asked so many questions, Fancy became quiet. "I went to the free clinic and still ended up having to pay fifteen dollars for a pregnancy test and consultation. The results came back positive and it's Byron's baby."

"Fancy this is not a game. Did you say Byron because that's what you want? Or is he really the father? And why did you go to the free clinic instead of going to Kaiser?"

"Oh, and I'm unemployed so I have no medical benefits." Fancy uncurled her feet, placing them on the floor next to her shoes. "Does it matter who's the father? Let's say someone broke into my house and stole all my things. Does it matter if I know the person? The point is my stuff is gone. Right? Maybe now Byron will marry me." Fancy didn't tell Mandy that Byron would have to get a divorce first.

"What makes you think it's Byron's baby?"

"We always spend time together. He's always there for me. Besides, he told me he loves me and he wanted me to have his kids."

"Fancy, a man should never ask you to carry his baby before he asks you to carry his last name. Besides, he's never there when you need him most."

"That's not true. Byron loves me. I'm going to tell him about our baby tonight over dinner."

"Does Byron know about the rape?"

"No. And I'm not going to tell him."

"How do you know it's not Harry's baby?"

"Of course it's not Harry's baby."

"Did you go to the hospital after Harry raped you?"

"No."

"Fancy, that's the first thing you should've done. That way the doctor could have taken samples of pubic hairs, semen, blood, or any other particles that transmitted from Harry's body to yours. The information would support your case as evidence in court. You never answered if you filed a police report."

"No, I didn't."

The receptionist buzzed Mandy. "Okay, give me five more minutes and tell the client I won't bill him for this session."

"Could it be Desmond's baby?"

"No way," Fancy said, slipping on her black heels.

"How's your mother?"

"You mean, Caroline. She's Caroline."

Maybe on her next visit Fancy would tell Mandy that Caroline would need a new place to live once her ex was released from prison. Thaddeus was another problem Caroline had created and another reason Fancy hated her. When Fancy was twelve, Caroline had convinced Fancy to lie to the police and say Thaddeus raped her. Thaddeus was charged with child molestation. Fancy had grown tired of Thaddeus beating on Caroline every weekend but the first time he'd hit Fancy and called her fat and ugly, Fancy never wanted to see him again. After he was sentenced, Fancy thought

Caroline would spend more time being a mother instead of chasing men. Fancy was wrong. Nothing changed except the faces. Caroline still drank too much, threw up too often, and made Fancy clean up the mess. Fancy would've run away, except she had no place to go. So she'd lied on Thaddeus and promised Caroline she'd never tell anyone. And so far Fancy hadn't told a soul.

Mandy took a deep breath and released it slowly. "Here's my home number. Call me if you need me. I'll see you next week. And please be on time. We need to talk."

"Yes, we do." Fancy hurried out of Mandy's office and headed home.

Most of the day Fancy lay in bed nauseated. She was sick but forced herself to shower and dress for her date with Byron.

Her reflection was not one of an ill woman. The halter-top dress exposed her cleavage. The short dress showed off her thighs. And her hair draped over her left shoulder, highlighting her toned back.

Byron's driver arrived early so Fancy took her time before going downstairs. Surprisingly, Byron was in the car, so Fancy smiled.

"Hey, I missed you. Where've you been?"

"You look nice. You always look nice," Byron said, kissing her on the lips.

Fancy shivered, then said, "So, you had dinner with SaVoy last weekend?"

Byron leaned back. He didn't respond. Well, at least he knew that she knew he'd taken out her best friend.

The view from their dinner table at The Claremont Resort was romantic. Byron ordered lamb chops for himself, duck for her, and a bottle of champagne.

"I have a lot on my plate right now. I brought you here to tell you this may be our last date for a few months."

The nausea in Fancy's stomach rose to her throat. She

swallowed air. "Why?" Her eyes searched his, trying to find an answer. "I love you. We can work out something."

Byron nodded at the waiter, acknowledging to pour the champagne.

Fancy lifted her glass and said, "A toast. To our unborn child." She smiled as she watched the smile on Byron's face disappear. Her smile vanished.

"What did you say?"

Fancy repeated the toast, holding her flute in the air, waiting for Byron's approval.

"This is not a good time. Look, I'll pay for the abortion."

"I'm not having an abortion!"

"Calm down." Byron motioned for the waiter to bring the check. "We'll talk about this later."

"This. You call our baby a this."

"Let's go." Byron stood behind Fancy, waiting to pull out her chair. He waited, then said, "You have ten seconds."

"Or what?" Fancy said, eating her vegetables, "you're going to call your wife?"

Byron stood behind her chair for exactly ten seconds, then he left. Fancy scurried behind him because she needed a ride home.

"Look, I'm not ready to start a family. Just be patient. I'll arrange for the abortion, and have someone stay with you for three days."

Oh, hell no. This wasn't foreign to Byron. How many women had had abortions for him? Byron had the driver pull over. He sorted through the floral bouquets at a roadside stand and bought a colorful assortment of sunflowers.

His phone rang so Fancy looked at the driver who looked at her. She looked at the caller ID. It showed home.

Fancy smiled and snuggled under Byron after he got in the car. "Spend the night with me."

Byron sat quietly, staring out the window. "There's

something I need to tell you," Byron said right before the red message light flashed on his phone. Byron listened to his message, then said as his driver double-parked in front of Fancy's building, "Sorry, I can't stay tonight."

"What were you going to say?"

"It can wait. I have to go. I love you," Byron said, waiting for her to get out the car.

"What about the money you still owe me?"

"I'll give you the money for the abortion this weekend."

"I'm not having an abortion. I mean the money for working at your fund-raisers."

"My accountant paid you months ago. Look, I don't like the way this conversation is going. I've already wasted too much time. I gotta go." Byron tipped the doorman and said, "Please, see Ms. Taylor to her door."

Fancy didn't want to let Byron know she was unemployed and that it was his fault she'd fired her regular sponsors to be with him. Before the driver closed Byron's door, he was on the phone.

With so many things happening, Fancy had forgotten to check her mailbox. She jumped with excitement. A familiar envelope from Washington and Associates only meant one thing. Harry's check had arrived. "You don't have to escort me upstairs, I'll be fine." As soon as the elevator doors closed, Fancy opened the envelope. Non-negotiable was watermarked across the front of her fifty thousand dollar check, and a bill for seven thousand dollars was enclosed with a letter.

The following expenditures in the amount of fifty-seven thousand dollars have been deducted from your settlement and your liability to Washington and Associates is due immediately. If you have any questions, please contact the attorney.

Every real estate course—principles, ethics, finance, escrow, property management—and the bleeding heart was deducted from her payment. "Fuck this! Harry's gonna pay me my money or first thing Monday morning I'm calling the cops."

CHAPTER 21

SaVoy was especially excited because after several dates, this was the first night Tyronne invited her to his place. She packed three DVDs, her cell phone charger, Nintendo and Play Station controllers, clothes for church tomorrow, and the lavender silk nightgown and robe she'd bought earlier. SaVoy was nervous and excited about spending her first night, all night, with a man. Scribbling on a blank five-by-seven note paper she wrote, "Papa, I'm staying the night at Tyronne's. His address and phone number are . . ."

Instead of wearing a ponytail, SaVoy finger combed her curls. How could she not over- or underdress for a house date? After changing several times, SaVoy wore her blue jeans, a tan asymmetrical cut blouse, black boots, and a short tan leather blazer. Her M.A.C. gloss shone between the chocolate lip liner.

When the garage door lifted she saw Desmond walking up to her door. SaVoy frowned. She tooted her horn, shifted into park, and got out of her car.

"Hey, you look nice. Where're you going?" Desmond asked.

"I'm headed to Tyronne's. I'm so nervous."

"Why?"

"Because I've never spent the night with a man before."

Desmond's eyes widened. "Tyronne's cool. He ain't trippin' on the fact that you're still a virgin." Desmond covered his mouth.

SaVoy slapped Desmond's shoulder. "No, he didn't!"

Desmond shrugged, then hugged SaVoy. "Look, I apologize. I shouldn't have said that. But you know Tyronne's good people." He released his embrace. "Don't trip." Desmond walked SaVoy to her car and said, "Leave now before you change your mind. I can come by tomorrow."

"What did you want?" SaVoy asked, rolling down her window.

"You," Desmond paused, then said, "to help me decide what colleges to apply to. I narrowed it down to ten." Desmond held up the paper.

"Are you serious? Let me see," SaVoy said, reaching for the paper. She unfolded it. "These are great. Think about Hastings and Harvard."

"What?" Desmond asked, sticking out his chest. "I get another hug?"

SaVoy kissed Desmond on the cheek and said, "Come by tomorrow. After church."

"For sure. I'm headed over to Carlita's to tell her the news. I know she's going to want to take me out to celebrate but a brother can't dress up until he gets an invite." Desmond kissed SaVoy on the cheek, close to her mouth.

SaVoy hopped in her car, rolled up the window, and drove off. She glanced in her rearview mirror. Desmond stood in the driveway watching her car.

The sweet fragrance of apple cinnamon escaped when Tyronne opened the door. SaVoy inhaled and peeped inside. No lights were on. Just candles burning. "Hey, woman. Come on in so I can close the door."

"You do have electricity don't you?" SaVoy said,
counting the candles. "Did you realize you have thir-
teen candles lit?"

"Get out," Tyronne said, placing his hand flat in
front of SaVoy's face. "You're fired!"

Before she realized what she'd done, SaVoy's M.A.C.
lip print was now in Tyronne's palm.

"Okay, you can stay, but let that be a warning." He
eased off her jacket. "Don't start, okay."

"Start what?" SaVoy asked, sitting on the fluffy white
rug. "You mean beating you at a game of Madden."

Tyronne smiled and tossed SaVoy the controller. "I'll
even give you the good one."

SaVoy glanced at the muscles in Tyronne's calves and
handed the controller back to him. "No, thanks. I
brought my own."

"Okay, I don't hear you talkin'. That's the best you've
got. Touch down!" SaVoy slid her controller across the
floor near the system. "That's game, baby! I win!"

"I see you have multiple personalities, woman. A
brother gotta watch you," Tyronne said, exiting the room.

SaVoy scanned the photos inside Tyronne's entertainment center. The photo of Tyronne with a little boy
was odd.

"Yeah, he's mine," Tyronne said, walking into the room.

"How come you haven't mentioned him? What's his
name? How old is he?"

"What you think his name is, woman? TJ's eighteen
months. That's my dawg. He's got a crazy ass mama,
though." Tyronne shook his head.

"Is that her?"

"Naw, that's his sister. Of course that's her."

Did Tyronne like the same type of women? The
woman resembled SaVoy. "What's her name?"

"Lisa."

Was she jealous of Lisa? Of course, not. "Who's the
people in this photo?"

"That's my mom, my heart, the only woman in my life who can do no wrong. That's my old man, the best dad in the world. That's my two sisters, my brother, and me. Now, before your water gets cold, you need to go take a bath."

"Do you do everything by candlelight?"

"When it comes to making love, if it's not by candlelight, it ain't right. I'll be in the living room."

"Practicing?"

"See, a brother was trying to do the right thing, but naw." Tyronne grabbed a decorative towel from the rack and whacked SaVoy on the butt. "I'm not going to tell you again. Take your bath."

SaVoy softly said, "Take one with me."

Tyronne resisted at first but eventually gave in saying, "Call me after you are in the tub."

SaVoy undressed alone by candlelight and eased into the water, then called out, "Tyronne."

When Tyronne entered, the silhouette of his hairy chest danced with the flickers of light. "Close your eyes, girl. I don't want to scare you. The shadow image is a beast."

Cupping her hands over her eyes, SaVoy was tempted to peep but didn't.

"If a brother didn't have dick control, you'd be in trouble."

"Maybe I want to be in trouble," SaVoy said, resting her back on Tyronne's chest.

Tyronne massaged her breasts. The sensation was ten times better than when she'd done it herself. He talked about his childhood. How his dad was always working, seldom home because he refused to have his wife work unless she wanted to. His mother's job was to take care of them and Tyronne sang his parents' praises.

Tyronne talked about how he tried creating the same type of family environment for his son, but Lisa was too insecure. One day Tyronne wanted his own business.

He hadn't quite figured out what type of business but he was confident his dream would come true.

SaVoy's hair unraveled from the ball she'd tied before getting in the tub. "Maybe you can own your own bottling company."

"No way. I hate jumping in and out of that damn truck all day long. I'm thinking maybe a meeting place for teens to hang out and have fun. Kids have more discretionary income than adults. Think about it. A working parent will give a nonworking kid an allowance. And when the child spends the allowance early, the parent gives the child more money. I just need to find an ideal location. I want it to be in Oakland but it doesn't have to be because the kids will find a way to get to wherever I open my place."

"Maybe when my dad buys the building you can convince him to lease you the other half."

"No shit? Actually, that's a great location." Tyronne became silent and gently teased her nipples.

SaVoy eased her hand over her clit and started massaging herself. Tyronne's dick slithered up her back like a snake.

"Let's get out of the tub before you turn into a raisin and I turn into a prune," Tyronne said, standing up.

"Turn on the light," SaVoy said.

"Nope." Tyronne wrapped the towel around his waist and walked out.

His bedroom was as immaculate as the living room, bathroom, and kitchen. SaVoy plopped down in the center of the bed and stretched out.

"Nope. You have ten seconds to get in the living room or else, young lady." Tyronne started counting backward.

SaVoy eased out of the bed and unraveled her gown. "Fine."

They played Scrabble. Tyronne beat her twice and she wasn't sure if he'd let her win the last game. "I want you," SaVoy said, looking deep into Tyronne's eyes.

"Nope. Chill out. Relax," Tyronne said.

"Well, at least let me see you."

"He ain't goin' nowhere. You'll see him in time." Tyronne threw several comforters and pillows on the living room floor. "You should've peeped when you had a chance. Let's go to bed. And if I catch you peeping"— Tyronne placed his hand in front of her face and said, "you're fired."

CHAPTER 22

Desmond watched Carlita gather her keys, purse, and *Black Issues Book Review* magazine. Carlita was an avid reader of African-American authors and religiously took two or three novels whenever she left the house. She bought most of her books from Alkebulan Books in Berkeley and Marcus Book Stores in Oakland.

"Whatcha readin' now, woman?" Desmond asked in a Jamaican accent.

Carlita stood erect and said, "Iz za show you when me gets back home from the salon ya know. Gets plenty of rest. Ya gonna need it, mon." Carlita lifted her leg, placed her knee next to her ear, and pointed her toes in the air.

Damn! Desmond pretended he'd passed out on the couch. Carlita was double-jointed and could twist her body in weird positions. The pose she'd struck was impossible for most but easy for Carlita.

"Do the damn thing, woman."

"Five dolla. You pay. Five dolla." Carlita wiggled her fingers in front of his face. Desmond dug in his pocket and pulled out forty dollars. "Thanks. Bye, baby. I should be back in about three hours." If he had any intentions on messing up Carlita's hair, he had to foot the bill in advance. Carlita secured the top lock from the outside.

Desmond glanced at his ringing cell phone on the coffee table.

"Holla," Desmond said.

"Hey, Desmond. This is SaVoy."

"Duh, I know that. What's up?"

"I was wondering if you've heard from Tyronne. I haven't been able to get in touch with him since . . . well, since I spent the night at his place."

"He's fine. Just chillin'. You must've scared him or something."

"Oh, please. Me scare him. I don't think so. Well, when you talk with him, ask him to call me, okay?"

"Sure. Hey, SaVoy. I need some more help with my pre-test. Is it okay if I come over tomorrow? Say around six."

"Okay, but don't forget—"

"Yeah, I know, to tell Tyronne to call you. I won't. I got another call. See ya tomorrow."

"Hello," Desmond answered. "Where've you been, girl?"

"Dez, I need to talk. Can you come over?"

Since Carlita wasn't due back for a couple of hours, Desmond said, "Sure, I'll be right there."

While driving, Desmond scrolled his cell phone book for Tyronne's number.

"Man, what's up? Why you not returning SaVoy's calls? She had to call me looking for you."

"Dawg, I don't know what to do with that feline. That girl is sweeter than honey."

Tapping on his brakes, Desmond asked, "So she let *you* hit it?"

"Why it gotta be like dat? Don't hate."

Desmond was jealous but didn't really know why. Maybe because Tyronne had busted several cherries and every feline Desmond had met was nowhere close to being a virgin.

"Man, that girl made love to me without givin' it up. Let's just say she's a fast learner. But she's too nice for me, dawg. That's why I haven't called her back. But I will. I don't want her giving me the evil eye when I show up at her dad's store on Wednesday. Where you at?"

"Fancy called—"

"Aw, here we go again. I told you, man. You shoulda left that ho alone a long time ago. Look, I gotta run. Peace. I'm out." Tyronne was gone.

Maybe that's why Desmond was jealous. Tyronne, as doggish as he was, could still pull nice girls like SaVoy. Desmond watched five minutes and one second flash on his display. "Damn," he said, trying to hang up before the next second of the next minute registered because his cellular company would charge him a full sixty seconds regardless. Desmond pressed star, two, talk, and requested credit for a dropped call. Every month he dialed in for his twenty minutes of credit, which added a ten-dollar savings to his bank account.

Desmond enjoyed having sex with Fancy but the thought of being with SaVoy turned him on even more. What would it be like to get with a virgin? Certainly he couldn't fuck her the same way he was hitting it from behind with Fancy. And truly not the way Carlita had taught him to make love.

Fancy answered the door wearing gray sweats and a white man's tank undershirt. "Hi, thanks for coming over," Fancy said, kissing Desmond on the lips.

"What's up? I know you need something." Desmond sat on the love seat, picked up the remote, and turned on the TV.

Fancy took the remote and turned off the television. "I need for you to listen to me, Dez. I'm pregnant."

"Whoa, why you telling me this?" Desmond sat on the edge of the chair.

"Because you're the only friend I have. Who else am I supposed to talk to?"

Desmond had never seen Fancy so desperate and it wasn't becoming. Fancy was always so strong and in control. He moved next to her on the sofa. Fancy laid her head on his shoulder.

"I want to have an abortion. And I want you to go with me. They said I shouldn't drive myself home afterward. My appointment is Tuesday at ten o'clock."

"I have to work Tuesday," Desmond said. Not because he didn't want to go. He wasn't sure if he supported her decision. She never said it wasn't his kid. He doubted that it was. And if it was, he was certain Fancy would not have his child. Fancy cried louder and harder.

"Please, Dez. I'll pay you to take off Tuesday. Just go with me. I can't have this baby."

"Whose baby is it?" Desmond asked, handing Fancy a tissue.

"Honestly?" Fancy sniffled. "I don't know."

"Then whose baby could it be?" Desmond asked. "You know. What I mean is . . ." Desmond sighed heavily.

"If you want to know could it be yours, maybe. But I don't know for sure."

"Who else?"

"Byron." Fancy paused, then said, "Adam." She paused again and said, "Or maybe it's Harry's."

"What! Damn! How many men you fucking?" Desmond stood and walked around the coffee table. "Byron, Adam, Harry, and me?"

"And let me guess. Neither Byron nor Adam will go with you. Damn, Tyronne was right. You are a ho. Why would you open your legs for so many men?"

Fancy started crying harder. "I knew I shouldn't have told you the truth. Get out!" Fancy pointed toward the door. "Get out now! I'll drive myself to the abortion

clinic. And I guess you fucking Carlita and me and whoever else makes you perfect! Get out!"

Desmond opened the door, then closed it. He stood
looking at Fancy and remembered how his mother told
him, "Baby, it's easy to be a friend when things are
going well. But if you're not there for a friend in the
time of need, then you're not a true friend."

"I'll take you Tuesday. But I won't let you pay me,"
Desmond said, hugging Fancy. "I'll call and check on
you later."

On his drive back to Carlita's, Desmond thought how
difficult it must be to live inside a woman's body. He
could easily have had sex with as many women as Fancy
had with those men but he could never give birth to
baby. Fancy was his friend. And she was pregnant with a
baby that could be from any of the four guys she'd mentioned. Suddenly Desmond realized he had a vested interest in making sure Fancy aborted the baby. He didn't
want a child under those circumstances and he definitely
didn't want to pay child support for the next eighteen
plus years if the baby was his. Carlita was still receiving
payments for her eldest son because he was living at
home while going to Cal Berkeley. The father was so
happy his son turned eighteen, but was disappointed
when the judge said he had to pay child support until
his son's twenty-second birthday.

Desmond unlocked Carlita's door using his key. He
had also given her a key to his place but found himself
spending more and more time at Carlita's. "Hey, your
hair stylist hooked you up."

"Yes, she did. Come here for a minute." Carlita went
into the kitchen and returned with two tall glasses of
cranberry juice. "I've been thinking."

Desmond stood immediately because whenever Carlita
said those words he was already at a disadvantage.

"Sit. We do need to talk. I'm happy with our relationship. I love you. You know I want you to move in. But I think it's time for us to get married."

Desmond scratched his neck although it didn't itch. "You think so. Why? I like things the way they are."

"You know I don't question you. Never have. Don't plan on starting now. But. You need to make up your mind. Either we're going to be together and you are going to stop running to rescue your immature friend Fancy every time she plays the damsel in distress, or we're not going to be together. It's as simple as that." Carlita never raised her voice.

"Can a brotha at least take some time to think about it?"

"Sure, take all the time you need." Carlita opened her hand and said, "Give me back my keys."

That's why Desmond didn't want to take the damn keys in the first place. He knew at some point she'd take them back. And he really didn't understand why Carlita had an attitude. She always seemed so easygoing. Desmond tossed the keys on the table next to his glass and walked out.

CHAPTER 23

Fancy parked her Benz in front of 14576 and turned off the engine. She couldn't believe she'd actually driven over forty miles, to Cupertino, to Mrs. Van Lee's house. Her knees quivered as the sunlight beamed between the redwood trees. Fancy took a deep breath, astonished at the two-story mansion. She exhaled, wondering if she should restart her engine and drive home. Naw, but she would leave the keys in the ignition in case she had to escape.

"You've come too far. Just tell her you're pregnant with Byron's child and he's going to divorce her." Fancy took tiny steps until she was standing before two spectacular cherry wood doors with brass door knockers on both sides. She stood in disbelief. This would one day become her home. How could she have not known the house Byron always took her to—the one where he'd changed the locks—wasn't his primary residence?

"Oh, shit!" Fancy jumped. A gray squirrel stopped within inches of her feet as if he were accustomed to humans. Perched on his hind legs, he curled his fluffy tail while his large curious eyes focused on her hands. She shushed him away whispering, "Get! Go! Move!"

"Oh, my gosh!" The creaking of the cherry wood doors startled her even more.

"May I help you?" A small-framed woman who looked like she'd swallowed a watermelon stood in the doorway. Short, wavy, coal-black hair. Pecan-brown skin. She wasn't nearly as gorgeous as Fancy. The woman was rather homely looking. She wore a blue slip-on long-sleeve dress with a hemline that rested above her blue slippers. Fancy wondered if the woman was having a boy.

"Are you Mrs. Lee?" Fancy asked, peripherally focusing on the woman's stomach.

"Yes, darling. How may I help you? You look overdressed to be from Molly Maids," she asked, then smiled.

Molly what? Who in hell did she think she was talking to? Molly Maids don't wear designer suits. The pantsuit Fancy wore, a salmon-colored two-piece with a silk rust camisole, was brand new. Her tan leather boots were worn once before. Fancy tucked her hair behind her ears to showcase her diamond teardrop earrings.

"Oh, I'm definitely nobody's maid." Fancy had enough of cleaning up behind Caroline to last her her lifetime. "I'm a real estate agent and appraiser. Just doing a comparison study in your area. A home similar to yours is listed and well, I was wondering if I could just look around outside before my client submits his offer," Fancy lied, hoping to get inside the house.

"Oh, you must be talking about the Latimores. We used the same contractor to redesign our kitchens and bathrooms but you won't find many similarities because our architectural developers were different." Mrs. Lee opened the door wider and stood back. "Well, what's your name? What company are you with? And where's your ID?" The short woman was still cheery.

Byron was obviously happily married and had no intention of divorcing his wife.

Fancy fumbled through her purse. "Oh, wow! I forgot my wallet at the office. I can come back if you prefer."

"That's okay, honey, I may not be home later. Come on in. I'll give you a quick tour."

When Fancy entered the house her mouth hung open and her eyes filled with tears as she held her stomach. Byron's home was exquisite. Marbled and cherry hardwood floors. Staircases to her left and right led to a row of rooms upstairs.

"Would you like some tea? We have black and green. We can sit while I show you the before and after rehab pictures." Mrs. Lee turned and continued walking into the kitchen.

Mimicking choking the woman, Fancy said, "Oh, no thanks. I have other appointments. I just came to see the amenities. Who's your interior decorator?" Fancy asked hurriedly, lowering her hands, pretending to appreciate the painting on the kitchen ceiling.

"Oh, my gosh!" Mrs. Lee faced Fancy, then cupped her hands underneath her stomach. "I've been in labor the past two days but I think this is it!"

In labor? For two days? What the hell? Fancy didn't have to stand because she'd never taken a seat.

The woman removed the cordless phone from the base. "I have to call my husband. Can you please stay with me until he gets here? He won't take long."

Fancy dropped her purse. Hurriedly she tucked her tan leather bag under her arm. "Um, I really have to go." Fancy shuffled across the hardwood floor onto the marbled foyer, and raced outside to her car. Her driver's license tumbled out of her purse, then fell in the grass. She swiftly picked it up, and hopped in her car. The engine wouldn't start. Her brand new car wouldn't start. Fancy opened, then closed her door again. She banged on the steering wheel. The car still wouldn't start. "This is an omen. I know it is." The cell phone fumbled in her hands as she called Desmond.

Hurry up and answer the phone! Desmond answered on the fifth ring.

"Dez, I need you baby. My car won't start!" Fancy heard sirens in the distance. "You gotta help me!"

"Where are you? And what do you mean your car won't start? It's a brand new Benz."

"I know what it is! Dez, this is serious. You're really not helping me!" Fancy worried more because the road she'd taken was one way in and one way out.

"Calm down," Desmond said. "Where are you? I'll come and get you."

"No, I just need to know how to get my car started."

"Well, what's it doing?"

"Nothing!"

Fancy hung up on Desmond when she heard a car coming up the driveway. She started breathing heavily. She desperately turned her key as far as she could in the ignition and pumped her accelerator several times. Byron pulled his car alongside hers.

Shaking his head, Byron frowned at Fancy. "What are you doing here?" he quizzically asked.

Mrs. Lee wobbled over to Byron. "I'm so glad you're here. Now I don't need the ambulance. You can take me to the hospital."

Byron kissed her forehead and said, "No way, Sis. You're going in the ambulance." Byron lovingly steered the woman toward the ambulance that just pulled up behind his car. "You know how crazy your overprotective husband is." They both laughed.

Sis? Mrs. Lee was his sister? Fuck! Fancy dropped her head and closed her eyes for a few seconds. When she opened them she could have kicked herself in the ass. One, for not trusting Byron. Two, she'd left her automatic gear in drive when she turned off the car.

Byron helped his sister into the ambulance, then walked over to Fancy's car. Fancy pressed the automatic lock button to secure all the doors.

Byron's arm rushed inside the car.

"Hey! What are you doing?" Fancy yelled, wrestling with Byron's arm.

He snatched the keys from the ignition. "Get in my car," he said forcefully.

Fancy sat staring at the house. She'd fucked up big time this time. Why couldn't she trust Byron? Or any other man for that matter? Maybe her inability to trust was the real reason she hadn't gotten married.

"Fine. Don't get out the car. I'll talk with you later," Byron said before dropping her keys into his pocket. Byron got into his car and backed out of the driveway.

Fancy opened her purse and removed her spare keys. Byron didn't honestly think she was that stupid. Fancy always kept an extra set of keys in her purse. When she turned the key, this time her car started. She sped backward out of the driveway onto the road and took off down the hill.

CHAPTER 24

SaVoy wondered if she'd done something to upset Tyronne. The last two Wednesdays another delivery person filled her orders. She didn't know what to expect this Wednesday. Why wasn't Tyronne returning her calls? Whenever she asked Desmond, all he ever told her was, "Tyronne's fine."

SaVoy heard the sound of a big truck, similar to Tyronne's, and leaned over the counter. Budweiser. Wrong truck. She walked to the door, stepped outside, and scanned down the street. First to her left. Then to her right. No Tyronne. SaVoy returned inside and aligned seasonings and boxed and canned foods along the edge of the shelves. SaVoy whispered, " 'Trust in the Lord with all your heart and lean not on your own understanding; in all your ways acknowledge Him, and He will make your paths straight. Lord, you know best.' " SaVoy continued arranging until each shelf appeared full although most of the items were only stocked two rows deep.

"What's up?"

SaVoy quickly turned toward the door.

Desmond strolled inside. "Need some help?"

SaVoy sighed, "No, but thanks. I need to keep busy," SaVoy said, kneeling before the detergents on the bottom shelf.

"Well, thanks to you"—Desmond opened his arms—"I'm ready to take my LSAT." When SaVoy stood, he wrapped his arms around her.

"That's great news. You've studied really, really hard; you should pass the test the first time around. Then you can apply for a scholarship with my church, too."

"Don't I have to be a member?"

"Nope. Pastor Tellings believes we're all a part of the same community. Member or not. Plus, lots of our members are very wealthy and even the ones who don't attend still tithe faithfully."

"Man, you are too close to my woman. You need to back up, boy," Tyronne said, opening his arms to SaVoy. "Come here, woman."

SaVoy gasped. Joyful tears welled in her eyes. "Where've you been? I missed you!" SaVoy was so excited she practically leaped into Tyronne's arms. "Desmond, could you watch the register for a moment?" SaVoy asked.

"Sure, no problem. But I gotta run in a few," Desmond said, watching SaVoy.

She squeezed Tyronne's hand, led him inside the office, and closed the door. "Where've you been?"

"Can a brother get a kiss before he starts kissing up?"

Tyronne's muscular biceps felt protective wrapped around her shoulders. He had the best kisses. Tyronne's warm and sweet tongue wavered inside SaVoy's mouth.

"I can't stay," Tyronne said, stepping back, admiring SaVoy. "You remember that little incident I told you about with my ex, Lisa? The one who spray-painted me in the restaurant."

SaVoy nodded.

"Well, I thought the company had forgotten about that shit but they didn't. My supervisor placed me on suspension for two weeks. Without pay. So I just chilled.

Handled my business, you know. Had some rough days. But a brotha's all right now. Back on the job. Had a lot of time to think, though." Tyronne kissed SaVoy lips, then said, "Especially about you."

"I thought I'd done something to upset you," was all SaVoy could think of to say. A minor in psychology and she was at a loss for words.

Tyronne kissed her lips again. "We need to talk. Can you come to my place around eight? Bring your clothes if you want to spend the night."

"Okay," SaVoy said. She beamed with excitement. All of her concerns dissipated the minute she saw Tyronne. She didn't want to waste time arguing or complaining, believing that would add to Tyronne's stress. SaVoy's plan, whenever she did have a relationship, was to complement her mate by being supportive. Not combative.

Desmond's hand was raised in a knocking motion when Tyronne opened the door. "Man, I gotta go." Desmond lowered his hand, then said, "Hey, man, you wanna go to the football game Saturday?" Desmond nodded. "I got two tickets and VIP passes, man."

Tyronne looked at SaVoy and smiled. "Depends."

Desmond frowned and said, "What? You must be kidding."

"Depends"—Tyronne nodded toward SaVoy—"on if SaVoy wants to hook up Saturday," Tyronne said, waiting for SaVoy's response.

SaVoy wasn't sure if this was a time to be selfish or selfless. Of course she wanted to spend time with Tyronne. Where was Vanessa when she needed her? "Why don't you go to the game. And we can get together afterward."

"I'll see you Saturday, dawg!" Tyronne yelled to Desmond as Desmond walked toward the door. "I gotta get busy. I'm running late." Tyronne tilted SaVoy's chin and kissed her lips, then added, "Um, um, um. For a very good reason." Tyronne shook his head. "Let me drop this order. I'll see you tonight, beautiful."

SaVoy watched Tyronne's biceps flex as he stocked the cooler and she became hotter.

"Peace. I'm out." Tyronne slapped the counter and left.

Tyronne could have taken her virginity but he didn't. That made him more special. SaVoy couldn't wait until eight o'clock to see him again.

SaVoy closed the store thirty minutes early and drove home. She replayed the song Tyronne had dedicated to them, "Everytime I Close My Eyes" by Kenny G, and sang along with Babyface, " '. . . every time I close my eyes I thank the Lord that I've got you. And you've got me too . . .' "

Papa's car was parked out front and Vanessa's car was in the driveway. SaVoy parked next to Vanessa's car and raced inside. "Hi, Papa." SaVoy kissed her father on the cheek.

"There's my Baby Girl. How's everything at the store?" Papa asked with a smile.

"Everything's fine, Papa." SaVoy looked at Vanessa and said, "Hello, Vanessa." Then she bit her bottom lip, and shifted her eyes toward her bedroom.

Vanessa patted SaVoy's dad on the knee and said, "I'll be back, big Papa."

That was the first time SaVoy witnessed her father slapping Vanessa on the ass.

SaVoy closed her bedroom door and sat on the bed facing Vanessa. "So, how are you?"

"We can skip the formalities." Vanessa squeezed SaVoy's hands. "How's Tyronne?"

"He's fine. I'm nervous because I like him so much. I'm going over to his place tonight. And I'm ready." SaVoy looked away from Vanessa.

Vanessa guided SaVoy's chin back in her direction. "Just remember this. Don't give up your womanhood for him. Having sex with Tyronne won't make him your man. Getting pregnant won't make you his woman or make him take care of a baby. What you should think about is sharing a special moment with a special person. And remember, it's okay to change your mind. Before. Or during. If you don't want to go all the way, honey, don't."

"I started taking birth control pills two months ago. And I had my first pap smear. The nurse told me I had to start my pills the first Sunday after my period and she said, 'Wait until after your next period before you have sex. If you don't, you could get pregnant. And always make him wear a condom.' And she said we should get HIV tested together. And get our test results together."

SaVoy opened her bottom drawer and pulled out a shoe box half full of condoms. "She gave me all of these. You think she gave me enough?"

Vanessa scooped a handful and tossed them in the air. "Hallelujah! It's rainin' safe sex all up in here!" Then she laughed heartily. "But Vanessa overlooked something, honey. You should've had your first pelvic exam at eighteen or if you would've had sex before eighteen you would've really needed to have an annual exam sooner."

SaVoy then commented, "That's what the nurse said too. But I don't think these prophylactics are large enough for Tyronne."

Vanessa left the bedroom and returned with her purse. "Here, take mine. These should fit. If not, honey, take a picture with your imagination and have a wet dream."

Those condoms must have been for Vanessa and Papa. SaVoy couldn't imagine using their condoms so she looked at the brand and size, then handed the condoms back to Vanessa. "Thanks. But I want to get my own."

SaVoy stopped at the twenty-four-hour Walgreens on

Telegraph and 51st and purchased two three-packs of condoms just in case some of them broke.

SaVoy arrived at Tyronne's exactly at eight o'clock. She put her overnight bag in his room. When Tyronne didn't come into the bedroom she went into the living room.

"You ready?" Tyronne asked, reaching for his keys on the end table.

SaVoy smiled. "For what?"

"Woman, let's go. I'm starving." His eyes darted to the corners toward SaVoy. "I sure hope you know how to cook 'cause a brotha loves to eat."

Cook? For him? SaVoy hadn't thought about that but since she was a terrific cook, the next time she was at Tyronne's house she'd cook for him.

Tyronne took SaVoy to Garibaldis on College Avenue. She had heard Fancy boast about the restaurant several times. Fancy was right. The food and service was extraordinary. So were the prices.

"So, let me guess," Tyronne said, munching on his vegetables. "You spent the rest of the day fantasizing about losing your virginity to me tonight." He glanced at SaVoy over his plate. "Right?"

SaVoy choked on her potatoes. "Tyronne. What makes you think that?"

" 'Cause, I know women." Tyronne looked into her eyes. "You can relax. That's not happenin'. At least not tonight."

What? Was he serious? "Why not?" SaVoy asked.

"The truth?" Tyronne polished off his cola and ordered another.

"Yes," SaVoy said hesitantly.

"I can get pussy anytime of the day or night. I can pick up my phone right now, and a feline would walk through that door before we finished eating. You're not like them. You're special, SaVoy. And I like you. A lot.

But as much as I like you, I'm not ready for you. Well, what I'm saying is, I think you deserve better." Tyronne's eyes didn't blink or waver.

If SaVoy had learned anything from college, she knew not to debate with Tyronne or anyone else over their own conclusive reasoning. Besides, she was outnumbered two to one—his thoughts and his words against her heart. "I disagree. But if you say so." This time Tyronne blinked several times. "How about going to church with me on Sunday?"

Tyronne smiled, then answered, "Oookay. Sure, why not?"

After dinner they returned to Tyronne's place. SaVoy prepared a nice warm bath. She entered the living room, holding a large towel that covered from her breasts to her thighs, and asked, "Can we at least bathe together again?"

Tyronne's succulent lips parted. "Woman, you cannot break me down."

SaVoy turned, then said, "I'm not trying to. Honestly." Her naked flesh was now facing Tyronne.

Tyronne changed to the vocal jazz blends on his digital cable, increased the volume, and followed SaVoy into the bathroom.

SaVoy waited until Tyronne was comfortably situated, then she eased into the tub, sat between his legs, and laid her head on his chest.

The more Tyronne massaged her shoulders the more relaxed she became. Tyronne's fingers teased her nipples, then slid up and over her shoulders. SaVoy placed his hands over her beasts again. This time he massaged them. SaVoy felt Tyronne's erection ease from between her cheeks and up her spine. Twisting her upper body to face him, SaVoy kissed Tyronne like all she wanted at that very moment was him.

Tyronne's wet sudsy hands held her face. "Let's get more comfortable."

SaVoy exhaled, dried him off as he dried her off, before making their way into his bedroom. Tyronne layered the comforter at the foot of the bed. Lit several candles. Lay atop the sheets. Spread his legs. The head of his dick rested on his navel.

"You are not ready for this, woman," Tyronne said, cupping his hands behind his head.

SaVoy wanted him so she teased his balls with her tongue, working her way up his stomach, slipping his head in and out of her mouth like it was a caramel-apple lollipop. Tyronne enjoyed the moment. SaVoy watched as his facial expression tensed. His eyebrows drew closer. His lower back started to arch so she stroked him a little faster and sucked a little harder.

"Damn, woman. You are doing the damn thing. Yesss. Yesss." Tyronne's head fell back against the bed. His hips thrust in motion with her strokes. "Aw, yesss," Tyronne whispered several times as his fluids flowed into SaVoy's hand.

SaVoy continued using Tyronne's cum as lubricant as she slowly massaged his subsiding erection.

"Woman, you're amazing," Tyronne said while SaVoy cleansed his private area with a steaming towel.

SaVoy straddled Tyronne and said, "Let's see how amazing you are."

"Ooh!" SaVoy yelled as Tyronne unexpectedly flipped her onto her back.

"How about I give you the beginner's package? And *if* you can hang, I'll advance you to intermediate. Next time."

Tyronne's tongue probed inside SaVoy's vagina. He eased up to her clit and gently sucked. First the tip. Then the tip and a part of her shaft. Then he wiggled the tip of his tongue all the way up to the base of her shaft. Down again. Up again. And back to her clit. Tyronne eased up to SaVoy's breasts and gently kissed each nipple. Softly he bit, licked, and sucked one nipple, then the other. As he alternated back and forth his dick hardened. Tyronne grabbed his dick, brushing the head against SaVoy's vagina and clit over and over.

SaVoy felt the warmth of his friction and said, "Um, that feels good." She moaned, trying to ease herself onto Tyronne's manhood.

"You think you slick, huh, woman. Now I'mma have to spank you." Tyronne slapped his penis against SaVoy's pubic hair several times. Then he buried his face in SaVoy's crotch and showed her how much he loved her.

SaVoy whispered, "Stop."

Tyronne kissed her lips, then eased her head under his shoulder, and stroked her hair.

SaVoy drunkenly said, "Was that really the beginner's package?"

"No, not really," Tyronne said. "That was the amateur's package. You ain't ready, woman." Tyronne threw his hand up and said, "You're fired! Relax, I'll be right back."

The warm towel felt good as he gently cleaned the crevices of her lips.

Afterward Tyronne snuggled his body behind hers. Their legs alternated against the mattress, his then hers, his then hers. Tyronne hugged her waist and rested his head on the same pillow right behind hers. SaVoy had so much fun experimenting she decided she'd definitely hold on to her virginity until after she'd gotten married.

CHAPTER 25

Fancy lay in her bed next to Desmond. She tossed and turned all night. Byron hadn't answered any of her calls. She'd phoned far more times than she'd left messages Saturday, Sunday, and Monday, telling him she was having the abortion Tuesday morning but he still didn't return her calls. When she blocked her number, he answered, "Hello," on the first ring. When she said, "Byron, it's me, Fancy," he said, "Grow the fuck up and stop playing games. Since you wanna play games, I have a surprise for you." Then he hung up. She tried calling back to apologize but each call never rang, not even once—all of her calls went directly into his voice mail. Fancy had stopped calling after Desmond arrived at her place last night.

Desmond rolled over and sleepily said, "Hey, you up already? How you feel?"

"Tired. I've been up all night. Couldn't sleep." Fancy looked over at Desmond. "I'm not sure I'm doing the right thing." Then she sat on her side of the bed.

"You'll be okay. I'll be here for you." Desmond reached over and massaged the small of Fancy's back.

Fancy stood up and said, "I'd better get dressed. If

you want something to eat, help yourself. They told me not eat anything this morning."

"What about water?" Desmond asked. "I can get you something to drink."

"I can have water. No juice, though." Fancy closed the bathroom door, sat on the toilet, and cried. She wondered if Caroline was scared and nervous before she had her first abortion. Was she being selfish? What if it was Byron's baby? What if it was Harry's or Desmond's? Why did that even matter now that another life was growing inside her? Her innocent unborn baby was getting ready to be killed because she didn't want to accept responsibility for her actions. Fancy cried in the shower. She cried while slipping into her yellow fleece suit and white jogging shoes.

Picking up her purse, she unwrapped a peppermint and grabbed a bottle of water. "Dez, let's go." Fancy sniffled and opened the door. "If I'm late they'll cancel my appointment."

"I'm ready. I thought you said you couldn't eat anything," Desmond said, pressing G on the elevator panel.

Stepping into the garage, Fancy pressed the unlock button on her car remote but she didn't hear a double beep. She looked around. "Where's my car?" She peeped through the wrought iron gate onto the street. Occasionally she'd park on the street but she was certain she'd parked in the garage. "Where's my fucking car!"

"Maybe dude took his Benz back," Desmond said, hunching his shoulders, looking at all the empty spaces.

"Byron wouldn't do that to me. He loves me." Fancy buried her face in her palms and started crying. "Why is this happening to me?"

"Yeah, dude loves you so much he's the one going with you to the clinic." Desmond clenched his back teeth and his jaw pulsated. "Let's take my car. You can worry about yours later."

Fancy cried all the way to the clinic. What was she going to do without a car?

Desmond dropped her off in front of the abortion clinic. A few people with picket signs yelled at her, "Murderer!" Fancy started crying again when she looked at the lifelike baby doll lying in a tiny wooden coffin. She ran up the six steps that separated her from those maniacs, and entered the freezing-cold building.

The woman behind the counter motioned for Fancy to come closer. Handing her a clipboard the woman said, "Fill out this form," then asked, "Did you have anything to eat?"

"No. Just a mint and some water."

"Well, that's something," the woman said with an attitude. "Nothing means nothing. So we're not going to be able to put you to sleep as you requested for the procedure. If you want, you can reschedule."

Fancy thought for a minute as she watched dozens of young girls complete the same form. There were maybe about four women that appeared older. Tears formed in Fancy's eyes as she fluttered her eyelids to wash them away.

Desmond walked up to the counter and said, "I can't take off from work another day so you need to do this today or have dude come back with you."

"Whatever. I'll just do it today," Fancy said.

Fancy completed the paperwork and silently waited until she was called into the nurse's office. The nurse handed Fancy a cup. "Urinate just a little, then I need you to hold this under your flow for a few seconds. Then set the cup in the cubbyhole over the toilet so the lab can verify your status."

A few minutes later Fancy was instructed to change in a small dressing room with several other patients. Each of them undressed and put on the open gown and went into a waiting area. Several of the girls were crying. Some were bragging like they were hurting the guy.

A woman wearing a white lab coat entered the room and called out, "Fancy Taylor."

When Fancy heard her name she thought about leaving like Caroline had done with her. Somehow she found herself in a smaller room with doors on both sides. She entered from the hallway behind the woman. When Fancy looked through the other door, hospital beds were lined against the wall occupied by women who'd already had the procedure.

The nurse closed both doors. The anesthesiologist injected medication into Fancy's IV. The doctor came in. He was friendly. He turned on a vacuum and began suctioning out Fancy's insides while talking to her at the same time. Fancy cried. She was too young and too old to be so careless. Fancy promised herself that was the first and last time she'd have an abortion.

Desmond handed her a bouquet of fresh assorted flowers when she exited into the lobby. "How you feel? You all right?" he asked.

"What kind of question is that? I just killed my baby. No, I'm not all right. I'm fucked-up, Dez. They said I should stay home a couple of days but considering I don't have a job, that's easy to do."

"Well, you know I'mma be here for you. I'm just a phone call away if you need me."

Desmond was always there for her. He stayed the rest of the day. Went to Walgreens and filled her prescription for Vicodin. Fancy thought about her car. She couldn't buy another one. What if Byron didn't take the car? What if he did? Since she never saw the title she wasn't sure who owned the car. She could take him to court because the car was a gift. Fancy decided tomorrow morning she'd call the police and report the car stolen.

CHAPTER 26

SaVoy knelt beside her bed and prayed. "Thank you, Jesus, for bringing Tyronne into my life. Thank You for letting Papa rent the unused space to Tyronne so Tyronne can start his business. Lord, please continue blessing Tyronne. You know his needs, Lord. Thank you, Lord, for leading Tyronne back into your house of worship. I, too, can see how much more focused he's become. And Lord, as always, I ask that you watch over Mama and Fancy and keep them safe. Amen." SaVoy always said a prayer for Fancy but lately her friend was struggling, so SaVoy prayed a little more often. Fancy's struggle was a good one because like Tyronne and Desmond, Fancy had accepted responsibility for her own success. But Fancy still refused to admit she needed anyone's help, including God's.

SaVoy admired her lemon-colored knee-length dress in the mirror. The canary sweater Vanessa gave her was a perfect match. SaVoy tossed her purse on the bed and answered the phone.

"Good morning, my friend. How are you this beautiful Sunday morning?"

"Great." Fancy replied. "On my way horseback riding. With Darius Jones."

"What? *The* Darius Jones? When and where did you meet him?"

SaVoy was curious because she and Darius grew up together in Sunday school. Darius was spoiled then and he was worse now that he owned a major corporation. But after Darius's Ma Dear passed he came to church once a year, each time with his stepsister Ashlee. Rumors had spread throughout the church. Supposedly Darius and Ashlee were kinder than kin. SaVoy never repeated gossip but Darius and Ashlee did seem awfully close to be related. Fancy's luck couldn't possibly be that good or that bad. Darius was way out of Fancy's league but at least he had one thing Fancy didn't. Religion.

"Girl, I'm just kidding. I wish I could get in touch with his rich fine ass. You sound like"—Fancy's voice lowered as she said—"you might know him."

SaVoy did one of Fancy's numbers and ignored her inquiry. "Tyronne's going to church with me again this morning. You wanna go?"

"I called because I wanted to know if I could borrow your car or if you would pick me up after class again this week."

SaVoy felt blessed supporting Fancy getting her real estate license. Although she could have told Fancy to catch the bus home, picking Fancy up every Wednesday gave them time to bond. The more SaVoy listened to Fancy the more she understood her. Although she wouldn't admit it, Fancy's ways were a lot like Caroline's and Fancy was simply living what she had witnessed most of her life.

"Of course I'll pick you up."

SaVoy didn't want to start any bad habits that might jeopardize their friendship. She knew Fancy couldn't afford to pay her deductible so SaVoy certainly wouldn't risk Fancy wrecking her car—her only source of transportation.

"Thanks, girl. I gotta go. Steven is here."

"I thought you changed your number to get rid of Steven months ago."

"Girl, sponsorships are scarce these days." Fancy laughed, then hung up the phone.

Fancy should've come to church because Darius's brother Darryl, who was better looking and had a slightly smaller ego than Darius, was visiting. Darius had named Darryl vice president and COO of Somebody's Gotta Be On Top, making Darryl a very wealthy man.

" 'Love thy neighbor as thyself . . .' " Pastor Tellings preached.

Pastor Tellings's sermons got shorter each passing year but the congregation loved him so they wanted him to deliver the message every Sunday morning. Instead, Pastor agreed to preach only on the first Sunday.

After service Tyronne said, "So you wanna go to Bible study for singles on Wednesday?"

SaVoy smiled and said, "Have I created a Holy Ghost?"

"Naw, you just helped a brotha return to his roots. That, and I wanna do right by you. I love you, woman. And since I'm gonna be a biznessman"—Tyronne tugged on his collar—"I need a strong black woman by my side."

"I'd like that, but—"

"But what?"

"Give me a minute. Wednesdays I pick Fancy up from school. So that means we'll have to meet at the church so I can pick her up on time. Or you can ride with me."

Tyronne responded, "That's easy."

SaVoy and Tyronne looked one another in the eyes and spoke in unison, "Separate cars."

CHAPTER 27

This time, instead of parking her car on University Avenue, Fancy exited the bus and waited for the light to change. She had to figure out a way to get another car because the caliber of men she liked were not bus drivers or bus riders.

SaVoy could have loaned Fancy her car. It was not as though she had someplace to go other than the store. Or over to Tyronne's—and he drove whenever SaVoy was with him. What was taking the light so long to change? Two Mercedes rolled by. Each driver flirted with her. Fancy ignored the first one. Broken-down Benz. Older than her mama. And the guy was butt ugly. Honestly, he didn't think she'd be interested in him? The second sports coupe was the same make and model as the one she used to have. Fancy leaned over. She lifted her eyebrows without cracking a smile. The man driving had on construction overalls and a wedding band. The last thing Fancy wanted was another Adam. What would she look like, sitting in his ride, a single woman with her Venice designer halter, matching black leather pants, and full-length coat? As soon as the walk signal flashed,

Fancy strutted across the street and pranced into Mandy's office.

"She's waiting for you, Fancy," Mandy's assistant said. "Go on in, Ms. Diva."

Mandy was scribbling notes. Perhaps from her last session or maybe in preparation for her talk with Fancy.

"You look nice, Fancy. You can hang up your coat and have a seat." Mandy jotted a few more notes.

"I feel salty," Fancy said, sitting in her usual place.

"Salty?" Mandy frowned, then asked, "Why?"

"Whew! Let's see," Fancy said, nervously rubbing her hands back and forth along her thighs. The leather felt baby smooth. "I followed through with the abortion. Byron took back the car he gave me so I reported the car stolen. I don't have a job. And I'm tired of borrowing money from Desmond and SaVoy."

Mandy nodded but Fancy couldn't tell if Mandy agreed with her or if she was simply acknowledging her statements.

Fancy continued. "But I'm actually enjoying real estate school. I'mma get my own properties. I'll show them. I don't need no man to take care of me."

"Did you ever find out who was the father?"

Fancy snapped. "What difference does that make? Desmond was the only one willing to take me to the clinic."

"How is Desmond?"

"What? Not today, please. This is about me. Don't waste my dime bringing up my past." Fancy breathed heavily.

Mandy shook her head. "You don't know a good thing when you have it, do you? Did you really want a baby? Or did you want bargaining power?"

"Bargaining power. Now. There. Are you satisfied? I wanted bargaining power." Fancy threw her hands up in disgust.

"Whoa, settle down. Are you looking for a job?"

"The next person I work for is going to be me." Fancy sat up straight. "I have a plan. I'm going to buy one of those HUD homes for a dollar, then I won't have to worry about rent. I can keep Steven and get a few new sponsors and keep on buying more houses until I'm rich. I don't know why I didn't think about this sooner."

"I hope you have a plan B because HUD doesn't sell one-dollar homes to the public. Those homes are sold to other government agencies. How's—"

"Yes, they do." Fancy twisted her neck.

"How's Caroline?"

Fancy stood and said, "If I leave now, can I get a refund?"

Mandy laughed. "Of course not. So I take it you haven't spoken with your mother. How about we invite Caroline to the next session? If you agree, I'll call her. You don't have to answer now. Just think about it."

"Whateva. Whateva. Do what you want. I gotta go." Fancy slipped on her coat and left Mandy's office fifteen minutes early.

Fancy rode the bus home. When she arrived a late notice was posted on her door where everyone could see. That bitch! It was only the sixth of the month and barely noon. Fancy snatched the paper, walked in her apartment, and slammed the door. She removed her black leather boots.

Fancy undressed and lay across her comforter. Life had to get better. Fancy hesitated on answering her phone.

"Hello."

"Hey, what's up? I snuck into my boss's office so I could check on you."

"I need a place to stay if I don't come up with two thousand dollars soon."

"What?" Desmond said. "What's going on? You late on your rent again?"

"Duh, yes. I got a late notice today." Fancy rolled onto her back. "Uuuhhhh."

"Don't stress. I can give the funds. I can drop it off after work."

"What? Man, are you serious, Dez?" Fancy sat in the middle of her bed. "I said I need two *thousand* dollars."

"I heard you. Look I gotta go. I'll call when I'm on my way. Get some rest. Bye." Desmond hung up the phone.

Fancy hung up and swung around on her dancing pole. She did the cha-cha-cha on her balcony. Where was Desmond getting that kind of money? Who cared? Fancy had been spared one of her nine lives once again.

CHAPTER 28

"**H**ey, man, what's up?" Desmond had phoned Tyronne because he hadn't heard from his friend in several days.

"Man, I'm so excited. Good things have been happenin' for a brotha left and right. Furniture is being delivered for my bizness today. Got a promotion at the cola company. I'mma a supervisor now, dawg. No more runs. Next week I start my training. And guess what?"

"What?" Desmond asked, pleased things were going well for Tyronne.

"Pastor Tellings asked *me* to be a deacon. Can you believe that shit?"

Desmond waited for Tyronne to correct himself but Tyronne didn't so Desmond said, "What you gon' do man?"

"I said I'd think about it. Just like a brotha is thinking about proposing to SaVoy. What you think?"

"Honestly?" Desmond said.

"Shoot, man. Don't hold back."

"I think you're not ready for marriage. Aren't you still seeing other women?"

"Man, that's the only way I can keep my cool around SaVoy. But I'mma bout to let them other felines loose. For real."

"Well, be honest with yourself, man. Don't play games and end up breaking SaVoy's heart."

"Yeah, you right. Maybe I should wait. Look, if you not busy Sunday, come go to church with us. Bring Carlita. But whatever you do, don't bring Fancy."

"Man, you can't tell me who to bring to church. I might just show up. Speaking of Fancy and Carlita, I gotta go, dawg."

"Peace," Tyronne said, and hung up the phone.

Desmond hopped in Fancy's old two-seater and cranked up the engine. It was so quiet, he restarted the car to make sure it was on. He'd recently tuned it up and figured it was time to give it back to Fancy. When Byron bought her the Benz, Fancy gave Desmond the car saying she didn't need it and he could do whatever he wanted with it. Desmond had stored it in his parents' garage and never mentioned it again.

He parked in front of Fancy's building and called her. "Hey, whatcha doing?"

"Studying for my real estate exam tomorrow. I could use a ride if you're available."

"No, I can't. Not tomorrow. I'm busy."

Fancy's voice escalated. "Too busy to drop me off and pick me up for my important test?"

Desmond hadn't told Fancy that in about two months he'd take the Law School Aptitude Test. Would Fancy be equally supportive of him? SaVoy helped him more than Fancy. Well, that wasn't a fair comparison because SaVoy helped everyone, including Fancy.

When Desmond went to his mother's house to get Fancy's car, his mom had said, "That there fast Fanny girl has got your nose wide open. One day you'll sneeze her out." Mom had lived her life. And although his parents had a beautiful marriage, Desmond knew there were things his mother had done to upset his father. But he guessed she'd forgotten about those days. But he sure hadn't.

"Can you come downstairs for a minute? I need to give you something right quick."

"Okay," Fancy said, and hung up the phone.

Desmond stood in the lobby and waited for Fancy. When she stepped off the elevator, he handed her the keys and eyed the car sitting in the driveway.

"Oh, my goodness! Dez, no you didn't. You kept my car?"

"No, I kept *my* car. You gave it to me, remember? But you can have it back. I never registered it in my name so you don't have to worry this time."

"Why didn't you give it to me sooner? Instead of having me begging for rides."

Desmond wanted to say, *Because you only want me when you need me,* but instead he said, "I need a ride back to my job so I can get my car."

Fancy went inside and returned bouncing happily with her purse in hand. "Let's go."

Desmond got out of the car. He gave Fancy a hug. "I love you. I know you'll ace that exam tomorrow. Remember, I'm with you even when I'm not with you."

Fancy wrapped her arms around Desmond, kissed his lips long and hard, then said, "I love you too, Dez."

Desmond worked the rest of the day thinking about Carlita and Fancy. He hadn't seen Carlita since he left her keys on the table. She'd called a couple of times but he didn't return any of her messages until this morning. Carlita was happy simply to hear his voice and know everything was all right. Law school was next year so he only had a few more months of leisure before he had to balance school, studying, and work. He wouldn't have much time for a social life so Desmond planned to visit Trina sometime after his test and before Christmas. He was grateful for all SaVoy had done and although he was happy for his boy Tyronne, Desmond wished SaVoy were his girlfriend because she was the perfect woman. Single. No kids. And a virgin. Desmond knew Tyronne wasn't going to do right by SaVoy. And Desmond knew the question was not *if* Tyronne would break SaVoy's heart, but *when*.

Parking in front of Carlita's house Desmond left his overnight bag in the trunk just in case things didn't go well.

When Carlita opened the door, Desmond said, "Hey, what's up? Good to see you."

"You too, baby. I missed you so much," Carlita said, massaging his back as she hugged him. "Oh." Carlita frowned. "You are so tense. Wanna talk about it?"

"Talkin' isn't what I really need but we can start there." Desmond passionately kissed Carlita.

Carlita smiled. "Let's take this inside."

Carlita gave Desmond a full body massage and fucked him so good he fell into a deep sleep.

CHAPTER 29

The money SaVoy loaned Fancy was dwindling. August first had arrived and it was time to pay her rent. Maybe Desmond would pay her rent again this month. Fancy decided not to stress over her lack of finances. She'd stopped handing out cards because hanging out in the East Bay she couldn't meet the type of men she wanted to date.

Fancy picked up her phone and dialed Adam's work number. "Hey, baby what's up? How are you?"

"Who's this?" Adam asked.

"Fancy. Don't act like you could possibly forget me."

"Hey, baby! I was hoping to hear from you. What happened to you that day? I thought you were going to the coffee shop."

"I left. I had to go take care of my mother," Fancy lied to gain Adam's sympathy. "She's sick. Not doing too well."

"Really? I'm sorry to hear that. You never really talked about your mother."

"You never asked."

"That's true. Look, you need anything?"

"Well, if I don't pay my rent by the fifth of this month, I won't have a place to stay."

"Hey, Big Adam can't have his baby homeless. As soon as I finish working on this house, I'll be by. How much you need?"

"Well, I need four thousand but—"

"No, buts. Big Adam will take care of his baby. I'll see you around eight o'clock. Gotta go. Bye."

"Bye, Daddy." Fancy hung up the phone and smiled.

The four thousand dollars had attachments but nothing Fancy wasn't accustomed to. Adam would get his money's worth tonight. Fancy picked up her car keys and drove to the JaHva House on Lakeshore to get a chai. Ordering her tea she stared at one of the men seated at the counter, trying to remember where she'd met him.

Unable to recall, she introduced herself. "Hi, I'm Fancy Taylor. You look awfully familiar. Have we met?"

The other four men became silent.

The man stood and shook his head. "I don't think so." Extending his hand he said, "I'm Wellington Jones."

"Oh, my gosh." Fancy gasped and covered her mouth and grabbed his hand. "You're Darius Jones's father?"

Wellington smiled and the other men roared with laughter. "Yes, that would be me." Wellington raised his palms toward Fancy. "Whatever Darius did, I don't want to hear about it."

"Excuse me, miss. Here's your chai," the cashier said, handing Fancy the tall white paper cup.

"Thanks. Just sit it there. I'll get it in a minute." She'd already paid the woman so Fancy redirected her attention toward Wellington, trying to figure out how she could get Darius's home phone number.

"I see where he gets his intellect from," Fancy said, smiling and moving closer to Wellington.

Wellington rubbed the back of his head, stretched his

neck left then right and said, "Excuse me. I don't mean to be rude but we're in the middle of our Socrates discussion. It was a pleasure meeting you, Miss Taylor." Wellington turned to a gentleman wearing a Kangol black leather cap, blue jeans, a sweatshirt, and a silver peace sign and said, "Rich, what does you being the last sugar daddy on earth have to do with what we're talking about?"

Fancy shook her head trying to figure out why a man like Wellington, with all his money, would hang out at the JaHva House. And why the man Wellington called Rich looked poor, according to her standards. Was he really rich or was that just his name? Maybe Fancy needed to rethink her strategy for meeting wealthy men. Maybe there were wealthy men in the East Bay.

Fancy thanked the woman behind the counter for her chai and drove to Top Notch Hair Salon on Seventeenth Street to schedule an appointment. She'd pay Raeshelle extra to squeeze her in tomorrow between clients. After begging and pleading Raeshelle agreed. Determined Adam was going to get the royal treatment, Fancy rushed to the nail salon for a manicure and pedicure. Tonight, for the first time with Adam, Fancy was unwrapping her exotic dancing pole.

CHAPTER 30

Desmond entered SaVoy's store looking down the street for Tyronne's truck. Damn, that's right. His boy was the boss now. Since SaVoy had helped him, Desmond decided he should help her by telling SaVoy the truth about Tyronne.

"Hey, woman. What's up?"

"Since when you started calling me woman? You know my Tyronne is the only one who calls me that. I was just about to close."

"Yeah, I figured as much. You wanna grab a cup of coffee? We can go to the JaHva House around the corner."

Desmond knew Tyronne kicked it at the JaHva every Wednesday night—after singles Bible study, after he dropped off SaVoy—for poetry. Usually he showed up or left with one of the female poets.

"Okay, I guess since there's no Bible study tonight. But I can't stay long."

Yeah. Desmond already knew, because Tyronne had told him, Bible study had been canceled due to a church retreat.

"Cool, let's go. I'll drive. You can leave your car here."

Desmond looked for Tyronne's car in Albertson's parking lot as he searched for a place to park. Tyronne's black SUV was nowhere in sight.

"We could have walked over here," SaVoy said. "Is it always this crowded in here?"

"You think this is crowded." Desmond ordered two ginger ales at the counter and said, "Let's go upstairs so we can get a better view. Wednesday is poetry night. In about an hour this place will barely have standing room. Have you seen or heard from Fancy lately?"

"Yeah, I called her this morning," SaVoy said, sipping her soda. "She was on her way to Mandy's. Then she had an interview with Howard Kees at Kees Realty in San Leandro. Fancy is really serious about real estate."

"Wow, that's great. I haven't heard much from her since I gave her back her car."

"Desmond, you are so nice. You know how Fancy is. At least she doesn't discriminate. She treats me the same way. She only calls when she needs something. But hey, she's still our friend."

Desmond carefully watched the door, waiting for Tyronne to walk in.

"You know, there's something I want to say but I'm not sure how to say it."

SaVoy looked at Desmond. "What? We're friends. You can tell me if something is bothering you."

"You're right. You remember when I first met Fancy?"

SaVoy nodded. "Yeah, I was there."

"Right." Desmond paused. "Well, I was really interested in you. But since Fancy did all the talking, I ended up talking to her."

SaVoy closed her eyes, then opened them slowly. "What exactly are you trying to say?"

"Nothing that matters I guess. I just thought you

should know. That's all." Desmond hunched his shoulders.

SaVoy smiled. "I was kinda diggin' you too. But Fancy always thinks every guy wants her and not me. She makes sure she's always in the guy's face. Even if she's not interested. She does all or most of the talking. Then, after the guy is gone she says things like, 'I'm not really interested in him' or 'He's not my type.' I really don't trip anymore 'cause if I say I like the guy, Fancy really acts like he's all hers and out of the kindness of her heart she'll hook him up with me only if she doesn't want him. Just like she did with you."

"Really? Like that? Damn. I had no idea. So you were feeling me too?"

"Yeah, but not anymore. I'm in love with Tyronne."

Desmond scanned the crowded downstairs area. He was so engaged in conversation he hadn't noticed Tyronne had slipped in. He was seated on the couch with a female on his lap. Now, *that* was the Tyronne he knew.

"Speaking of Tyronne, isn't that him down there?" Desmond pointed in Tyronne's direction.

SaVoy squinted. "I don't think so. That guy has some woman on his lap."

Desmond nodded. "Maybe you're right."

The first performer stepped up to the mic and said,

> *"A woman's first orgasm*
> *Should be by masturbation*
> *Or maybe from oral copulation*
> *But never strictly penetration*
>
> *She doesn't need permission*
> *To explore herself*
> *By herself*
> *She should try herself*

And hold on to her virginity
Not for infinity
But until he can prove
He's the one she should choose . . ."

"Wow, I like that." SaVoy clapped. "Felt like she was talking to me."

"Next we have Desmond Brown coming up to the mic."

Desmond made his way downstairs and up to the mic. Tyronne raised his fist in the air and yelled, "That's my boy! That's my boy! Do the damn thing!" The woman sitting on Tyronne's lap tongue-kissed him and Tyronne kissed her back.

Desmond glanced up at SaVoy. Her hands covered her mouth, she stood, made her way downstairs. SaVoy squeezed through the crowd until she stood directly in front Tyronne and said, "I guess I have no right to be jealous because I'm not your *woman,* but I am jealous." SaVoy turned, walking toward Desmond. "This was no coincidence. Thanks a lot. Friend."

Tyronne stood, damn near dropping the feline who was seated on his lap to the floor.

"Damn, Tyronne. Are you crazy!" she yelled, grabbing his waist and pulling herself up.

Desmond and Tyronne bumped into one another trying to get out the door first.

"Nigga, move out my way," Tyronne said, pushing Desmond aside.

Desmond squared his shoulders. "Don't blame me, man."

Someone else was spitting lyrics on the mic so Desmond waited, giving SaVoy time to leave Tyronne. He wasn't interested in showcasing his talent tonight. His mission was accomplished. Desmond weaved between the crowd and exited the back door, walked through the parking lot until he got to his Mustang. When he stopped at the red light by Foot Locker, across the street he saw Tyronne drying SaVoy's tears. By the time the light turned green, SaVoy was laughing a little bit. Desmond glanced in his rearview mirror and saw Tyronne passionately kissing SaVoy.

Desmond concluded SaVoy was naïve like most women. After what had just happened, there was no way SaVoy should have forgiven Tyronne that damn fast.

CHAPTER 31

SaVoy had managed to remain neutral, having two friends that didn't know and didn't like one another very well. She'd told Fancy to come over. Somehow Tyronne was in the neighborhood, and had called, so she invited him over, too. She was glad Tyronne didn't stay upset with Desmond. Desmond was wrong. But Tyronne was wrong, too.

SaVoy greeted Fancy at the door. Fancy arrived wearing a red suede skirt, a waist-cut sweater that displayed her navel piercing, and knee-high suede boots.

"Girl, don't you think you need to clean up," Fancy said, looking around the living room, then peeping into the kitchen.

Four clean plates were on the family room table along with a few glasses and silverware. Fancy put every dish away, then sat on the sofa.

"Fancy, you know we only use our living room for special occasions," SaVoy said, pointing toward the family room. "Let's go."

"Oh, live a little. You can't take it with you. Somebody needs to use this beautiful designer furniture. Besides, I can't sit on those cover-ups in the family room. My suede will get scuffed."

Maybe this was a special occasion. Fancy seldom came inside, so SaVoy sat on the love seat while Fancy continued lounging on the sofa.

"So, how are you?" SaVoy asked.

"Fine, except I don't have any money to pay my October rent next month." Fancy smoothed her hand over her hair down to the ends that stopped above her protruding nipples.

"So, what are you going to do?" SaVoy asked.

"Well, I was hoping you could help me out."

SaVoy knew Desmond had paid Fancy's rent several times and now he was worried about having enough money for law school, especially if he accepted an out-of-state offer. "How much do you need?"

"Two thousand dollars." Fancy picked up the *Essence* magazine and slowly turned the pages.

"Fancy, if this is a temporary solution, I can loan you money one more time. But if you're going to have a problem paying next month's rent too, maybe you should consider—" The doorbell interrupted SaVoy. She stood and looked at Fancy, and continued, "—moving in with us. We have a guest bedroom. But you can't have your men in and out of here." SaVoy peeped through the hole and opened the door.

"Hey, woman. What's up?"

"Just talking with Fancy. Come in."

Fancy rolled her eyes as Tyronne sat on the opposite end of the couch and clasped his hands.

Fancy looked at SaVoy and said, "Girl, I met Wellington Jones the other day at the JaHva House. I tried getting—"

Tyronne interrupted, "SaVoy, get me something to drink, baby, please, I'm thirsty." Tyronne motioned for SaVoy to come closer. He kissed her lips, then said, "Baby, I got the money to start my business."

"Fancy, you want something to drink?" SaVoy asked, sensing the tension building between Fancy and Tyronne.

Fancy rolled her eyes at Tyronne. "Excuse me, I believe we were having a conversation before you came in."

"Tyronne's just kidding. He's trying to agitate you, Fancy," SaVoy said, placing a glass of fresh lemonade in front of Tyronne.

"No, I'm not," Tyronne said.

"Girl, he probably stole the money. Nobody in their right mind would give him a loan."

"Fancy, that's enough. Look, I'll call you," SaVoy said. "We can continue our discussion later."

Fancy quickly turned toward SaVoy and said, "I know you're not choosing this—"

SaVoy frowned.

Tyronne spread his legs, put his hand behind his head, and lay back, looking at Fancy. "Is Miss Kitty's open today? I know a few executives who could splurge on a bed and breakfast."

SaVoy slapped Tyronne's knee. "You two cut it out! This makes no sense."

"Thug bitch ass nigga." Fancy got up in Tyronne's face.

SaVoy jumped from the love seat and eased between them, facing Fancy, and said, "Fancy, you need to leave my house. Tyronne is a king. My king. And our relationship does not require your acceptance or approval."

"What drugs are you on? I know you're not choosing this . . . him over me," Fancy protested, pointing her finger in Tyronne's face.

SaVoy backed Fancy up several steps. "No, I'm not." SaVoy escorted Fancy and opened the door. "You are. I'll call you later."

"Don't bother. The only reason you go to church so much is to find a man and since you couldn't find a decent one at church you fucked the soda boy."

"You're still welcome to go to church with me any-

time. Bye, Fancy." SaVoy closed the door. Most business-
men had some form of religion. If Fancy weren't so
stubborn, she could meet lots of them at SaVoy's church.
Fancy had so many issues, SaVoy knew not to take her
seriously.

"I'm glad you put that ho out. She's the type of female that makes a man just wanna slap her in the
mouth. Next time she puts her finger in my face, I'mma
break it off."

"Oh, no! I'm not going to listen to you talk bad about
Fancy. As much as I love you, Fancy is still my friend and
I will not give up on her. Just like I didn't give up on
you."

"Wait one minute. What are you talking about?"
Tyronne mimicked SaVoy, "Like you didn't give up on
me."

"Tyronne, I know you're seeing other women. It's obvious you're sleeping with 'em, too." SaVoy knew because Desmond had told her, but how she knew was
irrelevant.

Silence chilled the air. SaVoy wanted Tyronne to say
it wasn't true. She wanted him to hold her. To make her
feel secure instead of afraid. Afraid he'd leave.

Tyronne opened the door and said, "I call you later.
Peace."

What the hell just happened? Two of her closest
friends just left her home. Both of them upset. Neither
apparently cared enough at the moment to acknowledge her feelings. Not really knowing where to go,
SaVoy grabbed her jacket and left the house, too.

CHAPTER 32

Fancy lounged on her love seat. She'd passed her exam the first time. Some of the other people she'd spoken with had already taken the test several times. Fancy couldn't understand how they failed. Everything that was on her pretest was also on the actual test. Some of the financing problems she knew the answers to before she finished reading the questions.

"I don't need any of them. Desmond. Mandy. Harry. Caroline. Byron. SaVoy." Fancy wondered what had happened to Tanya. William was ruder each time Fancy had called. The last time he said, "Tanya's busy and don't call back because she'll be busy then, too."

Now that Fancy didn't have a date and no place to go, she realized she was so caught up in her own drama, she'd forgotten all about Tanya. "What the hell." Fancy leaned toward the coffee table and picked up the cordless and dialed Tanya's number.

She waited for the phone to ring. No ring was heard so Fancy said, "Hello."

"Hey, you."

Fancy recognized the voice, smiled and said, "Who is this?"

"Byron. Can you forgive me? I acted like a jerk."

"Me too, I guess," Fancy said.

"So can I pick you up in, say, about an hour?"

"Okay, I'd like that."

"Don't get all dressed up. I just want to go someplace where we can walk and talk."

"Okay, that's fine."

Fancy showered, curled her hair, slipped into her lime-green jogging suit and stroked on her red lipstick. When she heard the doorbell, she opened a bottle of her best perfume. Quickly she debated on whether to dab on the perfume, fearing it might attract insects. She recapped the bottle and tossed it into her purse.

Byron looked wonderful. His smile warmed her heart.

"Hey, gorgeous." He wrapped his arms around her.

The first thing Fancy noticed was that Byron wasn't driving her car. "Hi." She hugged Byron longer than Desmond usually hugged her.

"How about we go to *my* place, have lunch, then have fun working it off, and then watch the sunset from the mountains over the Golden Gate Bridge?"

"Sounds like you've given this a lot of thought. As long as we're together, I'm game."

Byron's place was redecorated with vibrant-colored flowers. "What are these?" Fancy asked, admiring the fuchsia and white ones and wondering if another woman had arranged the flowers. Byron didn't seem the same and Fancy realized she wasn't in love with him anymore. Maybe she never was.

"Orchids. My favorite. Every fall I travel to orchid shows throughout the Bay Area. And I only purchase the winners. So every orchid you see is the best in the bunch. Like you," Byron added.

Fancy sat on the sofa and Byron sat next to her. He held her hand, massaging her fingers. Did she ever really know Byron? She wanted to apologize for showing up at his sister's house.

Byron said, "Do you know how a woman can strip away a man's pride and dignity?"

Fancy shook her head. "No."

Byron stood and led her to his bedroom.

"Wow." Fancy covered her mouth. "This is beautiful."

Byron hungrily kissed her. She didn't deny him as he undressed her, then he undressed himself. Their bodies began to sweat.

"Turn over," Byron said, easing on a condom.

He entered her rectum.

"Slow down, baby, we don't have to rush. You're hurting me."

"I missed you so much, Fancy." Byron stroked deeper, then pulled himself out. He tore a fresh condom open with his teeth, rolled off the old one, and slipped on a new condom. Clearly, Byron wasn't taking any chances on making a baby. His huge dick felt wonderful entering Fancy's vagina doggie style. Byron took his time. He slapped her ass, then pulled her hair.

Fancy grabbed his hand and said, "Not the hair." Her weave tracks were loose enough. "Let me ride him, Daddy."

Byron lay on his back as Fancy mounted him. She eased down until it felt like Byron's head touched her stomach. Fancy licked her fingers and squeezed his nipples. She massaged her clitoris and continued teasing his nipples, alternating from nipple to nipple. She moaned. Byron grunted.

"Ooh, yeah, baby. I missed my pussy. She feels so warm. Let me taste her. Bring her to Daddy."

Fancy eased her pussy over Byron's lips, removed his condom, and started sucking his head. Byron reached over to his nightstand. Fancy watched him as he picked up a string of dime-size pearls. Byron licked and sucked her clit, simultaneously easing one pearl at time into her rectum.

"Oh, that feels good, Daddy. Give me another one."

Byron eased another pearl inside her and continued sucking her clit. Then he entered another and another and stopped, but continued eating her pussy. He reached over to the nightstand again and retrieved another string of quarter-size pearls. Byron slowly inserted the pearls into her vagina while sucking the juices from her clit.

Byron sucked continuously. Fancy couldn't hold back any longer. When she started cumming Byron slowly removed both strands, one pearl at a time. One from her rectum. Then one from her vagina. His mouth now covered her clit and shaft. When the last pearls were released Byron tossed them to the floor, slipped on a condom, and fucked her doggie style again.

"Whose pussy is this? Whose pussy is this?" Byron asked repeatedly, while Fancy thrust backward, bracing her hand against the headboard to keep from cumming and becoming unconscious.

Fancy kept on fucking without answering Byron. He slapped her ass until he started cumming. Byron pulled out, snapped off his condom, and came all over her ass.

Fancy collapsed in Byron's arms. That was not lovemaking. That was sex. Fancy dozed off and woke to KBLX playing in her ear. It was six o'clock.

"You gotta go somewhere?" Fancy asked.

"We've gotta go somewhere. We have to catch the sunset, remember?"

"My bad. That's right."

Fancy sleepily made her way to the shower. Byron showered in the other bathroom.

Byron drove along 101 and exited at San Francisco. He drove up the hillside and parked at the very end. A few cars were parked in the area. They hiked up the hill and sat on a bench overlooking the Golden Gate Bridge. Watching the sunset was beautiful, but with each setting the air became colder. Byron sat in silence like he was meditating. Fancy wondered why all she thought about was Caroline.

Now it was so dark visibility was about six feet. Fancy retrieved a miniature flashlight from her purse and squeezed the sides. "You ready? I'm getting cold."

Byron's eyes were glazed. He kissed her lips. His hands massaged her neck. Then he started choking her.

"Hey, you're hurting me. Let go."

Byron's hold became tighter. "Remember when I asked you, 'Do you know how a woman can strip away a man's pride and dignity?' and you said no?"

"*Gawk.*" Fancy tried inhaling through her mouth but couldn't.

Byron kissed her face. She felt her flesh oozing between his fingers. Fancy punched as hard as she could. Her eyes started bulging. Fancy felt like she was going to die on that hill and she didn't know why.

"Well, let me tell your sorry ass so you won't make the same mistake twice. The way a woman strips away a black man's pride is to call the fuckin' cops."

Fancy's body weakened. Her arms grew tired of fighting and now dangled by her sides.

"I spent the fuckin' night in jail because your sorry ass reported my car stolen. If I didn't hate that night in jail so much, I'd toss your ass off this cliff."

Byron shoved Fancy on the bench and left her there. She was too weak to yell or cry. Fancy sat on the bench until the sun started to rise. She found her purse and retrieved her cell phone.

Fancy whispered, "Dez, I need you."

"Fancy?" Desmond paused then said, "I'm busy. I'm at Carlita's. What's wrong? Where are you? I can't come right now."

Fancy struggled to make her words clear. "I'm stranded on the hilltop over the Golden Gate Bridge." Fancy rubbed her neck and felt broken flesh and crumbled particles. Her cell phone beeped, signaling her battery was dangerously low.

Fancy felt her eyes fluttering. "Dez, hurry up. Golden Gate Bridge. Hilltop." Fancy's arm collapsed, sending her phone crashing to the ground.

CHAPTER 33

SaVoy busied herself perfectly restocking and aligning groceries on shelves. Tyronne hadn't called since he'd left her home. It was Wednesday and her delivery was so late she considered closing early and going home but she was completely out of twenty-ounce Cokes, Vanilla Cokes, and Sprites. The new delivery guy finally arrived almost six hours late.

"What took you so long?" SaVoy questioned him before he finished unloading her order.

"Not you, too. Look, miss, I apologize. Through no fault of yours, I've had an extremely rough day and I still have three more stops. I'll be in and out as soon as possible," he remarked, motioning for her to stand aside as he tilted his hand truck. He quickly stocked the cooler and headed toward the door. "Have a nice day, miss."

"Hey, I apologize for snapping at you. You really *are* new, aren't you?"

"Yeah, that and my supervisor told me 'hands off' as far as you're concerned."

SaVoy smiled. "Really?"

"Yeah, really. You must be something special. I gotta run before he gets here."

"Have a good evening, um . . . what's your name?"

"I'm sure you can think of something to call me other than what my mother named me, Sylvester." He smiled, then waved. "I'm out."

The new delivery person reminded SaVoy of Tyronne in a few ways. SaVoy locked the door, raced to her office, brushed her teeth, washed her face, and replenished her lipstick.

Whoever was banging on the door, SaVoy heard the knocking all the way in the back. She raced to the front. It was Desmond. SaVoy unlocked the door.

"Hey, I knew you were still in here. What's up?" Desmond held his arms open, waiting for a hug.

SaVoy hugged Desmond lightly, patted his back a few times, then stepped back. "What's up with you?"

"Man, why every time I drop by the store you all up on my woman?" Tyronne said, walking in the door.

"What's up, man? Don't trip. I ain't gon' take your woman."

SaVoy casually said, "Can't."

"Whatever, y'all trippin'. I just came by to let SaVoy know Fancy had a terrible incident. She has no insurance. She refuses to go to Highland Hospital. So she's at home doctoring on herself."

"Oh, my gosh. Desmond, what happened?" SaVoy asked, staring at Desmond.

"Dude, old boy tried to kill Fancy for having him locked up."

"Hell, you can't blame him for that. Why in the hell would she do something stupid like that for anyway?" Tyronne asked.

"Man, she reported his car stolen. The one he gave her and took back. Cops picked him up from his house—"

Tyronne interrupted, "You mean that crazy ho called the cops for some indignant ass bullshit. Hell, I woulda—" Tyronne shook his head.

"Y'all get out of my store," SaVoy said with one hand

on Desmond and the other on Tyronne. "I can't believe my ears. Lord, forgive them."

"Us?" Tyronne questioned. "What'd we do?"

SaVoy couldn't believe how Desmond and Tyronne, especially Desmond, were bad-mouthing Fancy. Did they talk about her the same when she wasn't around? SaVoy drove as fast as she could to Fancy's. There were no parking spaces out front so she circled the block and parked around the corner. Fifty-five degrees. That was good November weather.

The doorman rang Fancy's phone several times but Fancy didn't answer.

"Please, I have to see her. She's sick," SaVoy pleaded with the doorman.

"Okay, but call me from her unit when you get upstairs."

SaVoy rang the buzzer, knocked on the door, and paced until Fancy answered, "Who is it?"

"It's me, SaVoy. Girl, let me in."

Fancy cracked the door so SaVoy let herself in and followed Fancy to the love seat.

"Desmond told you, didn't he?"

"I came as soon as he did." SaVoy sat next to Fancy. Fancy's neck was swollen and bandaged. "You wanna go to the hospital? I'll take you."

"I am not going to sit up at Highland waiting until all the gang bangin' drive-byers who done got shot, stabbed, or killed, been taken care of. I can take care of myself."

"Well, how about I take you to see my doctor in the morning and I'll pay the bill."

Fancy's eyes watered but she didn't speak.

"You don't have to tell me or anybody else what happened except Mandy. Have you talked with her?"

Fancy shook her head.

SaVoy placed Fancy's feet in her lap and began massaging them. " 'Be anxious for nothing,' Fancy, 'but in everything by prayer and supplication, with thanksgiving, let your requests be made known to God and the peace of God, which surpasses all understanding, will guard your heart and mind through Christ Jesus.' " SaVoy softly quoted scriptures from the Bible until well after Fancy was asleep. Subliminally perhaps some of the messages would become ingrained in Fancy's mind. SaVoy went upstairs, found a pillow and blanket, curled up on the floor by Fancy, and slept.

In the morning, SaVoy was taking her best friend to her doctor. And when Sunday came, SaVoy was taking Fancy to church.

CHAPTER 34

Yesterday, despite SaVoy's greatest efforts, Fancy was adamant and refused to go to church. SaVoy had said, "The Lord said come as you are," but Fancy was certain He meant her heart and did not mean come with broken acrylic nails and a worn-out hair weave.

Desmond said he couldn't loan her any more money and Fancy would rather be homeless than live with SaVoy or Caroline.

Fancy parked at a meter on University Avenue. She unraveled her plastic bag, covered the meter, and headed across the street. Mandy had agreed not to charge her for the thirty-minute session.

Fancy didn't speak to the receptionist. She walked into Mandy's office, took her usual seat, and began talking. "I'm cursed."

Mandy frowned. "My gosh. What happened to your neck?"

Fancy softly touched the remaining scabs on her neck. "Byron assaulted me."

"What happened?" This time Mandy didn't stare over her frames.

"Well, he claimed it was because I called the police on him but I don't think that's the real reason."

"Okay, why did you call the police? And what do you believe is the real reason?"

"I called the cops because he took my car."

"Your car? Are you sure it was legally your car?"

"He gave it to me so that made it mine. You don't just give someone a car, then take it back."

"Maybe part of that is true but, Fancy, can't you see? When Harry raped you, that was a crime and the appropriate time to call the police. When Byron took his car, if you felt the car was a gift, you should have taken him to court, not called the police. But when Byron assaulted you, that's when you really should have called the police."

"What difference does it make now? It's all in the past."

"But don't you see? Your past is your future. How you resolve this will determine how you handle future conflicts." Mandy paused, looking at the clock. "I'll make you a list of suggestions and send them to you in the mail. How's Caroline?"

"Fine, I guess. I don't know. I have my own problems to deal with. Like how I'm going to pay my rent and bills without taking on additional sponsors."

"How's real estate school?"

Fancy smiled. "I'm a licensed agent. Haven't sold any homes yet but I do have three listings and my license has only been listed with Kees Realty for ten days. Howard Kees says that's great for a newcomer, so I'm excited."

Mandy smiled. "You're headed in the right direction. You can come in for thirty minutes on Thursday. I'll bill you and you can pay me later."

"Thanks." Fancy left Mandy's office feeling better but

not much. She really wanted to get revenge on Harry and Byron.

Fancy drove by Desmond's house. His car was parked in the driveway so she parked on the street blocking his exit.

Fancy rang the doorbell. When Carlita opened the door, Fancy stepped back.

"Is Desmond here?"

"No, he's at work. But I'm glad you stopped by. Come on in." Carlita opened the door wider.

Fancy thought about it for a minute, then walked inside. Desmond's roommates were either gone or in their rooms asleep because the house was quiet.

Fancy headed to Desmond's room. Carlita turned and said, "Have a seat in the living room. I'll be in in just a minute."

When Carlita disappeared into the kitchen, Fancy entered Desmond's bedroom. His entire room was redecorated. Matching comforter and pillows. The new entertainment center had an eight-by-ten photo of Desmond and Carlita on the top.

"This room is off-limits to you. I said the living room."

Fancy sat on Desmond's bed. "Desmond's bedroom is never off-limits to me. So what did you want to talk about?"

"You know, that's why no one respects you."

"What are talking about? You don't know me."

"True. But I know enough about you. My only advice to you is to grow up. Start acting like the beautiful queen you are and stop trying to use men. Honey, you shouldn't want a man that'll let you use him. Trust me. I know. If you're using him, then he's definitely using you. Look, I'm in love with Desmond and Desmond is in love with me, but he's infatuated with you. If you're really Desmond's friend you won't make him choose between us. You could have given him what he needed a long time ago but you weren't woman enough."

"You—"

"Let me finish what I'm saying and then I'll listen to you. What I'm telling you, honey, is real women don't play games with men's lives or their livelihood. A man is going to be a man. You can't change him. But you can and you do set the standards for yourself and other women based upon how you treat your men. If you open your legs every time a man gives you money, then he thinks every woman can be bought. But if you have your own money, you're not in control of him but you'll never compromise your womanhood in exchange for his money. Keep your legs closed and enjoy him until you're ready to have sex. And don't have sex with him. Make love to him. Trust me, he'll know the difference."

"So is that why you have four kids by four different daddies? Because you kept your legs closed?" Fancy said as she bounced on the bed.

"No, and that's exactly why I'm talking to you. The same way I talk to other women. If someone had talked to me maybe I wouldn't have four kids. I love my kids. I used to be a lot like you. Dating rich men for money. I get paid very well by each of my children's fathers. Some are better fathers than others. But if I had to do it all over again, I'd trade all four of those rich men for a man like Desmond. One who cares about me. If you really want to learn how to make money, call me." Carlita reached into her purse and handed Fancy a card.

"I can handle my business. I've got three real estate listings right now."

"I have a client who's looking to buy her first home. Call me tomorrow, and I'll give you her number."

"You know, you're pretty and pretty cool," Fancy said, looking at Carlita's card. "I'll do that. I'll call you tomorrow."

Carlita must have subscribed to *Keep your friends close and your enemies closer*. Otherwise, why would she have offered to help Fancy?

"Remember, if you can't accept the man, don't accept his money." Carlita opened the front door. She yelled as Fancy unlocked her car door, "Do your own damn thing!"

Fancy repeated, "Do your own damn thing. Yeah." That was good advice, but Fancy was Desmond's friend whether Carlita liked it or not.

CHAPTER 35

SaVoy sat in her car outside Tyronne's apartment. What was so urgent that he requested she come over right away? "Lord, I know you won't give me more than I can handle so I'm going in. Cover me. And thanks again for blessing Papa with the deed to the store."

The lights were on. SaVoy placed her hand over her eyebrows.

"Woman, get in here. I have someone I want you to meet."

SaVoy sat on the sofa. "Where is she?"

Tyronne went into the bedroom and walked into the living room carrying Tyronne, Jr. on his shoulders. "This here is the man. Say hi, TJ."

"Hey, baby."

"Man, that's my woman. I told you to say hi."

"Hey, baby."

SaVoy laughed, holding her side. "What are you teaching him?"

"Life." Tyronne stood TJ up and said, "Go get in the bed. Nap time."

"Tyronne, he's adorable. He's two now, right?"

"Yeah, just made two. Now I have three adorable people in my life," Tyronne said, looking at his mother's picture.

SaVoy watched Tyronne bend on one knee. She smiled. "You are so silly. Get up."

Tyronne reached inside his pocket, and said, "No, this time I'm serious. SaVoy Edmonds, will you marry me?" Tyronne partially opened the blue velvet box, then snapped it closed. "You don't get to see the ring until I get an answer, woman."

SaVoy wrapped her arms around Tyronne's neck. "I love you, Tyronne. And I'd be honored to be your wife."

"See, that's why I love you. You always have my back." Tyronne opened the box and placed a square-shaped three-carat solitaire on SaVoy's ring finger.

"You lucked out. My old man told me a man should spend one month's salary on an engagement ring. And since I bought this ring after my promotion"—Tyronne held SaVoy's hand—"you got an extra grand."

"It's beautiful, Tyronne."

Tyronne checked on TJ and returned. "That boy snores worse than me."

SaVoy raised her eyebrows.

"Chill out. You know I don't snore. But seriously, woman, you don't know how relieved I was to finally find somebody who cares enough to make me take an HIV test. Who cares enough to wait to have sex. Who cares enough to help me pursue my dreams. Who cares enough to call me her king."

"That's because you are a king. Is TJ spending the night with us?"

"Naw, Lisa will be here in about an hour to get him. But you can spend the night with me."

SaVoy eyed the Play Station remote control.

"Aw, see. Now I'mma havta spank that ass. You will not beat me again." Tyronne stood and folded his arms high across his chest, and he was her superhero.

CHAPTER 36

For the first time in a very long time—years—Desmond put his relationship with Fancy in perspective. Fancy Taylor was just a friend. At the same time he realized Carlita was much more than a friend. Carlita was a woman. His woman. But moving in with Carlita wasn't what he wanted. If they were going to live together, Carlita would become more than his woman, she'd become his wife.

Desmond drove to Fancy's apartment. There was no place to park so he called her on the phone. "Hey, come downstairs."

"I'm on my way," Fancy said excitedly.

That meant she'd be another fifteen minutes. Women were never ready on time anyway, including Carlita.

Desmond wondered why Carlita never got mad or jealous or questioned him when he left late nights or early mornings. She didn't flip out when she saw him with Fancy at breakfast. Carlita never mentioned Fancy. Well, once, and when she did, Desmond realized Carlita was fully aware of his relationship with Fancy.

"Hey, Dez. So where are we going?"

"You'll see. You look nice," Desmond said.

Fancy always looked nice. Even on her worst days she looked good. The black hoodie sweatsuit with white stripes down the side was sexy. Desmond parked on Grande Avenue near Fairyland. The Orchid Festival Show and Sale was this weekend at the Garden House.

"Orchids? You brought me to see orchids?" Fancy questioned.

"You'll love them. Trust me. Besides, we won't be here long."

This was one of the few free events he'd taken Fancy to. Carlita loved the word free. She would've really enjoyed the festival. Desmond wanted to take Carlita but needed to take Fancy.

After viewing hundreds of orchids, Desmond picked out one for Fancy. "What do you see when you look at this flower?"

"My favorite color. Dez, can we go?"

Fancy probably had a date with someone she'd recently met. As a friend, Desmond refused to ask. He suppressed his feelings for Fancy.

"In a minute. Look closer," Desmond said, guiding Fancy's hips in front of the flower. "Oh, my bad. I shouldn't have touched you like that." Desmond moved his hands to his side.

"This ain't working. I'm ready to leave," Fancy insisted.

"It's you. It's the most sacred part of your womanhood. The orchid is like a," Desmond lowered his voice, then said, "vagina."

The autumn red orchid with red velvet lips resembled the beauty he saw in Fancy. The silkiness he remembered when he buried his face between Fancy's beautiful thighs. And the way she made him feel inside. Beautiful.

"Oh, okay. I can see that. The lips," Fancy said, pointing. "Hey! There's my clit." Fancy gently touched the flower. "So you want me to remember you every time I see my clit." Fancy laughed.

"No. I want you to remember how delicate and beautiful and sacred your womanhood is and I hope you find someone special to share your true self with, not just your vagina."

Fancy started to speak but Desmond motioned for her to be silent.

"Wait a minute. I'm not calling you no ho, Fancy. You're one of my friends but you have to stop selling yourself short in exchange for material things."

"Let's go." Fancy turned to walk away.

"One more thing. Then we can leave." Desmond picked up the potted orchid and escorted Fancy outside. They crossed the pedestrian bridge and stood facing the miniature waterfall. The flowing water calmed Desmond.

"Fancy, you're special to me. You know that. You also know how much I love you."

Fancy smiled and nodded.

"That's why I wanted to be the first to tell you."

Fancy glanced over her shoulder at Desmond in silence.

"I'm going to ask Carlita to marry me. If she says yes, then my relationship with you will have to change. I won't be able to come and get you every time you need me. I can still fix your car but not for free." Desmond turned Fancy around to face him, looked her in the eyes, and said, "I can't repair your broken heart."

"Now you trippin'," Fancy snapped, pulling away from his embrace. "My heart is just fine."

"If you say so. Come here. Don't pull away. Let me hold you." Desmond laid his cheek on Fancy's forehead. "I love you, Fancy.

> "If you only knew
> That I would die for you
> How many nights I've cried for you
> Looked my woman in the eyes
> And lied for you

*If you only knew
I'd never hurt you
I'd give my first to you
My last to you
I'd do without
Just to provide for you*

*If you only knew
I would share with you
Take care of you
Be there for you
Go anywhere with you*

*If you only knew
If you only knew"*

"You sure you wanna marry a woman with four kids?" Fancy asked, wrapping her arms around his waist.

"You a trip. If she says yes. Yes. That means you'll have to find someone else to take you out this New Year's Eve." Desmond pulled a small square white box from his pocket. He opened it slowly. Then he turned it upside down, shaking it until a plush black velvet box fell into his palm. He flipped it over and gently opened it. "This is the ring I bought for Carlita. You think she'll like it?"

He'd purchased the three-carat solitaire on credit. With the nice down payment, the pear-cut stone set in platinum would be paid in full before the end of next year. Desmond wanted to make Fancy jealous. A lasso made of burning steel slithered down his throat and captured his beating heart. Was he trying to hurt Fancy because she'd hurt him? Would a friend treat another friend so cruel?

"Whatever, I already have a date. Take me home." Fancy left the red velvet orchid by the waterfall so Desmond left it there, too.

"One more thing," Desmond said before Fancy closed

the door when they reached her apartment. "I was accepted to Hastings, Harvard, and Emory."

"Congratulations," Fancy said without looking back at him.

Desmond was hurting. He hoped someday Fancy would find happiness. Forgive her mother. Stop sleeping with men for money. Start worshiping her insides as much as she took care of her appearance. What woman wouldn't want a man who worshiped her mere existence? Flaws and all. A tear or two fell before he stopped the flow. He parked in front Carlita's house. He clasped his fingers and placed them behind his head. Why were relationships so challenging? The one he wanted he couldn't have. The woman he did have, he wasn't one hundred percent sure he wanted. Maybe he bought the ring out of emotional spending. The holiday spirit. Maybe he'd hold off on proposing to Carlita until after the New Year.

CHAPTER 37

Two days before Christmas, Fancy sat in her car waiting for the sunrise so she could roller-blade around Lake Merritt. Tanya had been on her mind for several days but Fancy was so busy, each time she remembered to phone, she also remembered there was something else she needed to do. The time displayed on her cellular phone, six forty-five. Fifteen more minutes before her peak minutes started. Fancy dialed Tanya number.

"Hello."

Oh, great. William had answered, again.

Fancy adjusted her ear bud and said, "Hello, may I speak with Tanya, please?"

"Tanya's busy. Who's this?" he questioned with authority.

Fancy heard Tanya's voice in the background. "William, who's that?"

"This is Fancy. Who's this?" Fancy questioned William back with the same attitude.

"Why you callin' on a Friday morning? Tanya's gotta go to work. I told you to stop calling here."

"May I speak with my friend, please? It'll only take a minute." Fancy smiled so she'd sound pleasant.

The next voice Fancy heard was Tanya's. "Hi, who is this?"

"Girl, it's me, Fancy. Are you okay? We were starting to think you're caught up like that author in the movie *Misery*."

Tanya's voice was barely above a whisper. "I'm okay, I guess."

"Your minute is up Tanya! Get off the phone so I can take you to work. I told you I need the car today."

"Look, Tanya. Listen to me. When William drops you off at work, don't clock in. I'll park in the lot across the street by Toys 'R' Us and wait for you."

"Okay," Tanya whispered.

"Tanya! Don't make me have to tell you again. Get off the damn phone. Now!" Tanya hung up without saying good-bye.

The sunlight was bright enough for Fancy to strap on her elbow and kneepads. *Swish. Swish. Swish.* Fancy took long strides around the lake, determined to complete three laps. Sweat poured from her forehead by the end of the first five-mile lap. Mandy's letter flashed in Fancy's mind. "Do something nice for three people in your life this holiday season." Fancy had selected Tanya, Desmond, and Caroline. By the end of the third lap, Fancy was just warming up so she spread her blanket on the grass and did five hundred sit-ups. Tempted to do five sets, running up and down the one hundred seventy-five steps across the street on Lakeshore, Fancy thought about Tanya and drove to Emeryville.

Byron entered her thoughts. Fancy wondered what he was doing and if she should call him and apologize for calling the cops. He hadn't called her to apologize for nearly killing her. Fancy decided if she honestly wanted closure, Mandy was right, she should never have contact with Byron again. Fancy searched her cellular phone book and reluctantly deleted Byron's home, work, and cellular numbers. Although Byron's assault wasn't her fault, she blamed herself for ruining a relationship with the man she could have happily married.

Fancy blinked several times. The woman trotting toward Fancy's car was smaller than her. Fancy got out the car and said, "Tanya? Girl, what have you done? You've lost so much weight. You look good."

"I wish I felt as good as I look. I'm stressed. I begged my supervisor for one hour so I have to be back by nine-thirty. The late holiday shoppers are crazy, girl. Look at these parking lots." Tanya pointed to Expo Design, Toys 'R' Us, Best Buy, and Pet Club. "Fancy, where did you get the new attitude? Since when did you start caring about me? Must be the holiday spirit." Tanya laughed.

"Oh, no, this is not about me. I am concerned about you." Fancy let down the windows.

"I don't know. I love William. And he doesn't hit me or anything but he yells a lot since he lost his job. He acts like it's my fault. Every bad thing that happens to him is my fault."

"When did he lose his job?" Fancy asked, stretching her arm out the window, motioning to the driver behind her that she wasn't leaving her parking space.

"Almost six months ago. Around the time I stopped calling."

"Girl, you stopped calling way before the summer. More like late winter early spring."

"I don't know what to do, Fancy." Tanya's eyes drooped and her head hung low. "I feel trapped. William talks crazy whenever I say I'm leaving. He says stuff like, 'You can't leave me. You're stuck with me for life.' "

Stuck? "Honey, Silly Putty doesn't stick forever. Nothing does." Fancy noticed Tanya didn't crack a smile so she said, "Well, if you ever need a place to stay, you're welcome at my home anytime." Fancy hugged Tanya.

"Thanks. I'll work something out," Tanya said, picking at her fingernails.

"If you don't have your own savings, girl, start stashing money on the side. Never let William know how much you make or how much you save."

"Thanks. I gotta get back to work." Tanya closed the car door and trotted back across the street.

Fancy drove home, showered, and headed over to Desmond's house. He wasn't home so she drove to his job. Desmond was in his blue cover-ups leaning over his Mustang.

"What's the matter with your car?" Fancy stood a few feet away.

"Hey, surprise seeing you here. I thought you weren't speaking to me."

"How could I not speak to my best friend?" Fancy said, opening her purse. She reached inside and pulled out a sealed card. "Here, I just stopped by to give you this."

"*You*, give *me* something. Whoa." Desmond wiped his hands on his cover-ups.

"You can open it later. How's school?"

Desmond's lips curved wide and long. "I haven't started yet."

"Where'd you decide to go?"

"Georgia. Going back home. Moving after the holidays."

Fancy felt sad for not supporting Desmond's dream. "I'm happy for you." Fancy paused then said, "I gotta go. Call me whenever you have a moment."

"Wait, don't leave. I can take an early lunch. You wanna do lunch?" Desmond's walnut eyes were warm and sparkling.

"I'm having lunch with my mother today."

"For real. That's great!" Desmond hugged Fancy, lifting her off her feet.

"Man, put me down."

"No way," Desmond said, swinging her around. He held her close and Fancy started to cry because she never realized how simple things meant so much to some folk. Desmond eventually placed her on her feet and said, "Let me open my card. I can't wait until Christmas."

When Desmond opened his card, a check for six thousand dollars fell out. "Whoa, are you serious? You—are paying—me back."

"Yeah, I figured you might need your money for your wedding."

Desmond didn't respond. He read the Maya Angelou friendship card, then hugged Fancy again. "Girl, I love you! Whoa! This is great!"

Gently pushing away Fancy said, "I love you, Dez," and walked away.

Fancy cried all the way home but this time she felt good inside. Fancy raced inside, showered, dressed, and got back in her car all within an hour so she wouldn't be late picking up Caroline.

Caroline was standing in the doorway waiting when Fancy parked in front of the house. Fancy looked at the blue house and froze. Her body wouldn't move. Haunting memories, things she'd never told Mandy or anyone else resurfaced. Fancy saw herself as a little girl on hands and knees as she scrubbed each step every Saturday until they shone. Now the steps were dusty. The bright blue paint was dim.

Caroline motioned to Fancy. "Come in."

Slowly Fancy placed her feet on the street's black asphalt and stood. The curtain-style skirt with ruffled trimming swayed in synch with her hips as Fancy floated up the dirty stairs to Caroline's door.

"Hey, baby. I'm so happy to see you. Come in for a minute. I'm almost ready."

When Fancy crossed the threshold her eyeballs traveled left without assistance from her head. Her old chubby elementary pictures still hung on the wall. The étagère with its numerous whatnots were blanketed in dust, but never when she lived with Caroline. Fancy stared at the blue couch. Her temples throbbed and her head ached.

"Fancy, come here, baby. Mama needs your help."

Fancy ran out the house. The metal screen door slammed behind her. She hated Caroline all over again. Fancy jumped in her car and started the engine.

"Wait, where are you going!" Caroline yelled from the doorway.

Fancy shifted into drive and sped down Seventh Street, turned onto Market, hopped on the freeway for about two miles, exited at Harrison Street, and drove home. When she dashed into the lobby the mailman handed her her mail. Fancy slowed down.

"Merry Christmas, Miss Taylor."

"Thanks." Waiting for the elevator, Fancy thumbed through the pile, counting the cards. The twenty-sixth envelope was from Byron. Entering her apartment Fancy tossed the entire stack in the trash. All except one made it across the rim. She picked it up and carried it to her bed. It was Byron's card.

Fancy sighed heavily. She inserted her finger and ripped along the edges. A letter and three more envelopes were enclosed.

Fancy,
   My accountant forwarded your checks to the wrong address. Merry Christmas.

Byron

P.S. I apologize. Your car is sitting in my garage collecting dust. If you want it, let me know before New Year's Eve. Otherwise, I'll donate it to charity. I'd love to take you to the gala this year. I love you, Fancy. Call me.

Each envelope was stamped "Return, Undeliverable Address." The street name was misspelled on each envelope. Fancy opened the first envelope. Her eyes widened when she saw a check for twenty-five thousand dollars. The second check was for thirty-five thousand, and the third was forty grand.

"Yipee!" Fancy danced. She sat on the sofa and scrolled the Bs in her cellular phone book. "Aw, damn." She'd deleted each of Byron's numbers and her detailed statement wasn't due until the middle of next month. "Damn!"

Fancy still needed to do something nice for one more person. Using her cordless phone, she dialed SaVoy's number.

"Hey, SaVoy. This is Fancy. If you still want me in your wedding, I'd be honored."

"Oh, bless you. Yes, I do want my best friend in my wedding."

"I love you, SaVoy."

"I love you too, Fancy. You wanna go to church with us this New Year's?"

"Thanks. But I already have plans. I'll talk to you later. Bye."

Fancy browsed through her last month's statement, found Byron's numbers, and reentered them into her phone. He didn't answer his cell phone so Fancy left a message accepting both of Byron's offers.

CHAPTER 38

New Year's Eve. Fancy sighed heavily. She gazed out the patio window at the stars. Big dipper. Little dipper. A mirage? Fancy fell onto her bed in tears and couldn't stop crying. The eve before her twenty-third birthday—an entire year had passed—and she still hadn't found the right man.

Each relationship with her best friends, Desmond, Tanya, and SaVoy, had changed. The most important man in Fancy's life was moving to the other side of the country. Atlanta, Georgia, was over three thousand miles away. William had isolated Tanya. And Fancy couldn't blame SaVoy for marrying Tyronne. Tyronne was a good man and Fancy believed, even though SaVoy and Tyronne were opposites, they were meant for one another.

Ruffling her down-feather comforter, Fancy scurried across her king-size bed in search of her ringing phone. One more ring and her voice mail would turn on. SaVoy's name registered on the display so Fancy quickly answered, "Hey, girl! What's up?"

"Just called to see what you're doing tonight." As usual, SaVoy sounded happy. Fancy could picture her best friend's bright smile.

"Going out. To a gala at the Ritz. No, I'm not going to church, so don't ask. Say a prayer for me and call me tomorrow. After three."

Fancy was happy and sad. Would some other woman flirt with Byron while she was on his arm tonight? Should she go out with Byron? Fancy insisted on meeting him at the gala because she was not going to be the same fool twice. Was she?

Dressed in a stunning designer turquoise gown, Fancy grabbed her shawl and went to the basement garage. Now she owned two cars. Fancy jiggled her keys and decided to drive the car Desmond gave her.

Mints. Mints. Stop at the store. No, go to the gala. It's early. Go to the store and get some mints.

Strolling inside the drugstore, Fancy purchased a small tin of breath mints. She cruised down MacArthur Boulevard.

"Damn, why aren't these lights synchronized?"

A light drizzle sprinkled across her windshield. At each light the raindrops splashed harder. Thicker. A few moments later, the downpour obscured her view. Fancy drove five miles an hour toward the Bay Bridge. The rain poured harder. A loud screeching noise pierced her ears. Fancy quickly pulled over and cupped her hands to her head. When the noise stopped Fancy noticed smoke rising from her hood.

"Shit! Why tonight? Dammit."

Not the timing belt, she thought. *Couldn't be. Not again.* Desmond had to have remembered to change it before he gave her back the car. The gas station across the street was closed. Every passing car stopped for the red light, then kept going. The only place in sight was the last place Fancy wanted to be on New Year's Eve. Church. SaVoy's church.

Fancy stood in the rain, then got back in her car. Her dress was soaked. Hair ruined. As she contemplated, the rain poured harder.

"I have no choice." Fancy raced across the street. Her shoes splashed in the puddles. Once inside she couldn't believe how many people were at church on New Year's Eve. Didn't they have a life?

A man seated in a folding chair next to the last pew motioned for Fancy to take his seat. Couldn't he see she was soaked and out of place? And as soon as the rain subsided she would go. Fancy tiptoed, then squatted on the edge of the seat, trying not to soak the cushion.

"Thanks," Fancy whispered.

When she bowed her head toward her lap, the person seated to her right handed Fancy a monogrammed handkerchief with the initials DL engraved in small gold letters. Fancy first noticed the locks, then Darius. *Oh, shit.*

Fancy whispered, "Thanks."

Although she heard the choir, Fancy focused on Darius. Why was Darius crying? Fancy reached for his hand. Darius immediately pulled away.

"Excuse me," Darius said, stepping over her wet feet.

Where was he going? Fancy quietly sniffed her clothes. No, that wasn't it.

Damn! Shoot! How could she follow him without being obvious? Fancy stood with the congregation. Sat. Then stood again. She noticed SaVoy and Tyronne. Tanya. Fancy's eyes roamed the surrounding pews.

SaVoy nodded and then smiled, acknowledging Fancy as if she were expecting her. Dez! There was Desmond. Fancy looked to his left. Carlita. They looked like the happy odd couple.

"Excuse me," Darius said, stepping over Fancy again to take his seat. His eyes were drier.

Fancy glanced at the preacher and bit her bottom lip to keep from laughing. His hair was shaped like a miniature Don King afro. Fancy frowned when the pastor began humming instead of singing.

After the song, Pastor Tellings preached, "Call if you

will, but who will answer you? . . . Darkness comes upon them in the daytime . . . Blessed is the man whom God corrects . . . We have examined this, and it is true. So hear it and apply it to yourself. This is from the book of Job. From henceforth know that you cannot outthink, outsmart, con, nor get over on God. Resentment kills a fool, and envy slays the simple. Don't be simple. Don't be foolish . . . Let us pray."

When Darius wrapped his hand around Fancy's, Fancy felt an instant connection. She was embarrassed because she didn't know how to pray or what to say to God, so she remained silent inside, waiting for everyone else to finish. Then she heard Darius whisper, "Lord, thank you for blessing this queen and bringing her home. If she has any burdens, Lord, I ask that you remove them from her heart . . ." Then he prayed for Ma Dear. He must have missed her a lot. Then he prayed for Ashlee, Maxine, and his brothers. And fathers? Wellington and Darryl. He prayed for his mother. She was the only one he didn't call by name. Fancy wasn't sure Darius was conscious that he spoke aloud. But other people mumbled too. Fancy remained silent and said a special prayer for Caroline. Darius broke her concentration concluding with "Amen" so Fancy said, "Amen."

Fancy was elated when church ended. She blocked Darius's exit, extended her hand, and said, "Hi, I'm Fancy Taylor. Remember me?"

"Pleased to meet you. I'm Darius. Darius Jones."

Fancy frowned, then straightened her eyebrows. Was this the same arrogant guy she'd met or a clone? "Why the initials DL?"

"The DL is for Darius's Law. That's how I'm living. I make the rules. I don't follow them."

Fancy smiled, then frowned as SaVoy, Tyronne, Desmond, Carlita, and Tanya invaded their space.

SaVoy smiled wide and bright, then said, "We're going

to my house for appetizers and socializing, you guys care to join us?"

Before Darius could respond Fancy replied, "I can't. My car just broke down outside."

Desmond extended his hand to Fancy. "Give me your keys. I'll pick your car up tomorrow."

"Looks like you need a ride, young lady. I can handle that for you if you can trust me," Darius said.

Fancy's night was just getting started. "Sure. Thanks."

SaVoy raised her eyebrows twice. No, she was not telling Fancy not to sleep with Darius. This was a new year and one of the wealthiest men in Oakland was by Fancy's side.

Darius flipped open his cell phone, then pressed his speaker button. "I'm ready." He hung up and said, "If you're rolling with me, let's go."

"Not so fast, mister," SaVoy said. "Tell your mother I said hello."

"Ready?" Darius asked, still ignoring SaVoy.

What was that all about? Fancy thought.

Fancy walked out with Darius. The driver opened the door to a black stretch limousine.

Fancy smiled and waved good-bye to her friends. Desmond turned toward Carlita, holding Carlita's arm tighter.

"My place or yours?" Darius asked.

Fancy smiled and replied, "Mine."

After Darius dropped her off, Fancy reflected upon her last year's resolutions. Her New Year's resolution, to find the right man: tall, rich, and handsome, was the same. Darius was definitely Fancy's type. But unlike his predecessors Fancy would take her time and get to know him.

Fancy stood on her balcony. SaVoy had told her it was never too late to call upon the Lord. So this year, for the first time in over ten years, she prayed. Fancy thanked God for her mother and promised to stop calling her Caroline. Fancy thanked God for making her complete, realizing everything she needed she already had. And Fancy prayed for God to give back her friend. And if for any reason Desmond should be out of Fancy's life, Fancy promised God that she'd never refer to Desmond Brown by saying, "He's just a friend."

Who knew? Maybe God had blessed Fancy with a new friend, Darius Jones.

EXPECTATIONS

We expect
Someone driving on the freeway
In front of us
To keep the same pace
So that we may keep the same pace
Or we expect them to get the hell out of our way

But they don't do
Even though
they don't
have a clue

We expect strangers to give us
Three feet of space
And not be in our face
Listening to what we are saying
Although they may not be paying
They may be praying
Because their loved one is dead
And they don't even notice
We are alive

But we expect them to do
Even though they don't have a clue

We expect our spouses to do
What we want them to do
Even though they sometimes don't have a clue
What if they
Were you

We expect our children not to make
The same mistakes
We've made
Because we've paved

Their way
They should not stumble
Nor fall
Yet we cannot remember
Yet we cannot forget
We too
had to
Learn how to crawl

I hope
I hope
I hope
After reading Soul Mates Dissipate
If you only understand
We are not perfect
And will never be
And we must accept responsibility
For the actions of our plans

We do have a plan
Right
There is a purpose
in life

I hope
After reading He's Just A Friend
We will stop
Using the word friend
So loose
And learn to untie the noose
That we have placed around each other's necks

I hope
After reading Never Again Once More
We discover the core
Is forgiveness
Forgiveness is key

Oneness in love is the key
For true love can never be
Separate and equal

So I hope
The next time you
Have expectations
That you have them of yourself
And no one else
Or you will be disappointed
By who
No one

But you

CHRONOLOGY

Soul Mates Dissipate, Never Again Once More, He's Just A Friend, and my next four novels are intertwined. I recommend reading the series in order. Hopefully, this brief background will help the reader better understand the connections.

Soul Mates Dissipate
Soul Mates Dissipate is, for now, the beginning. This page-turning drama takes you on a journey with Jada Diamond Tanner and Wellington Jones, aka . . . soul mates. Wellington's mother Cynthia Jones, who has a history of her own with her sister Katherine, friend Susan, and ex-lover Keith, invites another woman, Melanie Marie Thompson, to break up Wellington's engagement with Jada.

Never Again Once More
This sequel to *Soul Mates Dissipate* spans twenty years into the lives of Jada and Wellington. Jada marries Lawrence Anderson. Wellington marries Simone Smith. Darius Jones, Jada's son, is born and matures to twenty years of age by the end of this story and he's climbing

on top of his mother's corporate ladder and her female executive staff.

He's Just A Friend

Fancy Taylor is a beautiful but not so brilliant woman on the move to conquer a rich husband by any means necessary. Along her journey she'll meet several friends, some of which become foes, and eventually Fancy will meet Jada's son Darius Jones.

Somebody's Gotta Be On Top (the next release)

Regardless of the situation, Darius Jones is always on top. His motto is: "If it doesn't make money, it doesn't make sense." That includes the women in his life. That is, until he meets Fancy Taylor.

If you've read each novel, as I mentioned before, Cynthia Jones has a history so moving, trust me, her story is worth the wait. Cynthia's story creates the beginning and concludes my seven-book series. After Cynthia's novel, I promise not to keep you waiting for *Kiss Me: Now Tell Me You Love Me*, a chilling drama about Harrison and Angela Gray.

AUTHOR'S MESSAGE

Here's my take, spin, belief, on life, love, and relationships. Change is constant but some folk want to change the people and things around them, but not themselves. They believe their values and concepts are more valid than others, thereby having a need to mold and clone offspring and mates. If I had a dollar for every time I've heard a man say, "I want to get married, and I really don't expect that much of my wife, all I want is blah, blah, blah," I'd be richer than Oprah. Okay, maybe not Oprah, maybe her friend Gail, but you get my point. So here's the deal. Change the way you think. Change the way you feel.

Relationships are emotionally based for both men and women. Yes, men, too. The public or outward display differs depending upon gender but the suffocating thoughts of betrayal and abandonment can psychologically paralyze a couple rendering both numb to their true feelings of love. Breakups are seemingly devastating because mentally people permit themselves to experience a tremendous loss. A loss so grave some individuals take their own lives and/or the lives of loved ones. Change the way you think and you'll change the way you feel.

Understand that separation anxiety manifests in numerous ways from infancy to adulthood. Children are comforted as long as they can see their parents. Adults feel secure when they know their spouses are constructively present and in their corner—emotionally, spiritually, financially, and so forth. Kindergartners cry when their parents leave them on the first day of school. Parents cry when their children go off to college. Lovers argue and sometimes fight, wishing their partner would just go away. The same individuals cry themselves to sleep, praying their fleeing mate will soon return.

When the ties that bond begin to tear, lovers panic. Why? Because they perceive the problem cannot be resolved even before they've attempted to effectively communicate, therefore adding pressure and stress to an already deteriorating relationship. When times are challenging, take a deep breath and ask yourself, "What is the real issue at hand?" Not problem. But issue. Perceive your dilemma as a resolvable issue. The answer always resides within because you are the hammer, the driving force, equipped to repair or condemn your relationship.

Change the way you think. Change the way you feel.

Grow in love as one. Oneness in love is key. Oneness in love is *the* key. Conceptualize that the man is the soil and the woman is the seed. One cannot flourish without the other. True love can never be separate and equal. Independently, neither man nor woman is complete. Jointly the halves become a whole, but only when the two fuse as one. Immediately begin replacing the I, me, mine with us, we, ours.

Never allow others to pollute your garden of love and solidarity. If you conclude the soil or seed is incompatible, first seek to find what nutritional supplements are deficient. Then gradually add each element. Don't expect an overnight change. Only after you've given your best, if you still haven't reaped a ripe harvest, you can move forward with a clear conscience. If you decide to uproot to find a more compatible mate, discard the weeds that plagued your garden, lest you contaminate your new soil or seed. Once you realize you already possess everything you need to cultivate a healthy relationship, only then will you experience the joy and happiness of giving and receiving the love you deserve.

Change the way you think. Change the way you feel.

Think positive. Smile at your mate. Lovingly stroke your mate. Whisper kind and kinky thoughts to your mate, especially in public. I did say whisper, right? Okay. Reflect on the good times. Let go of the bad times. Generally you won't forget but you must learn to forgive—forgive others as well as yourself. Share your dreams. Embrace your fears with faith. Fear is faith twisted upside down. So learn to turn fear around. Absorb one another's tears in the soil. Collectively the tears will cleanse the soil and both souls. The water will fertilize the seed and revitalize the spirits.

Never take life for granted. And don't assume you'll always have the love of your life. A relationship is a commitment that requires dedication just like operating a successful business, being an outstanding employee, and lovingly parenting children. Develop a passion for a healthy relationship. And when you use the word friend, never use it in a complete sentence with the word "just" as a qualifier. Because no friend is just a friend. And when you marry, marry your friend first and become his or her lover second. For a friend will always be a true love. But a lover won't always be a true friend.

Peace and Blessings
And so it is
Mary B. Morrison

If you desire to learn more about making healthier relationship choices, purchase a copy of my relationship workbook entitled *Who's Making Love* and/or attend one of my Who's Making Love workshops.

Website: www.MaryMorrison.com
E-mail: AskMaryBMorrison@aol.com

AUTHOR'S NOTE

The other side of what I do that many are unaware of is I'm the Founder and President of The RaW Advantage™. The RaW Advantage™ is a business dedicated to avid readers and aspiring writers. I conduct self-publishing workshops for writers and host author receptions for readers.

The RaW Advantage™ also encompasses The SHIFT Program and Who's Making Love workshops. I created The SHIFT (Supporting Healthy Inner Freedom for Teens) Program to help teenagers build self-esteem and make healthy relationship choices. Anyone who hasn't listened—I mean truly listened—to a teenager speak from the heart concerning their views on love, let me tell you, society has stripped away many of their hopes and dreams of having healthy relationships. I strive to show teenagers—especially young ladies who set the tone and establish the bar for relationships—how to use their inner strength to assist with their decisions. Decisions that parents, teachers, and friends can influence but cannot make for them.

I'm taking an additional step to provide references. The rest is up to you.

Spiritual Guidance	Meditate and ask God or your spiritual leader
SHIFT Program	*www.therawadvantage.com*
Free Testing for HIV/AIDS	1-866-RAP-IT-UP
Rape Crisis Hotline	1-800-656-HOPE
Teen Pregnancy & Prevention	1-800-BABY-999

The following is a sample chapter from
Mary B. Morrison's novel
SOMEBODY'S GOTTA BE ON TOP.

It is available wherever
hardcover books are sold.

ENJOY!

Somebody's Gotta Be On Top

Stop!
Somebody's Gotta Be On Top
How much are you willing to pay
To live another day

What are you afraid of. . . .

Money isn't keen
It's the realization of a dream
In the color green
Envy
Slime
Slipping
Tripping
Through time
Exchanging hands
Yours
Mine

What are you afraid of. . . .

Wishing
Wanting
Never daunting
Taunting
Your faith
Or taking a risk
Or waiting for break
To take a piss
Shit!
Piss on
Those who sing
Piss off
Those who scream
I'm living my dream!

Stop!
Somebody's Gotta Be On Top
How much are you willing to pay
To live another day

What are you afraid of. . . .

Success
Achieving your best
Willing to live with less
In order to attain more
Are you afraid to open the door
Before you knock
Or maybe you're content
Shoulda
Coulda
Woulda
Only if. . . .
You'd spent
Time Time Time
How much are you willing to pay
To live another day
Frivolous chatter
Doesn't matter
Settling
Meddling
Gabbing
Back-stabbing
Shattering hope
Slippery slope
Walking a tightrope

What are you waiting for. . . .

An invite
When the time is right
Not tonight

Tomorrow
Sorrow
Today
You'll borrow
Someone else's
Money
Honey
Hopes
Dreams
Anything
Sign an I.O.U.
Promise to repay
In dismay
That which you haven't earned today
Belongs to someone else
Isn't that funny
Yesterday is gone
You're sitting at home
On a diminishing throne
Of hopes
Dreams
Envy
Green
You scream
Money ain't a thing!
That's a lie
Can't miss what you never had
Lad
Your slice of the pie
Is on someone else's table
You're able
But. . . .
Unwilling

What are you afraid of....

Stop!

Somebody's Gotta Be On Top
How much are you willing to pay
To live another day
No pain
No sweat
No blood
No tears
Just fears
Who cares
What's new
What are you really going to do
Successful people are the same as you
Living with fears too

What are you afraid of. . . .

How much are you willing to pay
Today
Or Not
Regardless
Somebody's Gotta Be On Top

CHAPTER 1

Monogamy wasn't natural. Monogamy was a learned behavior that Darius couldn't be taught. When would women realize sex wasn't a bed partner of love? Besides, who would teach him how to be faithful? Jesse Jackson? Bill Cosby? Willie Brown? Bill Clinton? His dad, the ménage à trois king? All the men he respected, all the men he knew, were men. Fornicators. Adulterers. Players. The distinction of a real man was a real man kept his family in the foreground and his females in the background. Like backup singers. Once the song was over, their job was done. Thanks for having made him cum. Now go. With Darius, not many of his lovers deserved an encore.

"Ha!" Darius laughed, then said aloud to himself, "You a fool boy." His office was quiet all morning. No constant phone calls or interruptions by his secretary, Angel.

Any woman who wanted Darius Jones had to commit to him and only him. His woman had to have a job. Not any job. A high paying job. Preferably her own business. So what if he had enough money to take care of her. Her mama. And her grandmama. A woman without a steady income was venomous. A woman with too much idle time was lethal. No piece of ass was worth his millions of dollars. He was the only heir to his mother's empire and one day would split his father's fortune with one sibling who was barely four years old.

Those broke leeches in thongs, jiggling their asses on beaches or benches, at the bus stop, were the ones who were constantly plotting and planning—pregnancy, rape, battery—on how to become rich off of a man. For sex. For real. Any wealthy man would suffice. Mike. Kobe. Deon. Including him. Bullshit conniving tricks. They weren't privy to suck his dick.

Rich pussy like the Vivica A's, and Mary J's, Halles, and Janets of the world needed stroking too. But they also had reputations worth protecting. Lawsuits to them translated into bad publicity. Lost revenue. They'd end the relationship before bringing forth charges. That's the kind of woman Darius wanted. And if Darius ever caught his woman cheating, she didn't need to waste his time explaining. Or packing. Because he'd personally have all of her shit moved out of his house. Immediately! With Darius, no one got a second chance to make a bad impression. Except his mother.

Darius pressed sixty-nine on his speed dial. His lungs expanded. The warm air escaped his nostrils, grazing his smooth upper lip.

"Hey, you," she answered.

Her voice penetrated his soul. Chill bumps invaded his skin. The hairs on his arms stood tall. Darius wasn't cold. He swallowed the lump clogging his vocal cords and said, "So, you packed yet? I can hardly wait to see you tonight. Make sure you arrive two hours early at the airport." Darius deepened his voice then emphasized, "I don't want you to miss your flight this time."

Darius rolled his leather high-back chair until his abdomen pressed against the edge of his glass-top desk creating a crease in his wool jacket. Slowly he smoothed his finger over the photographic image of her naturally pink-colored lips. Thin and seemingly oh-so-very soft. She looked ravishing in the family picture they'd taken a month ago at Thanksgiving dinner with his parents.

"Are you still in the office?" she asked.

His hand traveled from her temple and traced the outline along her straight black hair, which cast a strikingly beautiful contrast against her nearly white complexion. His eyes fixated on hers.

Loving someone more than himself, more than life, more than making money, was absurd and not what Darius had planned. But this special woman—naw, she was more than a woman, she was a lady—had stolen his heart. First she'd become his platonic childhood playmate. Now she was his best friend. His only friend.

The honeysuckle scent of her hair, the subtle movement of her hips when she walked, the provocative melody of her voice each time she innocently laughed while calling his name, the gentleness of her touch whenever she groomed his dreadlocks, the taste of her words lingering on his palate as he gasped into the receiver consumed his thoughts. Nervous energy growled in the pit of his stomach reminding him he'd forgotten to eat lunch again today. Consciously he erased his boyish grin. She evoked feelings Darius swore he'd never harbor for any woman after having been betrayed by his ex-fiancée.

"Of course I'm still in the office. And my staff too. Just because it's Friday and New Year's Eve, doesn't mean they're entitled to leave early. I might let 'em go at three. Maybe. Now answer my question."

"Don't worry. I packed last night. And my dad is dropping me off in a few. I'll call you when my plane lands in Oakland." She paused then whispered, "I miss you, brother."

Darius remained silent. Damn. Although they spoke every day, three to five times each day, he'd practically forgotten about the incident with her dad. Darius hadn't seen her father since the day, over two years ago, when he'd beaten her father's ass for causing his mother to hurt her arm and leg. In retrospect, Darius understood Lawrence's frustrations with his mother because after that physical altercation Darius's mother gave him the shock of his life. Thereafter, his feelings for his mother numbed his compassion toward women even more. If his mother were a liar, then every other woman was too. Except his lady on the opposite end of the phone. But the feasibility existed, so he couldn't completely trust her either. What a fucked-up world to live in, Darius thought, when the only person he could trust one hundred percent of the time was himself.

Forgetting about her dad and his mom, Darius massaged his erection through his pleated slacks hoping she'd continue talking, but hopefully not about her dad. Her voice had him so turned on he wanted to make love. To her. For years. *Say something. Anything. Please,* his dick urged, her tone repeating in his mind. *I miss you.* He'd missed her too. But silence lingered in his ear.

New Year's Eve this year would be unforgettable. He wasn't going to propose, but he'd finally gathered the courage to logically express the depth of his love. His birth parents weren't hers so factually they weren't related. And since his mom was remarried to her soul mate, Wellington Jones, the man his mother should've married instead of Lawrence, Darius felt Ashlee and he were two consenting adults capable of making their own decisions.

Darius's flight from Los Angeles would arrive into Oakland International Airport one hour before Ashlee's plane from Dallas was scheduled to land. His luggage would remain at baggage claim because he wanted to surprise Ashlee by waiting at her gate with a dozen of her favorite long-stem white roses.

Breaking the silence she finally spoke, "Did you hear me?" Lightly she articulated, "I said, I miss you."

Ashlee's delayed response made Darius believe she was also thinking about him. The cordless phone slipped from between his ear and shoulder so he quickly activated the speaker. "Of course I heard you. I just wanted you to repeat it. That's all." He placed his fingers against his thick lips then laid the same two fingers atop the glass frame over her mouth.

She inhaled then softly said, "I miss you. I miss you. I miss you. I miss you. I miss you. How's that? Turn on your cam so I can see you."

No way, Darius thought as he unzipped his pants and squeezed his head suppressing the cum vowing to escape his hard-on. He imagined what she looked like in the nude. Although they'd visited one another for more than ten years—he still had no idea if her nipples were lighter or darker than her breasts. If her pubic hairs were curly or straight. If her clitoris was small or large.

"Hey, lady. I've gotta run. I'll see you later." Darius stood. Securing his relaxed muscle into his black silk boxers, he then watched the tiny metal clamps overlap until the last one reached the top.

His lungs suctioned in the much-needed oxygen for his brain when she exhaled an intoxicating, "Bye."

Darius waited until she hung up then removed his tan coat, tossing it onto his chair. He entered the private rest room connected to his office and vigorously rinsed his face with cold water. While staring at his reflection in the mirror, Darius wondered why his mother had lied to him about his biological father? Why she'd waited twenty years to reveal the truth? Why didn't his biological father, Darryl Williams, Sr., display the same love for him as he did for Darius's two half brothers?

Darryl was a former NBA all-star whom Darius had overtly idolized most of his childhood, including the four years Darius started on the varsity basketball team in high school. Darryl was his college basketball coach at Georgetown, which explained why his mother never came to any of his college games. His mother apparently had an epiphany when her mother died and decided it was time for a damn confession. A truth that mentally scarred him. Possibly for life.

Fuck Darryl Williams! Darius Jones didn't need anybody but Darius Jones. His beloved grandmother, Ma Dear, the only woman that had never lied to him, would've said, "Don't waste time disliking people who don't like you when you can appreciate the many people that do love you." Darius knew Ma Dear was right, but after Ma Dear died disappointment and resentment befriended him.

Although sometimes Darius drowned in his waterless tears, real men, when their hearts ached with sadness and their souls suffocated from failure, didn't show signs of weakness. Darius remembered because Ma Dear's husband, Grandpa Robert, whom she'd joined in heaven, told Darius when Darius was four years old, "Boy, looks like you been crying. Crying is for girls and sissies. Remember that." Darius never forgot. Tears. Confessions. There was no way Darius would ever let Grandpa Robert down by displaying a wimpish attitude. Sensitivity belonged to losers like Rodney, the undercover bisexual brother who infected his ex-fiancée with HIV. Anger and outrage were more acceptable. Darius thought again, what a fucked-up world to live in.

Buying his office building and loaning him a million dollars was just another one of his mother's ways to compensate for her guilt. And he had every intention of making her suffer for the next twenty years or at least until he felt she'd repaid her debt. Everyone was indebted to something or someone. But if his mother hadn't married Lawrence, Darius would've never met his number one lady. So perhaps he should've been grateful, but gratitude required expressing feelings.

Shifting his thoughts back to his lady, he smiled in the mirror, running his fingers over his locks. He gathered each shoulder-length strand in a ponytail then admired the sweet brown succulent flesh hundreds of women had enjoyed feasting upon. Her flight would arrive at ten o'clock tonight. What would she wear to his parents' ball tomorrow? Hell, it didn't matter. Possessing the same qualities as his mother, his stepsister always looked great. Just like his ex-fiancée, Maxine. Ladylike. Feminine.

Why was his childhood so innocent and his adult life so skeptical? As a child he could do no wrong. Women adored him. Fantasies of having his own family. A loving wife who'd only love him and he'd exclusively love her. At one time he believed that was true. Until those two fifth graders told him he could have both of them or his boring girlfriend. She wasn't boring. She was quiet. There was a difference. But two were definitely better than one. Darius once believed marriage was sacred. Until he witnessed his mother divorcing Lawrence for no good reason other than she wanted another man.

Why did grown-ups lie about simple shit? Santa? The Easter bunny? Who was this dude Cupid? Someone who was supposed to make him believe he was in love? Most people weren't. Most people were lonely or afraid of being alone so, good or bad, they clung to the familiar. Not Darius.

Darius walked out of his corner office, one flight down the back stairway, entered the exit door, stood over his new employee and folded his arms high across his cashmere shirt. Quickly she clicked on the minimize box at the top of her computer screen and the game vanished.

"Naw, put the screen back up," Darius insisted, staring over her shoulder. "I wanna see how good you are because obviously you're no good for my company." Darius waited. "You've got ten seconds. Ten. Nine. Eight . . ." he always counted backward so when he stopped, he was at number one because he was number one. The best at business, politics, economics, sports, and sex. Especially, sex. Darius's eyes focused on the digital clock at the bottom of the seventeen-inch flat screen monitor. Two hours remaining before his driver would take him to the airport.

When the screen came into view, Darius pointed toward the door and said, "Get your shit and get the fuck out of my office."

"But, it's the holidays and there isn't any work to do. I can ex—"

"Don't waste any more of my time or my money." He'd warned her in the orientation last month not to use his company's equipment or services for personal reasons. At the top of the items listed on the acknowledgment form by his Human Resources Director was the computer, followed by the telephone—both cellular and office—supplies, beverages, and so forth. "What's my mission statement?" Darius asked, watching the woman hesitantly remove his company's cell phone and credit card from her purse.

She mumbled, "If it doesn't make money, it doesn't make sense."

"So, what? You thought I was joking?"

"But, I can ex—"

"Explain what! Explain why I'm paying you thirty-five dollars an hour to waste my electricity!" The back of his hand slapped into his opposite palm repeatedly as he continued. "Occupy my space! Drink my coffee! Eat my bagels! And play games on my computer!" Darius threw his hands in the air then said, "That doesn't require an explanation. The only thing I want to know is how you're playing a sorry-ass losing hand of three-card draw," his pointing finger landed next to her score, "solitaire made me money? Prove that and you can stay."

The twenty-two-year-old recent college graduate, who was the same age as Darius, silently stared at him, then said, "But everyone in the entertainment business is on vacation except us."

"That's right! And you should be studying the screenplay I gave you yesterday because I specifically told you I need to hand this to my inside contact at Parapictures and give a copy to Morris Chestnut first thing Monday morning. Am I supposed to pay you and someone else to do your job? Huh? Answer me!"

Calmly she replied with a frown, "Why are you so upset? You're the one who said your mother's best friend, Candice Morgan, wrote the screenplay, so obviously Candice will select you as her agent. What's the big deal?"

"I don't care who wrote the damn script! Unless I secure the best deal possible before anyone else—" Darius shook his head. "You just don't get it. You may have graduated cum laude but you sure as hell flunked basic comprehension." He grumbled, "Damn, it's hard to get good help." Darius paged security from his mobile phone and said, "Escort my new employee out of my building. Immediately," and went back upstairs into his office.

How in the hell was he going to maintain an advantage over the other nine companies that were also given a non-exclusive right to shop the hottest screenplay on the market? As much as he wanted to attend the ball, he had no choice. He had to stay home and work. Darius speed-dialed his mother's number.

Candice and his mother had fallen out when Candice produced an unauthorized biography of his parents' love life including all the graphic juicy details his mother had shared with her so-called best friend. That's what his mother deserved for telling all her business to her so-called trustworthy girlfriend. Women. They all spent too much time analyzing every damn thing, talking too damn much, and complaining all the time. Maybe women were the ones responsible for fucking up the world. First Eve. Then his ex-fiancée. And of all persons, his mother.

Sighing heavily Darius said, "Hi, Mom."

"Hi, baby, I'm glad you called. I was just thinking about you." His mother whispered, "Stop, Wellington. I'm on the phone with Darius." Returning to a normal tone, she asked, "So what time is your flight getting in?"

"Hi, son!" Wellington's voice cheerfully resonated in the background.

Wellington Jones, although he wasn't Darius's biological father, was the only male man enough to raise Darius from birth until now. When Darius's mother revealed the truth, Wellington had said, "You are my son. A very brave man stepped up to the plate and raised me as his own." Darius recalled how Wellington had shared his adoption history. "I don't wish this type of devastation on any person. Honestly, I'm disappointed in your mother. But God wants us to learn the importance of forgiveness. You have every right to be mad. Just don't let your anger destroy you . . . I love you no matter what." Darius wondered how Wellington could be so compassionate without losing his masculinity.

"Sorry, Mom. I'm not going to make it. Gotta work. Something important just came up." Darius couldn't dare tell his mother her life was the greatest story roaming throughout the industry, because his mother was livid with Candice while Wellington thought how wonderful it would be if another black person could join the ranks of becoming a millionaire. His dad felt there was no direct harm to them. Wellington's only request was that Candice change the names.

"Darius, you work too hard. You just started in this business. Give it some time, honey. You'll get the next movie deal and I bet it'll be a more lucrative contract."

"Mom, you don't understand. There's no such thing

as working too hard. If I get this deal, my reputation will soar internationally. Mark my words. Darius Jones will instantly become a household name because this is a script all nationalities can relate to. Mom, somebody's gotta be on top. There's those who do and those who don't. And those who don't never come out on top. Gotta go. Gotta work. Happy New Year, Mom, and tell Dad I said the same."

"Well, honey, if you insist. But before you go, how's your proposal coming along?"

"Not as well as I thought. I just fired the person assigned to put together my presentation. The meeting for selection of an agent is Tuesday morning. Every interested agency is going to pitch why they should represent Candice. I have a meeting with my inside contact person at Parapictures on Monday. And if I'm lucky, Morris will show up as promised to the meeting."

"Okay, baby. Now, I've got to go. Your dad is trying to—never mind. I'll call you tomorrow. I love you."

"Yeah, Mom. I know. Bye."

Darius gazed at the family photo, dialed his travel agent, and arranged for Ashlee to take a flight into Los Angeles.

The following is a sample chapter from
Mary B. Morrison's eagerly anticipated upcoming novel
NOTHING HAS EVER FELT LIKE THIS.

It will be available in August 2005, wherever
hardcover books are sold.

CHAPTER 1

A woman didn't have to stand on the corner to become a prostitute. All women at some point in their lives have exchanged pussy for goods and services. The best tricksters could barter for homes, cars, diamonds, furs, and enough cash to maintain a five figure bank account. The unsophisticated females, oblivious to how much men would pay to bust a nut or have their dicks sucked, were happy with a movie, a meal, and a few lies about how much the man loved her. The naïve chickenheads came out of their pockets with top dollars, leasing their showcase men, not realizing that gigolos were always on auction awaiting the next highest bidder. No matter what the circumstances or consequences were: Men needed to get laid. Women wanted to get paid.

"Females! Fuck!"

Darius yelled, thrusting his fist, parting the gushing water with the force of his hand. Starting the New Year masturbating in the shower wasn't his idea of pleasurable sex but it was safe. At least he didn't have to worry about allegedly getting another feline pregnant. Tricksters spelled financial security *b-a-b-y*.

"The next female kickin' it with me better not have

the word baby in her vocabulary," Darius said aloud to himself, massaging his dick under the water. "Darius, please baby, just put it in one more time. Baby don't leave, I'm not finished cumming yet. Oh, baby, your dick is so good," Darius mimicked. "Please, baby, please my ass." Stroking his dick with each syllable, Darius said, "I'll beat my shit every day befo' I get suckered in by another leeching-ass woman."

Warm streams of water, pounding against Darius's muscular neck and shoulders, drenched his locks. Darius admired his caramel reflection, illuminated by candle-light, that danced on the glass shower door. Massaging the creamy body wash onto his well-defined chest, Darius's hand slid along the crevices on his abdomen, over his inward navel, then teased his curly dark chocolate pubic hairs. Cupping his balls, Darius squeezed his nuts, watching his dick grow longer.

"Damn! Women are straight up scandalous."

Didn't matter if the fe-fe was a VP, VIP, stay-at-home wife, his wife, his sister, a lover, an employee, an associ-ate, a groupie, a counterpart, smart, fine, dumb, ugly, dumb and ugly, a model, a hooker, a Christian, his best friend, or his mother. The one thing Darius knew women shared in common was placing an invisible price tag on their pussies.

"If I give you some, what you gon' do for me?" Under-cover prostitutes in denial like he owed them some-thing. If anyone was getting paid, it should've been him. Hell, Darius did most of the work most of the time. Darius didn't mind working for his, but the lazy females were history. The next woman he met had to be physi-cally fit, no exceptions. Females unable to ride Slugger for five minutes straight without falling off or holding on had to get up off of his dick and out of his bed. He'd cum within five minutes and if she didn't get hers, oh well, she could work for it or take her lazy ass to a gym and learn how to work it out.

Women were simple and Darius didn't mean in a basic kinda way. Ignorant. Shysters. Dick-headhunters. The sweeter the pussy, the higher the ransom: Husband Wanted, Medical Benefits Needed, Rent Overdue, Children Gotta Eat, Desire a Trip to Paris, Pussy Needs Recreational Lickin' and Stickin' While Man is Away.

And the tag lines were consistent, "Here's my number Darius, call me on my cell. Hit me on e-mail, Daddy. Oh, what the hell, you can come on over to my place." On the first date? Damn! But if all he wanted to do was hit it, Darius was down for banging a female's cranium against the headboard so hard that he cared less about remembering her first, last, or nickname, never taking her public, and never seeing or calling her again. The easier the woman, the cheaper the pussy. Cheap pussy was not on his list of chicks to do. Some females—just because he was rich—were so dumb, they'd do anything to lay with him. Those were the ones who got nada, nothing, zilch.

Darius's large thick fingers and manicured nails wrapped snug around his slippery shaft as his dick penetrated an imaginary womb. "Aw, yes. Make your pussy suck this dick, gurl," Darius moaned daydreaming about the one woman he was in love with. Ashlee.

With numerous hidden agendas, women, including Ashlee, refused to have sex when they were mad, teased him with sex if they were interested, and gladly fucked him unconscious whenever he surrendered his money or his time. But when Darius treated a woman like a whore, even if she wasn't a ho, that was when her ass became transformed into a black widow—fucking, devouring, then killing him—defacing his personal property, determined to strip him of his dignity, cash, or whatever else she could sap out of him all in exchange for pussy and sometimes bad pussy. Like his wife, Ciara.

"*Huuhhh,*" Darius exhaled releasing his grip. "I'm not wasting an orgasm on feline frustrations. I might fuck around and impregnate some sewer animal."

Layering his wet skin with baby oil then toweling dry, Darius covered his locks with a terrycloth silk lined cap, sprawled his naked flesh atop his oversized king comforter, then clamped his hands behind his head, gazing in the mirrored ceiling, admiring his sexy body.

"Damn, you look good, boy-ie."

Darius's sexy physique and manly facial features were a blessing and a curse. It wasn't Darius's fault women couldn't resist surrendering their pussies to him, but, unfortunately, their troubles had become his. Today was one of those rare days Darius didn't feel like doing a goddamn thing. Seeing anybody. Talking to no damn body on the phone. Not even his mother. Especially, not his mom.

After all he'd been through last year, almost losing his life in a fire that destroyed his business, and supposedly getting three women pregnant, his mom had the audacity to exacerbate his problems and side with his stepfather insisting that he, Darius Jones, the only child of a self-made millionaire woman, Jada Diamond Tanner, sole owner of Black Diamonds, get a job? What a joke.

Taking in the entire view of his lean six-foot-seven, two-hundred-twenty-pound body stretched atop the royal blue-and-gold suede comforter—the colors that represented his future college, UCLA—Darius closed his eyes and prayed.

"Dear God, I know I don't deserve Your mercy, but as Your child, I have Your permission to ask. Right? Please, Lord, please send me a sign that those unborn children aren't mine. I'm still a kid at heart myself and, well Lord, honestly, I'm not ready to be a father. Yes, I know You spared me from contracting HIV from my ex-fiancée, Maxine. And, yes, You did deliver me from almost committing suicide when I thought I had HIV. And I'm so grateful you've given me an opportunity to play professional basketball. Well, almost. So You can see with so many positive things in my future, there's no way I can deal with any negativity. Thank you, Jesus for listening. But as I lay here today, needing You again Lord, I beg You to deliver me once more from having to get a job, deliver me from being broke, and please, Lord, please deliver me from being a father. Amen."

Darius's grandma, Ma Dear, had taught him how to pray for what he wanted. That God answered prayers. Well, right now, lying in the midst of loneliness, Darius certainly hoped Ma Dear was right when she'd said, "No matter how down you get, pray. And don't forget to pray when God blesses you with good fortune, my child, because just like the Lord giveth, the Lord also taketh away. God is forgiving. But you can't outsmart Him." Yeah, Pastor Tellings spoke those same words New Year's Eve while Darius sat in church on the back pew next to a fine woman.

Tears escaped Darius's closed eyelids, rolled down his temples, and into his ears. The only woman Darius respected was dead. Ma Dear, no matter how upsetting it was, always kept things real by telling him the truth. So why didn't Ma Dear tell him that Wellington wasn't his biological dad. But Ma Dear never said that Wellington was his father. Cupping his hands over his face, Darius wished his grandmother was alive. "Oh, shit." The side of his bed closest to his ribs moved slightly. Lifting his head, Darius saw an imprint in his mattress next to his torso.

"Couldn't be," Darius thought laying his head on the pillow. "Chill out man. Stop trippin'. It's all good. Ma Dear, if you're here, I need you."

Ma Dear also told him, "Never kick a man while he's down." Darius wished those words would've held true for him last year when he was hospitalized.

Through watery eyes, Darius gazed at his ceiling vividly recalling the night he was incapacitated—the night his life changed for the worst—his stepdad, Wellington stood over his hospital bed preaching, "Son, lay back down. The only thing you're going to do right now is listen to us. We've decided that the money we loaned you must be repaid by the end of the year. And, since we already know you can't afford to repay us, we're taking over your company. And you can't work for us, son. You're going to have to get a job. Working for someone else."

Wellington was twisted. Confused. Who in hell Wellington thought he was talking down to. Instantly, Darius had rebelled and said, "Oh, hell no!" then pleaded with his mother, "Ma! You can't let him do this!"

What a joke. Standing in his hospital room, Moms didn't say a word that night so Wellington had continued his soliloquy, "Son, you don't respect your mother. You don't respect me. You don't respect your wife. You don't even respect yourself. So why should we contribute to you using other people? We won't. Never again. And if you don't get a job, we're taking your name out of our will. You'll inherit nothing."

What made Wellington a sanctified authority on Darius's behavior? Judging Darius when Wellington should've been confessing to Darius's mother the affair he was having. But Moms wasn't any better than Wellington. They deserved one another. That same night at the hospital Wellington couldn't leave the conversation alone. No, seemed like he was just getting warmed up.

Wellington had insisted, "Darius, you owe Lawrence an apology for misleading Ashlee."

Misleading Ashlee? Darius had thought, lying in that hospital bed glancing over at Ashlee who was lying in the hospital bed across from him. Ashlee's second-degree face wound was wrapped in bandages. Darius felt sorry for her wounds but he'd risked his life to save Ashlee. Seems as though he was the one who deserved a thank-you.

Besides, Ashlee wasn't a kid. She'd made her own decisions. At first Ashlee didn't want to have sex with Darius because his mom had married Ashlee's dad, Lawrence. But, to Darius, their parents' commitment could never make Ashlee his biological sister so Darius explained to Ashlee, after they'd made love, that there was no incest.

Since Wellington wouldn't back the fuck up, Darius caved Wellington's chest in with a backlash and replied, "Maybe your wife owes Lawrence an apology for aborting his baby."

Darius's mom stood there like she was the one shocked. But having aborted her ex-husband's baby when Lawrence never knew she was pregnant was wrong. Hell, just like his mom had waited over twenty years to disclose that Wellington wasn't his biological father, maybe Darius's mother wasn't pregnant from Lawrence. Maybe she'd aborted Wellington's child. Darius's mother wasn't perfect, but she seemed innocent, so no one had ever questioned her motives, actions, or whereabouts. But Darius knew his mom never stopped fucking Wellington, even while she was married to Lawrence. Darius knew a lot of secrets his parents assumed he had no knowledge of. As screwed-up as his life was at times, Darius didn't hate on other people, but if Wellington didn't stop trying to control him, Darius would tell his mother about Wellington's other woman. What a fucked-up world to live in when Darius couldn't trust anyone but himself.

Picking up the remote and pressing a few buttons, Darius's circular bed elevated three feet above the hardwood floor then rotated one hundred and eighty degrees clockwise. He started to see if the indent in his bed was still adjacent to his side when unexpectedly, a damn near foot-long erection distracted Darius, so he blocked Ma Dear from his mind and began stroking his dick.

Darius didn't have a problem working for his mom

again, holding down her Executive VP position or working for himself at the company his mother had given him, Somebody's Gotta Be on Top Enterprises. But Darius should've known his company was subject to takeover by his parents when they insisted on holding sixty-six and two-thirds percent ownership.

Now instead of organizing, funding, and producing film projects in Los Angeles, Darius was home alone in his Oakland mansion jacking-off his frustrations. On the verge of cumming, Darius said, "Fuck this bullshit," pissed that his parents were jocking him to sign over the multimillion dollar insurance claim check from when his office building burned to ashes.

Wellington already had plans to keep *all* of Darius's settlement money, expanding Wellington Jones and Associates' two office locations—Los Angeles and San Francisco—to include the Somebody's Gotta Be on Top two offices. While Darius was hospitalized, Wellington had secured three new film options for *Never Again Once More, He's Just a Friend,* and *Player Haters.* And Wellington had planned to take credit at the Premier for the release of Darius's first film, *Soul Mates Dissipate* and stated, "If you find yourself a job, I might invite you to the Premier."

"Fuck, him!" Darius yelled. "This is bullshit!" What a trip. What a goddamn trip.

Damn, Darius's dick was functioning independent of his brain. His dick was hot from the friction and hard as steel ready to explode in his hand. Pumping Slugger several times, Darius slowed his pace to prolong his ejaculation.

"Fuck 'em! Treating me like some orphan. Shit! I'd starve before kissing their asses or work for "the man." That's not how Darius Jones gets down. I'm a man. The man."

And that fine sistah Darius had met at church on New Year's Eve, what was her name, Fancy, yeah Fancy

Tyler or Taylor or somethin' like that, she was all woman. Picturing sliding his dick between Fancy's nice large perky breasts with firm nipples beckoning him to suck 'em, Darius stroked faster.

Sexy teasing cocoa complexion. Beautiful brown eyes. Immaculate physique. From her pedicure to the top of her head Fancy was without question the most beautiful woman Darius had ever met. They'd make a great-looking couple. He'd wanted to hit that pussy for almost a year, and Darius would be straight lyin' if he said he cared that Fancy was dating his boy Byron. She'd mentioned something about being single when they'd met so maybe she was no longer dating Byron. Either way, Darius wasn't trying to take Fancy from Byron, be her man, be her sponsor, marry her, or any ig'nant shit like that. Why did females take him seriously? He just wanted to bang her a time or two 'til the backed-up cum inside his balls rumbled through his big-ass nuts and blasted inside his jimmie, then he'd move on to the next female.

"Whoa!" Darius watched his thick white cum squirt in the air like a fountain landing in the crevices of his stomach. "Wheeww. Oh, my gosh. Damn, that shit felt good." Massaging the semen into his balls, Darius's erection wouldn't subside so he continued stroking his shaft. Forget Fancy, today wasn't a good day for anything except putting his life in order.

Three expecting women were liable for Darius's fucked-up mood: Ciara, Ashlee, and Desire. Ciara had it coming. Any woman who tried to date like a man could only blame herself for getting caught up in the game.

Darius was lucky, and luck did have a way of protecting his ass from the dumb shit he'd done, but he hadn't been very fortunate since Ma Dear had died. Ma Dear was his foundation. His salvation. The edge of his bed moved again. Cool air swept his feet. Darius lifted his head to witness a different indent, only this time the imprint was at the edge of his bed, closer, seemingly holding his feet. Darius smiled.

Every man needed a woman that he cherished. If Ma Dear were alive instead of visiting him in spirit, Darius was positive she'd convince his mother to give him back his business. Death was inevitable and having his grandmother was impossible. Or so he'd thought until now. He knew she was there with him. Darius was a survivor but hopefully his mom wouldn't let him suffer much longer.

With a measly quarter of a million dollars in his combined accounts, Darius could sponge off of that until he started college at UCLA in the fall, about seven months from now. Around the same time all of those money-consuming brats were due to arrive, crying, eating, shitting, and sleeping all day long. Fortunately child-rearing was a woman's job. The only dependent Darius wanted to treasure was Ashlee.

Ashlee. Darius thought he could trust his stepsister. They shared everything from childhood memories to walking down the aisle in their parents' wedding to a hospital room after they were injured when Darius rescued Ashlee from the fire that Ciara had set to his office building. But when Ashlee's nurse handed Darius that small brown paper bag with a bottle of prenatal vitamins inside prescribed for Ashlee Anderson, that's how Darius had discovered Ashlee was carrying his child. Ashlee was the one woman who wouldn't fuck around on him.

"Huuhhh." Sighing heavily, Darius couldn't imagine another guy nibbling on Ashlee's pink nipples, gently kissing her small clit, or bringing Ashlee to a sweet, savory release of vaginal fluids that he'd grown to enjoy tasting. Narrowing his eyes, Darius couldn't envision another man's dick roaming inside Ashlee, spitting seeds inside his woman. No man could love a woman better

than Darius. Leaning on his side, Darius held his dick at the base of his shaft, smiling. Slugger was nine and three-quarters of an inch long, four inches thick, skilled in pussy satisfaction, and certified triple platinum. A dick made to share.

Thinking of dicks, the corners of Darius's mouth retracted as he rolled onto his back. If his half-brother, Kevin, hadn't stolen over a million dollars from his company, well the company wasn't his anymore but that nigga had done righteous to get out of town overnight. Kevin wasn't slick. But Darius blamed himself for going against his main principal, to never trust anyone except himself. After Darius announced Kevin as his Executive Vice President at Somebody's Gotta Be on Top, Kevin had gotten closer to Ashlee, and Darius had foolishly appointed Ashlee as his Finance Director. No woman would ever manage his money again. Kevin was clever enough not to steal any checks. Instead, Kevin had copied one check then ordered duplicates.

Kevin had probably flown the red-eye back to Harlem to beg for that old janitorial position he'd had before working for Darius. Lots of shit fell apart last year, all in one day. That same night Kevin left L.A., Ashlee's father picked her up from the hospital in Los Angeles and flew her back with him to live in Dallas like he was her knight in shining armor and shit. Darius hadn't seen nor spoken with Ashlee since that night because Lawrence kept answering her goddamn phone. When would Lawrence realize he couldn't protect his grown-ass daughter from Slugger? No man could. With or without Lawrence's blessings Darius would fulfill his desires of divorcing Ciara and marrying Ashlee.

Desire. Now that was a bitch who had a slither of faith so shallow it could effortlessly slide underneath the belly of a dead snake without touching a thing. Darius was too drunk to remember to put on a condom and Desire was too eager to claim her baby from a twenty-two year old multimillionaire. Trickster. That's why she'd raced back to London, so Darius wouldn't confront her and make her have an abortion. Desire's baby probably wasn't his anyway. A one night stand and passions for hardcore sex was all they'd shared in common.

The way Desire circled the outside of Darius's asshole with her tongue then tea-bagged his balls into her mouth before squatting down onto his thick chocolate bar as she wrapped her pussy muscles around his shaft, suctioning the cum from his nuts, made Darius yell her name twice, and that was a first. If he could remember all that shit, why couldn't he remember to wrap up Slugger? Wait a minute. Sitting up in his bed, Darius suddenly recalled he had put on a condom. But it was nowhere in sight the next morning. "That trickster pulled my protection off." Otherwise how could she possibly be pregnant with his baby?

The hell with females. Darius decided to chill at his Oakland residence—his home away from his Los Angeles home—for a few more days until after his half-brother's funeral. Darius didn't mean to sound as though he didn't give a damn about Darryl Jr., but *"Ou-wee,"* Darius was relieved like a muthafucka when Kevin clarified that the Darryl who was shot and killed on New Year's Eve wasn't their father.

Answering his phone on New Year's Day, Darius was ready to hang up as soon as he'd recognized Kevin's voice then Kevin yelled, "Darryl's dead!"

Immediately Darius thought it was Darryl Sr., his father. The dad he'd never known. The dad who'd finally accepted responsibility for being his father. Darius was speechless.

"Man you still there?" Kevin had asked.

Darius recalled whispering, "What happened?"

"On that corner, mein. Wrong place. Wrong time."

"You mean DJ? Not Dad?"

"Yes, brother. Our brother. DJ."

Inhaling through his nostrils for what appeared to be a full sixty seconds, Darius's lungs had inflated. Slowly the warm air escaped his mouth. "Where are you?"

"Don't worry about me, mein. I gotta run. I'll see you at the funeral."

Darius was relieved because his biological dad, a former NBA All-Star had become more of a friend than a father, and Darius was so happy to have Darryl Sr. acknowledge him as his son.

Irrespective of age, every man needed his father just as much as his mother, if not more. And hearing his real dad say, "I love you, son," allowed Darius to shed tears of forgiveness for Darryl Sr. not being a part of his childhood. Now that Darius's funds were dwindling, and his Mom and Wellington were trippin', Darius desperately needed Darryl's continuous help. Darryl Sr. had single-handedly gotten Darius the full basketball scholarship to UCLA with the promise of Darius entering the NBA draft within a year or two.

The lubricant had dried to a crust but Darius's dick was still on swole. He hadn't had sex in over a week. That was ridiculous.

Let me call Fancy, Darius thought. I know we just met a few days ago but I need to bust this second nut before my balls erupt. All I really need is a warm pulsating pussy. And since I'm in Oakland, based on proximity, Fancy happens to be option number one.

Lowering his bed, Darius retrieved Fancy's business card from his nightstand which only contained her first name, e-mail address, and phone number.

Fancy answered on the first ring, "Hello."

"Hey, Ladycat. What's up?"

"Who's this?" Fancy replied.

Yeah, right. Women. Like she didn't have caller ID. "Darius, you wanna hang for a minute?"

Fancy snapped, "I don't just hang. You need a desti-nation. Call me back in five."

"Whateva nigga you talkin' to on the other line can wait. You've got a real man now."

"Apparently not, because a real man would respect my choice to call back. Hold on."

"Yeah, she's no fool," Darius mumbled, waiting for Fancy to click back over.

"Hey, I apologize. I've had a pretty hectic day. I was just finishing up scheduling an interview for a job and earlier I was surfing the employment section."

"Okay. That's cool, I guess," Darius said pretending to be interested. "So when do you start work?"

"Who knows? You know how bad this job market is. I would've started at this property management company today if they'd offered a managerial position. Hey, maybe you can give me a job with your company. I've got great skills."

"Well, let me invite you over for a private screening. Who knows? Maybe I'll cast you in one of my films."

"Thanks, but I'm not that easy. I don't do bedside in-terviews. Besides I already have plans. In fact, I need to start getting ready for my date, but if you'd like, you can take me out this Saturday night and we can talk. Call me tomorrow. Bye, Darius."

"Talk?" Darius shook his head. "Bye, Ladycat."

"By the way, I like that nickname. I'll keep it. Good-bye."

Ladycat was just like all the rest of the women and Darius knew Fancy wasn't independent. But she was a fool if she thought Darius would pay her bills and give her money like Byron. Kimberly Stokes was the only pussy Darius ever had or would pay for. Women. Thinking of tricksters, he was still holding the cordless in his hand when his mom's name popped up on the caller ID.

Reluctantly, Darius answered, "Hi, Mom."

"Hi, sweetheart. How are you?"

"Depressed," Darius lied. "Can't believe my brother is actually dead. But," Darius sniffled, "I'll be okay. Eventually. I guess."

"Oh, honey, I know it's so sad. When are you coming back to L.A.? Your father and I need to sit and talk with you about finding a job. And you still need to sign off on this check."

Forcing tears, Darius cried, "I just said I was depressed. I can't think about anything right now. I need time to myself."

"Okay, honey. Don't cry. But Wellington is threatening to—"

Darius cried louder.

"Never mind. It can wait. I'll deal with Wellington. Just let me know when you can make it back to L.A. Sometime this week or at least before the end of January would be good."

Sniffling, Darius replied, "Sure, Mom. Whateva you want."

"Okay, sweetheart. I know you're sad but you really didn't know Darryl that well."

"What?!" Darius yelled, "I don't believe you! I'm suffering and as usual you're being selfish."

"You'll be all right. I've got to go. I love you, sweetie. Call me tomorrow."

"You sure don't act like you love me. Bye." Darius lay the phone beside his thigh. The person his mom truly loved was her husband and anything Wellington said went, even if it was against her only child.

"Fuck 'em!" Darius didn't need his mom. Or Wellington. Looking up in the mirror, Darius's dick stood alone, lonely with no playmates, pointing toward the ceiling. Darius had to release his frustration so he picked up the cordless and dialed option number two, Kimberly Stokes.

Darius felt his bed move again. This time the imprint had vanished. Ma Dear was gone. Hopefully his grandmother hadn't given up on him. Dead or alive, Ma Dear was still the only woman he could trust.